A *Choice* of *Captors*

Also by Jane Shoup:

*Down in the Valley*
*Spirit of the Valley*
*Will of the Valley*
*Knightfall*
*The Restoration*
*Zan, Birth of a Legend*
*The Key*
*Ammey McKeaf, Book 1~ The Chronicles of Azulland*
*Heirs to the Throne, Book 2 ~ Chronicles of Azulland*
*Into Shadow, Book 3 ~ The Chronicles of Azulland*
*Charity Cases*
*Santa:2020 The Final Ride*
*The Time Tunnel of August Kaplan*
*An American Baroness, Book 1~ Sons of Barons*
*Nearly a Marquess, Book 2 ~ Sons of Barons*
*Christmas at Manoria, Book 3 ~ Sons of Barons*
*The Barretts of Crimson Hall*

Copyright © 2017 by Jane Shoup

ISBN 9780692831373

# Prologue

*16 April, 1746*

Observed from a distance, through the eyes of a dispassionate foreigner, it might have been seen as a virtual ballet of death. It should have gone differently and smoother for the badly outnumbered Jacobite army, given the number of rehearsals involved — battles both won and lost, but it was nightmarishly confusing in the ferocious action and the deafening noise, primal screams, and volleys of musket fire.

Iron flashed, blood sprayed, and men screamed and dropped as an exhausted, blood spattered, Adrian McGoldrick once again raised his broadsword to cut into a charging man. It never made contact because the tip of a bayonet from another direction caught Adrian the chest, just below the heart, ripping downward to his hipbone. He collapsed and another man fell on top of him, also struck down. The redcoat who'd struck the second men positioned himself to drive his bayonet down to finish the job, but a Lochaber axe hit between his shoulder blades and cut through his body, exploding his heart. He arched forward and fell atop his victims.

Badly wounded and bearing the weight of two dead or dying men, Adrian turned his head and stared at the blood-drenched soil. So, this was it. The end. In the midst of defeat. Worse than defeat, slaughter. Adrian closed his eyes and thought of his sisters, who would be widowed now, and of their children. He would never see them again. He would never see his home again. How would they manage? He forced his eyes open.

*How would they manage?*

He couldn't breathe and it suddenly mattered. It mattered more than the pain. He drew his arms back, his fingers dug into the blood-soaked earth, and he attempted to pull free of his encumbrance. Inch by inch, gasping for air, he pulled and scooted until he was finally free of the dead men. He looked around the carnage-littered field, searching for the cover of trees. It was too far, especially as the victorious enemy chased and hunted down the wounded to finish them. Adrian was losing too much blood. A strange, pain-free lightness of being overcame him and he recognized it as death. But when he lost consciousness, an angel hovered. *Hope*, she urged.

Hope? Hope for what? He couldn't survive this. He stared at her beautiful face, her flowing dark golden hair. Her sense of otherworldly serenity. "Hope," she whispered, beckoning him.

How strange, he could have sworn he felt warm breath on his face.

"Dinna cry out," a deep voice whispered in his ear. "Wiv go' yeh."

# The Predicament . . .

*Jedburgh, Scotland*
*17 July, 1746*

Sara Anne Aldridge took rigid steps to the closest barn wall, and then sat and leaned against it, her knees too weak to continue standing. Across the badly decaying old structure, the others, all except Ginny, sat in hunched in fear and speaking in whispers. Ginny, Sara Anne's cousin, had just been taken to be interrogated by the Scottish rogues who had abducted them, and who now stood only yards away under a lean-to as dilapidated as the barn.

A tremor went through her body. Sara Anne bent and then hugged her knees knowing she had to think. She would be taken before the tribunal next and what would she tell them? To think, it had only been a matter of weeks since she'd escaped Charles Town. When she thought back on how hard she'd worked at it and the risks she'd taken, this predicament was almost humorous.

Almost.

In a bitter, ironic sort of way.

Charles Town to Middlesbrough, England to wherever they were now in Scotland. Three countries in under two months' time. It was nearly as mind boggling as having been snatched by bandits bent on holding them for ransom.

*Ransom!* If that wasn't ludicrous given what she'd had to go through to get to England.

So, what to do now? Be truthful or lie to protect herself? Was she truly protecting herself if she lied? But if she did not, if she admitted who she was, and *if* the abductors spoke truth about their intentions, she would be sent straight back to Middlesbrough with Ginny where Aaron Waldron would be waiting to lay claim to her.

Her breath caught as she pictured his patrician face with its cold, victorious expression.

*No!*

That was not the path she would take. There had to be another. She squeezed her eyes shut, determined to reason her way beyond the fear and emotional turmoil. She managed to take a deep breath and exhaled slowly. A breeze ruffled her skirt and hair, smelling of rain, but she was hardly aware of it. She was recalling the Shaw's summer social right before her life began unraveling.

# Chapter One

*Charles Town,*
*7 May, 1746*

Sara Anne inspected herself in the full-length looking glass in her room. The pale moss-green gown she wore matched her eyes perfectly. It was one of four new gowns her father had commissioned for her after blustering endlessly over the dreadful state of their finances. She had no idea what he was thinking – ever – but the gown was exquisite.

She lifted her skirt, swept around in a small circle and then curtsied. She began the steps to the minuet with an imaginary partner who was amazingly graceful. Come to think of it, so was she. She stopped and curtsied again. "You hardly seem out of practice at all," she complimented her image, although it wasn't true, She looked out of practice, and she felt it. It had been just over a year since she'd attended a gala. Just over a year since Caroline's death.

*A year.*

But now, because of a date on a calendar, the period of mourning her sister had ended, or so it was said. Now, it was time to put on a good face and attend functions and be displayed like a prize horse at auction. In the back of her mind, Caroline whinnied at the analogy and then laughed. "If only," Sara Anne mouthed.

She pressed a hand to her middle knowing that she would soon be watched and evaluated for her fitness as a wife and mother. Well, not so much fitness as a *mother* with all the loving skills that implied. No, it was more her fitness to produce an heir that would be considered. Charles Town men put a lot of emphasis on carrying on their bloodline. How well would she do?

Sara Anne edged closer to the mirror wishing she could displace herself into the room beyond the wavy, silvered glass. Certainly, it looked identical to the one she stood in, other than being backwards, but it had a vastly different feel to it. Cool and quiet and free of strife.

As a child, she'd conjured a fantasy world around the looking-glass room. Her secret friend, Hope, had lived there and, just as their rooms looked almost the same, so too did Hope look nearly identical to her. The big difference was their eye color. It was how Sara Anne had always known Hope was real. Hope's eyes were brown with gold flecks that looked lit from within. She also had a slight auburn cast to her hair that Sara Anne did not. "Are you still in there, Hope?" she murmured.

She wasn't, of course. Hope hadn't appeared in more years than Sara Anne could count. *She's only an imaginary friend,* Caroline had insisted. Sara Anne had argued fiercely and tearfully that it wasn't true. Alright, yes – she did sometimes conjure her up in her imagination, but not always. Sometimes she could sit in front of the mirror and eventually summon her. *Then you're dreaming her,* Caroline had insisted. It was maddening not being able to convince her sister otherwise.

Alright, yes – she did sometimes fall asleep while in a sort of mirror trance, but she hadn't made Hope up. Or so she'd believed with all her heart. Now, she didn't know. Nor did it matter since Caroline was no longer around to argue the point. That was the saddest thing, really. Caroline had not only been her sister, but her closest friend and confidant. So, now, all their childhood secrets and traumas, all the shared knowledge and experiences were hers alone. It was as if they'd meant nothing, and that realization left emptiness so deep, it ached. It ached all the time.

"My, my, chile," Bet said as she walked in. "You is a sight."

Sara Anne turned to face her with her arms held out for inspection. "It took Sally a quarter of an hour to do the laces."

Bet smiled as she turned Sara Anne back around to face the mirror. "You always look beautiful to me, but that dress. Lawdy!"

"Well, the girl needs to look good if she's to land a rich husband and rescue the family finances."

"I wouldn't be lettin' *them* hear you talk like that."

Sara Anne nearly replied, *Who me? Think you done raised some addlebrained white girl,* but that had been Caroline's comeback to Bet, not hers. And now there was silence because Caroline wasn't there to spout it, and then be chased around the room by Bet, laughing mischievously the whole time, her laughter infecting everyone within earshot.

Sara Anne sucked in her bottom lip and struggled to maintain her composure. It was so foolish how a silly memory could reduce her to tears. She cleared her throat and walked away from the mirror. She was fixed and ready, there was no sense in allowing herself to fall apart. She picked up her gloves and tugged one on. "I suppose I'll go downstairs. Do you know who's going?"

"Miz Dora Leigh," Bet replied regretfully as she fussed with the lay of lace on the neckline.

*Damnation!* It was nearly an hour's ride to the Shaw's plantation, and Sara Anne would rather have endured the company of anyone over her aunt. She started toward the door with the other glove in her hand. "Wish me luck," she said, trying to keep her voice light and free of quiver.

"You know I do."

~~~

Bet watched Sara Anne go with a silent sigh. She understood the pain she felt. How could she not? She'd been there when both Caroline and Sara Anne had come into the world, and she'd watched over both of them all their lives. To have watched Caroline waste away and pass on had been even more agonizing than watching the girls' mama die, torn apart in childbirth. She had truly loved Opal Aldridge.

Caroline had only been four years older than Sara Anne at the time, but she'd become a surrogate mother to her. Sara Anne, not quite three years old at the time of her mama's passing, had no memory of her, so Caroline had been everything to her. Sara Anne still wasn't herself after losing her sister. Her confidence had utterly diminished. She had just been looking into the mirror, but not in appreciation of the beauty others saw when they looked at her, but in search of flaws. That was the influence of her father, Delbert Aldridge, whom nothing was good enough for. "Damn him," Bet mouthed.

7

~~~

Dora's eyes raked Sara Anne over neckline to hemline. "Very nice," she commented, dispassionately. "Seamstress did an excellent job."

"Ought to be an excellent job," Delbert groused. "For what she charges."

Sara Anne could have groaned from the worn-out topic, but she wisely refrained. "What time shall we leave?" Sara Anne asked her aunt.

"Now," Dora replied. "I was only waiting until you removed the stench of that place from your person."

Dora was referring to the Charles Town Home for Orphans that Sara Anne helped at a few times a month. Dora was hoping for some sort of a reaction, for which she had already prepared several clever and cutting lines, but Sara Anne recognized the baiting, and she wasn't about to play that particular scene again.

"Shaw will spend a fortune on this evening," Delbert commented as he poured himself another drink. "To show he can do it, I suppose."

"Why aren't you going?" Sara Anne asked him.

"Have no desire to go. These things are for young people."

She could tell by the slur of his words that he'd been at the drink for some time.

"Go on," he said, dismissing her with a wave of his hand. "Go … represent the family."

Sara Anne dutifully followed her aunt from the house, mulling over the statement. It needled her. Not the word *represent*. No, it was the word family that bothered her. He hardly had the right. Caroline had been her family. Bet was her family. Her father and aunt lived on the fringe of her existence. They were there, they were blood, and yet there was no meaningful connection between them. Was there love between them? Affection? The uncertainty she felt was disturbing.

As always, Sara Anne paid close attention to the steps as she descended them. They were crumbling in places. They needed to be torn out and replaced, and they probably could have been for the amount of money spent on her new gowns. She had pointed that out, assuring her father that she was perfectly willing to either make do with her current wardrobe or forgo the season's festivities altogether. It had been the wrong thing to do, which seemed to be her special talent as of late. Her father had grown red in the face and railed at her. How did she think they would keep up appearances, he'd demanded to know. He'd been so angry that she simply dropped her gaze, kept very still, and waited for the tirade to end.

Lately, he'd been prone to throwing unreasonable tantrums. It had to be his grief over Caroline making him behave in such an erratic way. Emotionally distant and disapproving was characteristic of him, belligerent was not. Still, people grieved in different ways. After the death of her mother, he had forbidden anyone from mentioning her. Caroline explained that it was wildly romantic; that he must have loved her so much that even the mere mention of her name reminded him of the pain. "I think if it hadn't been for us, Papa would have killed himself when mama died," she'd confided.

"But he couldn't leave us?" Sara Anne asked in an awed whisper.

Caroline confirmed it with a wise nod, and they'd decided that day their father was both romantic and noble.

*Go represent the family*, he'd just said. She was the future of the family. She'd been told that, as well. That was why her aunt was here, to escort her to functions in order that she might attract and land a suitable husband. They hadn't said so exactly, but they didn't have to. Since there was no son in the Aldridge family, her husband would inherit Riverbend, the four-hundred-acre Aldridge plantation located nine miles northwest of Charles Town. The plantation, named for its location on the Ashley River, had been built by her great-grandfather nearly sixty years ago in 1690.

There had been more than a thousand acres, but her father had been selling it off for years. To the best of her understanding, they'd suffered financially because of an overabundance of rice and cotton grown in the region. Still, it was vitally important that Riverbend remain in the family and prosper, he declared.

A good marriage contract would have been expected of Caroline, only she had contracted a fever when she was not quite seventeen and never fully recovered from it. Her illness hadn't been a constant factor in their lives. She had been perfectly fine for months at a time, during which time she and Sara Anne had attended balls, picnics, and all sort of functions together. Caroline was so lovely that she'd always had admirers, although her fragile health precluded any from becoming too ardent in their pursuit.

So, it was up to her. Perhaps this would be the evening someone snagged her fancy. She only wished Caroline was there with her.

~~~

Dora Leigh Aldridge Maynard had married well enough due to a sizable dowry, but she had never possessed the beauty, wit or confidence her nieces had been given. They'd received those assets from their mother, Opal, whom Dora had detested with virulence.

Opal was the youngest daughter of a nobleman who'd been granted land from the king himself. She was long dead now, of course, as was Caroline. Only Sara Anne was left, and it was time for her to be of some use to the family.

Beautiful women always had more choices and opportunities than plain women. Dora had recognized early on that her choices would be limited. Herbert Maynard had seemed worthy enough early in their acquaintance and more than a few of her friends and rivals had been desirous of landing him, but appearances had proved deceiving in the cruelest of ways.

He'd been dead and gone for five years now. Dead from heart failure after a long and debilitating illness the physic had never been able to accurately diagnose. Fortunately, widowhood suited her. She now had the freedom to travel and visit as she wished. She wasn't tied to Maynard Hall in Beauford overseeing Herbert's care and meal preparation. She could be here, making sure Sara Anne was placed in a marriage where she would do her family the most good.

~~~

10

When the Shaw home, a grand red-brick mansion with a half dozen twenty-foot white pillars, came into view, Sara Anne tried to conceal her nervousness. Their carriage fell into line, halting several times before it stopped. The door was opened, and Dora was assisted from the carriage first.

Inside, wigged gentlemen and matronly ladies had gathered in the main hall, most of whom turned from their animated conversations to look over each new arrival. Bella Shaw approached. She was past fifty, but still attractive and vibrant. She'd had two sons and three daughters, all married adults now with their own children whom the Shaws doted on. Mrs. Shaw was the very model of a happy, well-satisfied lady, and she was unfailingly gracious.

"Sara Anne, dear, don't you look lovely?" Mrs. Shaw said, reaching for her hands. "It is so good to see you."

"It's lovely to see you, as well. I've been looking forward to this evening."

Mrs. Shaw gave her an understanding smile before turning to her aunt. "Mrs. Maynard," Bella said. "Are you enjoying your stay at Riverbend?"

"It's always pleasant to return for a visit," Dora replied cordially.

"Is your father here?" Bella asked Sara Anne.

"I'm sorry, no. He wasn't feeling quite up to it."

"I'm sorry to hear that. We were looking forward to seeing him. Pass on our regards?"

"Yes, ma'am, I most certainly will."

"If you'd care to freshen up or simply visit, many of the young ladies are congregated upstairs. You know the way."

"Thank you," Sara Anne said, anxious to get away from her aunt. She started toward the staircase but was stopped several times by people inquiring after her father. She'd spotted a clear path when she noticed Lance Harriston making his way toward her. Caroline had always teased about how appropriately he was named. "Anyone who looks like Prince Charming should be named either Prince Charming or Lance. You don't suppose his middle name is Lot, do you?"

"I'm so glad you're here," Lance said when he reached her. "Come and take the air with me?"

"I'd be pleased to," she replied with a smile.

He led her toward one of the many sets of French doors standing wide open. They stopped to retrieve a glass of champagne and taste it, and she looked around the large open room with an appreciation of its elegance. The walls and the base of the high, coffered ceiling were blue, the wood trim stark white. The furniture was new since she'd last been there. There were gleaming, cherry-wood tables and upholstered settees and chairs in tasteful paisley and solids in blues and gold. It made her realize how shabby Riverbend had gotten over the years. Nothing had been updated in decades.

"So, tell me," Lance said discreetly, "Is the venerable Widow Maynard as dreadful as she looks?"

"Only if one multiplies that by ten," she returned under her breath.

He grinned. "That is a shame. Some people mellow with age."

"And some cheeses get stronger and stinkier with age. She's more of that variety."

His eyes twinkled as he chuckled. "Your father didn't come this evening?"

"No. I alone am to represent the family."

"Well, you do it beautifully."

"Thank you, sir."

They walked on, stepping through one of the pairs of open doors onto a wide veranda where her senses were assailed by the scent of magnolia. A vast, green lawn stretched before them. Beyond it were gardens sparkling with fireflies. It looked enchanted.

"I see you still love lighting bugs," he commented with a grin.

"Of course, I do. Look how magical they make it look."

"They only started twinkling when you got here."

She smiled. "If that's true, I'm obliged to them."

They descended the steps and strolled slowly, enjoying the cooler air and the music of a stringed quartet on the veranda. "Did you hear that Miss Turner accepted Travis Strong?" Lance asked.

She had not, but that made three engagements that had been announced in as many weeks. "Elizabeth?"

"No. Maisie. Elizabeth is betrothed to Samuel Hollifield. That happened last winter."

She frowned thoughtfully, wondering if she'd been told that and simply forgotten.

"It's been a difficult year," he commented sympathetically.

Yes, it had.

They segued to a servant circulating with a tray and he exchanged his glass for a fresh one. He lifted his glass to her. "And I'm so glad to have you back amongst us."

"Thank you." She couldn't raise her glass in a toast; it didn't feel right. "I miss her," she admitted.

"I know," he sympathized. "Shall we go see that fountain you like so much?"

She smiled. "The mermaids?"

He nodded. "Indeed." He lifted his glass once more. "To mermaids and fireflies."

This time she touched her glass to his with appreciation that he'd lightened the moment. They walked on, strolling past brilliantly colored azaleas and softly blooming dogwood trees. He led the way toward an arched opening in a tall hedgerow. Once through it, paths diverged, all of them empty of people for the moment. When he stopped and moved in for a kiss, it took her by surprise enough that bracing her hand against his chest was instinct.

"The hedge blocks us from view," he reasoned.

She hesitated, and a second later, his lips were on hers. He pulled her close, trapping her hand between their bodies. Her other hand was also trapped, holding the champagne flute, but she didn't feel truly ensnared. It was, in fact, a wonderful feeling, and there was nothing terribly wrong with kissing him since she probably would marry him. She felt certain he would ask before long and she would say yes. It would be a perfectly pleasant life and they would have lovely children.

He pulled back and his gaze roamed her face, lingering last and longest on her lips. She wondered if he could feel her heartbeat. With a slow smile, he bent his head to kiss her again, but stopped at the sound of footfalls approaching. He managed to take a step away from her before a dark-haired man came into view. Aaron Waldron.

"Harriston," Waldron said with a tip of his head.

"Waldron." Lance returned the gesture.

Aaron's gaze shifted to Sara Anne and intensified. "Miss Aldridge."

"Good evening," she returned.

Aaron Waldron's gaze caressed her neckline before seeking out her eyes. "I hope I'm not intruding."

"Not at all," Lance replied easily. "We're just taking the air."

"It is agreeable," Aaron replied stiffly. "Small wonder so many of us are beginning to spill outside."

He seemed to be implying more than he was actually saying, and Sara Anne felt a pang of puzzlement at the almost proprietary air he exuded when he looked at her. She looked back to the blue eyes of Lance. Behind his straight face, he looked as though he found the exchange humorous. "I believe my favorite fountain is just up ahead," she said.

"The mermaids? I believe you're correct," Lance replied. He looked back to Aaron and gave another tip of his head. "If you'll excuse us," he said, before leading Sara Anne on.

How bizarre. She could have sworn she felt Aaron Waldron's eyes blazing into the back of her, but that made no sense. They had never shared one single moment of closeness, not even of the friendship variety, so was he thinking to look at her in that overly direct manner?

"I do believe Waldron has eyes for you," Lance ventured.

"That is ridiculous," she stated a bit too forcefully.

"Why ridiculous? It's not. In fact, suddenly I'm wondering if I should be worried. After all, the man is considered to be the most desirable bachelor around. And everyone assumes this'll be the season he chooses a bride."

"I have no idea what people assume," she said, highly aware of the hot tingling of her face.

"What I'm wondering is why you would think it's a ridiculous notion," he pushed.

"What I'm wondering if when you became so enamored with tittle-tattle," she rejoined.

"It behooves a gentleman to have ears, just as it does a lady."

The fountain was in front of them. It featured dolphins and mermaids, and Sara Anne studied the serenity on a mermaid's face, determined she would mirror it. "While admittedly out of touch with local gossip, the last I heard, a match was expected between Mr. Waldron and Miss Lucy Young."

"True. That may yet be," he admitted. "After all, what other young lady could possibly have a dowry to match what the Young's can offer?"

As if the Waldrons needed money. "Should we be getting back?"

"So that Mr. Waldron won't be stewing in his jealousy?" he teased.

"I refuse to even dignify that with a response."

"You have to admit, though, that was, *uh,* a rather odd encounter back there."

"It was odd and it made me uncomfortable."

"Good," he exclaimed.

She looked at him sharply. "Good?"

"Yes. He makes me uncomfortable, too. Especially when he looked at you that way."

She blushed and walked on without wait for him to lead the way. When they entered back into the courtyard, Aaron Waldron was standing in a group near the steps leading to the house engaged in conversation, but he was watching her. At first, Sara Anne made a concerted effort not to meet his gaze, but then she decided not to play mouse to his cat. She would not be toyed with. She would look where she chose to look and go where she chose to go, and with whom she chose to go with. She looked at him and he cocked his head just so as if to acknowledge that he'd made her look. How galling!

Some considered him handsome, and he did exude confidence and power and authority that made one take notice, but Sara Anne felt nothing of a romantic inclination for him. She didn't personally think of him as handsome. He was tall with a lean body and square shoulders. His dark eyes were a little too deeply set and his features were a bit too sharp and patrician for her taste. Plus, he exuded that raw, male power that put her on edge. He was not the sort of man she would ever be comfortable with. Not like Lance. Lance exuded charm, not power. And, while he was somewhat self-absorbed, he was immanently capable of kindness and gentleness. He would make a fine husband and father.

~~~

At midnight, Waldron walked back into the ballroom after meandering about the grounds in search of Sara Anne. He hadn't seen her since dinner. He finally spotted her across the crowded dance floor, talking to an older couple of no consequence.

"She is a beauty, isn't she?" someone said.

Aaron turned to Oliver Welborn who had spoken. He looked back to Sara Anne across the dance floor, wondering if he should attempt discretion in his reply. "She is."

Oliver waved a servant over and plucked a glass of wine from the tray. "Want one?" he asked Aaron.

"No."

"You interested, then?" Oliver asked when the servant had walked on.

"Maybe I am."

"Shame about her sister. She was a beauty, too."

"Yes, she was."

"What intrigues you about her?"

Aaron felt no inclination whatsoever to explain his interest in Sara Anne for Welborn's amusement.

"Her flawless skin?" Oliver asked lustily. "Those green eyes? Her golden-brown hair that curls so prettily?"

"Sounds like you've given her some thought, yourself."

"One can think." Oliver's gaze raked over her form. "One can think all sorts of things."

"Keep it to yourself," Aaron warned.

Welborn guffawed. "I thought you were fixed on Miss Young," he said.

"I don't recall being *fixed*."

Oliver shrugged. "My mistake. One would know if one was fixed or not."

"Yes," Aaron said coolly. "One would."

"I doubt there's a decent dowry there," Oliver mused, still watching Sara Anne. "But she's quite something. Her beauty is so natural and clean."

She was something, Aaron agreed. Besides lovely, she always seemed less constrained than other young women. It was said she lacked a proper upbringing, being motherless from an early age and all, but she seemed passionate and freer than most and he found that exciting.

~~~

Dinner had been delicious, but Sara Anne had enjoyed a bit too much champagne to fully appreciate it. Alcohol always diminished her appetite to practically nothing. She made herself eat some of every course because she could not appear to be inebriated or foolish. Her aunt would pass it on to her father, and he would be difficult to live with for weeks.

She was tired and hoping they could take their leave soon. She looked around the ballroom for her aunt, finally spotting her talking with none other than Aaron Waldron. A sense of foreboding seized her, and she clenched her gloved hands, trying to reason away a panic. What would they be talking about? Surely, not her. Not marriage.

Lance returned to her side after being dominated by the Bell sisters the last quarter of an hour. They'd shared three dances but hadn't spoken a great deal since before the six-course meal. "I was hoping they would seat us together at dinner," he complained. "I suspect there was an attempt at matchmaking going on there."

17

Sara Anne's concentration was on the conversation going on across the hall. Although dancers kept getting in her line of sight, she could tell that Aaron was doing most the talking and he seemed serious and businesslike. They were not discussing the weather.

"Sara Anne? Matchmaking at dinner. What do you think?"

"I hadn't considered it," she replied absentmindedly.

Waldron was seated next to Miss Young, of course, and Nat Drummond next to Miss Crofton."

"Those matches do seem inevitable," she replied, hoping it was true.

"They had me pinned in between Miss Bell and Miss Newbury," Lance went on.

"Which Miss Bell?" she asked.

He looked hurt. "You didn't notice?" Before she could respond, he replied, "Hannah." He glanced around before adding, "The lesser of two evils, I suppose."

"Mr. Harriston," she chided playfully. "What a perfectly dreadful thing to say." Not that she didn't agree. She did. Viola Bell could be a nasty piece of work, always gossiping viciously about someone.

"Whom were you seated next to?"

She blinked, feigning hurt feelings. "You didn't notice?"

He grinned. "Could it have been Peter Garrity on one side and old man Pence on the other? I may have noticed."

She looked back to where her aunt and Mr. Waldron were last seen, but they were gone.

"Are you looking for someone?"

"I was curious as to where my aunt was."

"I have no idea, but I am standing right here before you."

She turned her attention to him. "Of course, you are and I'm glad of it."

"Good. Then shall we dance again?"

"I'd like that very much."

# Chapter Two

Sara Anne didn't notice Aaron Waldron anymore that night and he wasn't mentioned on the way home, which was a relief. Furthermore, Dora must have given her a good report of the evening because her father didn't seem any different than usual over the next few days. If anything, he seemed more cheerful than he had in weeks.

A week to the day later, she was on her way out of the house for a late morning ride when she saw Lance emerging from her father's study. Her heart took a wild leap wondering if this was it. Had he come to ask for her hand? She felt almost shy as she bid him good morning.

A flash of something that looked like acute embarrassment crossed his face. "Good morning," he returned.

It wasn't normal for Lance to appear awkward and embarrassed — unless, perhaps, he'd been discussing a tender subject. "What are you doing here?" she asked quietly.

He shook his head and looked away. "I was talking with your father about something. Nothing important."

*Nothing important?* Then either it hadn't been about asking for her hand or it hadn't gone well for some reason. She wanted to know which. "I was just going out for a ride. Would you care to join me?"

He drew in a sharp breath. "I'm sorry. I have some business to attend to. I…I thought you went into town every Thursday to help at the orphan home?"

It sounded almost accusing, and she frowned in confusion. He was already skirting around her to leave, and she turned with him. "Is anything wrong?" she asked, suddenly positive there was.

"Of course not," he answered quickly. "What could be wrong? Will you be going to the Alvey's gala next week?"

"Yes."

"Good. I shall see you there."

He walked on, leaving her stymied. She looked down the hall toward her father's study. She wanted to know what their meeting had been about, but the strangest things could set him off. She'd have to think of a way of drawing him out without being too obvious.

She walked on and made her way to the stable. "Men are strange, aren't they, Ladyfair?" she murmured to her mare as she saddled her. "What business would Lance have with my father, other than me? And why did he seem so strange today?"

She mounted, left the barn at a trot, and then rode hard, past the fields and to the riverbank. Colors and shapes flew past her muted by motion. She always rode past the fields that way. The image of slaves at work stirred bothersome emotions. Likely, her mother had planted something in her mind a long time ago because she hadn't believed in the institution of slavery. Caroline had told her so.

"Mama said it was fine to have servants," Caroline had explained when Sara Anne was young. "As long as they had choice in the matter. That's what Bet is. She's a servant, not a slave."

Truth be told, it was all a little confusing—slaves, servants. She wasn't even sure what those things were. All Sara Anne knew was that Bet took care of them and loved them. "What is a slave?" she finally asked.

"Oh, we buy them," Caroline answered. "They're people who don't have anywhere else to go."

That made sense. "Their houses aren't very big," she observed.

"They don't need much," Caroline replied. "I heard papa say so. I guess they don't have many things. Mama said she wouldn't have any slaves in the house. I don't think she wanted us to have any at all, but papa said how else could we make do? I heard them."

Sara Anne's adult understanding was more accurate, of course, and more conflicted. It was better not to think about it. It wasn't as if she could control anything, anyway. She slowed Ladyfair to a walk, pondering marriage again. She'd thought about it a great deal and she could only think of four men who were truly viable prospects for a husband, Lance, of course, Walter Holland, James Beckwith and Peter Garrity. All were from good families; all had enough wealth to support a family, and all seemed reasonably healthy and Christian. If only she felt something more. It ought to be that one felt something unique and truly special for one's husband.

Walter was mild-mannered and, well, a follower. That was her biggest bone of contention with him. He didn't seem to have any thoughts or ideas of his own. He wasn't unattractive, although he did have a gap between his front teeth that was off-putting.

James might do. He was attractive with dark hair that he parted in the middle and slicked down. He had a tendency to drink too much at social events, which was a singularly unattractive characteristic, but perhaps she could be a good influence in that regard.

Peter had red hair, which didn't really bother her, although she didn't think she would care for having redheaded children. He seemed shy, which wasn't a terrible thing, of course. Truthfully, she didn't really know him well. She also didn't feel an inkling of interest in getting to know him better.

What was it men thought about when they went about selecting a wife, she wondered? Attractiveness and intelligence, surely. Health. Bloodlines.

*Money.*

Her throat suddenly felt tight. She reined in Ladyfair without realizing she was doing it. Perhaps Lance *had* come to discuss the prospect of a proposal and he had expected her to have a larger dowry. That would have explained his strange mood and his embarrassment. How much was her dowry, anyway? If it wasn't much, would that stop him from asking for her hand? The thought made her queasy.

*It wouldn't come down to money. Would it?*

~~~

Dora's jaw went slack as her niece walked into the morning room. "*What* are you wearing?"

Sara Anne's bombazine gown was well worn, but no cause for the horror-stricken look on her aunt's face. She wasn't wearing a burlap sack, for Heaven's sake. "I'm helping clean a dormitory today," she replied. Dora was garbed in a high-necked lavender gown that looked ghastly on her. The color was remarkably wrong for her olive complexion, but did Sara Anne look horror-stricken about that?

"Properly bred young ladies do not go into town on their own," Dora remarked in a scathing tone. She set her teacup down with a loud clank. "And they certainly do not go wearing rags!"

Sara Anne could have groaned at the familiar refrain, but instead she went to pour herself a cup of tea, which is what she had come for in the first place. She added a spoonful of sugar. "It's hardly rags, Aunt Dora," Sara Anne replied calmly as she stirred her tea, enjoying the bell-like sound the spoon made as it touched the side. "I go into town every week by myself."

"I am *painfully* aware of that."

This constant bickering was wearing. "As you know, we don't have servants enough to drive me around and wait on me hand and foot. Caroline and I always—"

"Caroline is dead," Dora snapped.

Sara Anne nearly gasped, stunned by the coldness of the statement. She had been intending to say that she and Caroline had always gotten themselves where they needed to go and had never encountered any problems in doing so, but her aunt's declaration had been spoken with such vitriol that she had no more intention of reassuring her of anything. She set her cup down and walked from the room, sorry for the tears that stung eyes.

She was still seething as she hitched the buggy and loaded up a box of early vegetables and a case of blackberry jam. Why couldn't she just ignore her aunt's criticism? She had certainly heard enough of it over the years. She and Caroline both had, although Caroline had never taken it to heart as much as she had.

"Proper young ladies do not climb trees," Aunt Dora had berated them once.

Later, when they were alone, Caroline had mocked her in a shrill voice. "Proper girls do not climb trees," she had mimicked.

22

"They *sit* and they *sew* until they *want* to climb a tree. But they do not! Which builds character."

"Oh, dear," Sara Anne had played along. "We won't have character?"

"That's right," Caroline had replied sadly. "But we climb trees and swim and ride horses better than a lot of people, which makes us characters." She shrugged. "Almost the same."

Wen Sara Anne was seven, she had been chastised for poor table manners. "Young ladies do not eat in such a slovenly fashion," Dora had declared.

"Who's a young lady?" Caroline had countered, only to be slapped hard and sent from the table for insubordination.

Sara Anne had tried to leave with her, but she had been made to stay. Later, when she was excused, she went upstairs, smuggling a yeast roll for her sister. There was still a mark across Caroline's cheek, and Sara Anne could see the telltale signs of crying on her face. She offered the roll, feeling terrible about what had happened since it had been her fault. Caroline thanked her ever so quietly and then gobbled the roll up like a noisy monster. They'd dissolved into peals of laughter. Caroline got, "Now, *that's* slovenly fashion," out, spewing breadcrumbs.

"The only good thing about Aunt Dora," Caroline had frequently said, "is that she eventually goes away. Never soon enough for us, but eventually. And then we are without her, and that it a wonderful thing."

The Orphan Home was a sore point with Dora, although Sara Anne could not fathom why. Whatever the reason, Sara Anne was not about to let it affect work that had become important to her. She had been helping there for six years now, ever since she was twelve. Caroline had been the one to discover the place, and she'd begun going a few years before allowing Sara Anne to join her. They'd always felt a connection with the orphans because they'd lost their mother. They'd been fortunate enough to have a father and a home and enough to eat and decent clothes to wear. The little ones who came to the Home had nothing.

Being involved with the Home made Sara Anne feel good, and it kept things in perspective. It made her problems and any

pettiness around Riverbend less significant, and it gave her
something worthwhile to do with her time and considerable vigor.
The truth was, she had too much vigor for a woman. Aunt Dora
had always said so. Until Caroline got sick, she'd had too much, as
well.

Sara Anne drove past Mulatto Alley, a street lined with
bordellos, including the infamous Pink House, and imagined what
her aunt would have to say about driving through *that* district. It
was relatively quiet on this late morning, but a few women were
about. They were used to seeing her pass by and didn't pay her a
moment's heed. As girls, she and Caroline had avoided the area,
until it occurred to Caroline how foolish it was to go out of their
way to avoid passing a few painted ladies.

Sara Anne had been fourteen the first time they drove through,
and nervous. She'd kept her eyes straight ahead, especially when
women called out bawdy remarks to them for the fun of it.
Caroline found humor in it and sometimes called back. After a few
trips, Sara Anne relaxed. The painted ladies weren't going to
charge them. They didn't exhibit any real rancor toward them.

One winter morning, as they passed through, Sara Anne
noticed a scantily clad, light-haired girl close to her own age. The
girl had seen her, too, and turned away in embarrassment. She
started to walk away, and Sara Anne noticed her pronounced limp.
The sight had affected her tremendously. "Caroline," she cried,
taking hold of her sister's arm. "She's so young."

"Yes. It's hell to be penniless and female," Caroline had
replied passionately.

"Can't we do something?"

"We can get ourselves to the Home and help. Perhaps we can
help the girls there, so they won't end up here."

"What about her? Caroline! Stop ignoring me!"

Caroline reined in the horse and stopped the wagon in the
middle of the street. "What do you think we can do for her? Do
you think for one minute our father would allow us to bring her
back home?"

"No," Sara Anne admitted.

"No," Caroline repeated. "Besides, she's gone."

"We can find her," Sara Anne pleaded. Her eyes filled.

Caroline gave in with a sigh. "Alright, we'll look. I suppose I don't mind an impossible cause if you don't."

But the girl was not to be found that day. When they did find her, a few weeks later, she pleaded with them to leave her be. It broke Sara Anne's heart. Afterwards, she made a point of not looking at the painted ladies again. Like the slaves working in the field, it was just too painful and degrading, and nothing she thought or felt would change a thing.

# Chapter Three

The ivory silk gown Sara Anne had donned for the coming out of Miss Sylvia Alvey was a favorite but, admittedly, rather too low-cut. That wasn't an altogether bad thing. This evening, she had to be her sweetest, most charming and most appealing self because she was determined to find out the truth about Lance's intentions.

Surely, he wouldn't let the matter of a paltry dowry stop him from asking for her hand if that's what he really wanted. And it was! He'd been flirting and hinting for two years. It's just that, with Caroline's passing, the timing had been wrong.

All week long, she had tried unsuccessfully to broach the subject of suitors and dowries with her father. Talking to him shouldn't have been as difficult as it was, but she feared his volatile temper. Being yelled at put her stomach in knots.

Bet appeared at her door. "They ready to go."

Sara Anne was more than ready. "I'm surprised my father is going."

"Hurry, now," Bet urged. "Won't do to keep 'em waitin'."

"Wish me luck," Sara Anne said as she passed her.

"Beautiful as you are—"

The sweet words kept Sara Anne company as she rode to the Alvey's home across from her father and aunt. When the carriage neared it, Delbert cleared his throat and remarked, "Going to be an announcement this evening."

Sara Anne wondered how he would know such a thing. He wasn't privy to a great deal of local gossip as far as she knew. "Oh?"

"Miss Alvey is becoming betrothed."

"Miss Alvey? Meaning Susan?"

"Yes."

At her sister's coming out? She was surprised, but perhaps it wasn't that strange. "To whom?"

Delbert pursed his lips and threw a quick, sideways glance at his sister before replying. "Harriston."

Sara Anne's mouth went painfully dry. "L-Lance?" she stammered.

"That's right."

"Susan Alvey is marrying Lance?" she repeated, certain she must have misunderstood.

"Yes," Dora spoke up, her tone sharp. "It is a good match, acceptable to both families. He was never a worthy candidate for an Aldridge."

Sara Anne fought for breath and control of her emotions. Thankfully, the elder Aldridges gave her a moment of silence to adjust to the shock, but, rather than acceptance, she felt the beginning of hot, prickly anger. *A worthy candidate for an Aldridge?* Shouldn't she have been one of the judges of that? "Why didn't you tell me?" she asked.

"We're almost there," Delbert warned. "Pull yourself together, girl."

She gaped at him. He had no compassion for her. None whatsoever. In fact, he had no compassion at all. He'd probably ruined everything for her. "Why was Lance at the house last week?"

"To find out if your dowry could match hers," Del replied in a scathing tone.

The words hit their mark and Sara Anne squeezed her eyes shut. It *had* come down to money. He'd rejected her based on her dowry. God help her. They were almost at the Alveys. She could feel the distance closing. Everyone would be watching for her reaction. Lance had been so attentive to her for so long. It only he hadn't been so attentive. "I can't go," she whispered, praying they would not make her.

"Tell her," Dora said.

"Cheer up, Sara Anne," Delbert said smugly. "Just so happens that I know something else." He paused before continuing. "Waldron desires your hand in marriage."

Sara Anne's eyes flew open. She felt dangerously sick to her stomach. Her instinct had been correct. About Aaron, and Lance.

Her throat felt so tight she wasn't even sure she could force enough air through it to make an intelligent argument. "He asked for my hand in marriage and I am just now hearing of it?"

Delbert's eyes narrowed. "If you think I won't slap that look off your face and send you right back home again, you would be mistaken."

She looked out the window to avoid seeing the look of enjoyment on her aunt's face. The Alvey's home, a sprawling Georgian plantation, was in sight, and guests were milling about the front and side yards. How would she face everyone? She looked at her father, careful to guard the expression on her face. "I would like to return home," she pleaded. "Please. This has been a shock and I don't feel well."

"Best thing is to be here," he said. "Stand by Waldron's side. We're not announcing it yet, but—"

*Announcing it!* "Did you—" her breath ran out before she could finish the question and an involuntary shiver shook her. "Have you given your consent?"

Delbert leaned forward squinting so hard, it looked like he was in pain. "Do you know what this marriage could do for us?"

The knowledge that her fate was sealed jarred her at the same moment the carriage came to a halt, jerking them all. Silence filled the cab. "I don't even know him. Why would he want this?"

"I don't know why," Delbert replied, "but I'm not about to look a gift horse in the mouth. A better match could not have been made. You will be taken care of as you never have been. Gowns, jewelry, fineries. You'll want for nothing."

Love, she thought. What about love?

"Everyone will be watching," Dora said coldly. "Present yourself in a way that will bring pride to yourself and to your family. What is done cannot be undone, and you are not a child any longer. Do not act like one."

Sara Anne averted her eyes so the hatred she felt for her aunt wouldn't be revealed. She had often been accused of giving her every emotion away through her expressions. Her father was probably not above striking her, although she doubted that he would do so in public. Still, if he did, it would be her who was utterly humiliated, and she had quite enough humiliation to contend with. The door opened and a welcome breeze rushed in. Tears sprang to Sara Anne's eyes. She really did feel ill.

The elder Aldridges exchanged a look before Dora scooted forward and climbed out. Sara Anne fanned herself frantically, willing the tears away.

"Sara Anne," Delbert said.

Reluctantly, she looked at him, halfway expecting a tender word, but he gestured toward the open door and the footman waiting with an outstretched hand.

The next few minutes lasted a very long time. She felt an unchristian loathing for her father and aunt, but kept pace with them. Since he had not been seen a great deal since Caroline's passing, several people made a point of speaking with him. Their progress was slow, and it was not unexpected for her to remain by his side with a somber expression on her face. She looked the dutiful daughter, although the truth was, she needed time to prepare for what lay ahead.

Lance – engaged. To someone else. Her Lance. Perhaps her father was wrong. And Aaron Waldron claiming he wanted to marry her? It was preposterous. Did no one see how preposterous it was?

Sara Anne's knees had felt weak before she alighted from the carriage, and the weakness spread as she began to sense people's eyes on her. She tried to convince herself it was merely her imagination playing tricks on her, but guests yanking their gaze away after being caught staring convinced her otherwise. She was obviously the object of attention. Was she the object of pity and ridicule as well?

Everything had a slanted, unreal quality to it, and she found herself noticing the oddest of details; the way the breeze softened the appearance of everything. The way a person's expression altered when the person to whom they were speaking glanced away. A butterfly fluttered in front of a woman with the tallest pompadour Sara Anne had ever seen and the woman attempted to chase it away with her fan.

Sara Anne made an effort to appear normal, but she was anything but. She dreaded seeing Lance, and yet she found herself looking for him. *Are you going to the Alveys?* he'd asked. Why hadn't he said he was betrothed?

At what seemed an appropriate juncture, she broke away from her father and the group that surrounded him and made her way toward the house in hopes of finding some privacy to collect her thoughts and her composure.

"Sara Anne Aldridge," Viola Bell called from the center of a group.

It was too late to avoid them now. She had carelessly ventured too close, and the circle had opened to her. She attempted a smile. "Good evening, Viola."

"Don't you look lovely?" Viola said, raking Sara Anne up and down with her gaze. "We aren't trying to impress someone, are we?" she asked with barely concealed amusement.

"Not at all," Sara Anne replied, innocently. "But thank you."

Viola's expression darkened.

A quick flick of a fan drew Sara Anne's attention to a friendlier member of the group, Judith Pitt. Sara Anne could tell by Judith's crinkled eyes that she was smiling behind her fan. "That is a lovely fan," Sara Anne commented. It was hand painted to match her gown.

Judith pulled it away from her face. She didn't hide her smile because now there was an appropriate reason for it. "Thank you," she replied as she stepped closer to Sara Anne.

"I admire a talent for painting," Sara Anne said to her. "I don't possess one myself."

Judith took her arm and they strolled away from the rest of the group. "You have other talents and wit and beauty."

Judith's kindness was harder to endure than Viola's viciousness, and Sara Anne felt a lump form in her throat.

"It is such a fine evening," Judith said, looking off. "I'm grateful for the breeze." She leaned in closer and spoke *sotto voce*. "I declare, some gentlemen should endeavor to bathe more frequently."

Sara Anne had often wished so, herself.

"I am also grateful for the reprieve you offered," Judith continued. "Thomas was going on and on about some bad turn in his business affairs. It's so tasteless to discuss business in front of ladies. Don't you think?"

"It's thought to be," Sara Anne replied carefully. She didn't find it offensive in the least, but some did.

"What bothered me more was the way a few of the others seem to take delight in the misfortunes he was speaking of." The two of them came to a stop under a towering cypress tree. "It seems wretched when one person derives pleasure from another's failure. I kept wishing he would stop talking." Judith smiled in a bemused fashion. "I really don't know why I led you off. That was so silly of me. Would you care to join us?"

"Thank you, but I think I'll go inside for a bit."

"Perhaps later, then." Judith started back to the group, but turned back. "You really do look lovely."

"Thank you." Sara Anne watched her go, realizing that Judith had only strolled with her those fifteen yards or so to ease her away from the acid-tongues in the group.

Beyond Judith, one of the male members of the group, Will Forrester, caught her eye, bowed to her and then blushed beet-red. She nodded politely at him, and then started off hurriedly before he could make a move to join her. Unfortunately, her foot caught on a raised root of the tree, and she tripped and stumbled, ending in the outstretched arms of Aaron Waldron. Despite the horror of the moment and the color that flooded her face, a terrible, uncontrollable bout of laughter burst from her. As if she hadn't have been the object of ridicule before!

Aaron was holding on to her arms and smiling – no, laughing, as if he were part of a private joke. He had prevented her from falling on her face and now he was attempting to make her blunder less humiliating. That filtered through her consciousness and sobered her with both surprise and gratitude. She dabbed at the corners of her eyes, which were damp from either her outburst or her humiliation.

"Are you alright?" he asked, watching her carefully.

She was unable to look into his face. "You rescued me and I thank you."

"It was my pleasure. But you missed a spot." He withdrew a handkerchief from his pocket and touched a spot near her right eye.

It was a highly personal gesture, and she felt the shock of it reverberate through her body. She watched him as he drew back and glanced around casually. She couldn't help herself; she did the same. Just as she suspected, they were being gawked at with unabashed curiosity and a mixture of other things.

Judith looked pleased.

Will looked distraught,

Viola Bell and Mabel Riggs were both glaring at her as if they hated the very air she breathed.

"Have to watch the knees," Aaron said.

"Excuse me?" she stammered. How could he possibly know how weak her knees were?

"The Cypress knees," he explained with an amused look on his face.

The raised roots. She knew to be careful of them. She hadn't been thinking.

"Perhaps you should take hold of my arm," he offered, extending it.

She accepted and they moved toward the house. Now that the humiliating moment was over, she felt oddly drained.

"You've heard about Harriston?" Aaron said conversationally, without looking at her.

His directness took her by surprise. "Yes."

"And my proposal?"

The front door was standing open and the covered porch and the foyer beyond looked filled with people. This did not seem the right time or place for this discussion. "I was told everything as we arrived here this evening."

He stopped and turned to her with piercing dark eyes as if searching for her reaction.

"I haven't had a moment to myself to think about it," Sara Anne admitted.

Aaron leaned in slightly. "Harriston approaches without his bride-to-be." He gave a discreet movement of his head to indicate that Lance was approaching from their left. "I have the distinct impression he's making for us." He paused. "For you, that is."

She wasn't ready to see Lance. Not now. Not in front of all these people.

"You have the most beautiful eyes I've ever seen," Aaron observed. "They're such an unusual shade of green."

The compliment came out of nowhere and she blushed.

"But I stray from the point. Do you wish to talk to Harriston, or walk?"

She swallowed. "Walk. Please."

He smiled and guided her in the opposite direction of Lance and the house.

~~~

Several yards away, Lance stopped. His eyes narrowed at Waldron's back, knowing the son of a bitch had finagled that. He'd finagled everything. Lance wasn't going to lower himself and chase after them so he changed course and was admitted into the group of friends and acquaintances Sara Anne had encountered only minutes before. Viola Bell grabbed his sleeve. "Are they—"

It took restraint not to shake her hand off him. "He has asked for her hand," Lance replied bitterly.

The combined gasp from members of the circle drew stares from everyone in the vicinity. Viola's looked horrified. Her mouth moved, but no sound came out. Mabel burst into tears and a few other young ladies bit their lips to avoid doing the same thing.

~~~

Aaron navigated a path toward giant oaks in the side yard. It was an appealing spot because no one was within listening range. He waved over a servant with a tray of colorful drinks and took two. Handing her one, he said, "Let us discuss the future, Miss Aldridge."

"Why? If my input doesn't make a difference?" Her tone wasn't angry as much as resigned.

33

"Who says it doesn't?"

The words shocked her. They walked on, stopping in front of a bench encircling the massive trunk of an ancient tree. "Does it?" she asked, hardly daring to hope.

"Of course."

He seemed so sincere; relief flooded through her. She sat and took a sip of the rum punch. "We don't even know one another," she stammered.

"An odd comment. What don't you know about me? Charles Town isn't that large of a place."

"I don't know your thoughts on religion or politics," she began.

"I'm Episcopal, like you, as you well know since we've attended the same church all our lives."

"We rarely attend," she rejoined. Her family had never attended more than twice a year that she recalled.

"And politics?" he said as he sat beside her. "Women should never attempt to understand politics."

She wasn't about to argue the point because, like most men, he would never concede any ground on the matter. "I don't know what you enjoy doing in your leisure time."

"Oh, I'd wager you've heard stories."

A breeze blew her hair back and a loose curl tickled her neck. He reached out and touched it. It was another intimate gesture that shook her composure. "I've heard you enjoy gambling."

"Indeed, I do. I relish a challenge and I play to win."

His words had an edge that made her wonder at his meaning.

"What else do you know?" he asked.

"Your family raises horses—"

"Thoroughbreds," he corrected.

"And you're involved in that."

"I am. I am involved in all aspects of our several businesses. You see? You know quite a bit about me. Now, my turn. You're beautiful, goes without saying. Intelligent, which I personally value. Passionate." Her green eyes widened, and he smiled. "I'm guessing at that, of course, but I think I am correct." He looked away. "I think you might enjoy getting *involved*, as you say, with the horses." He cocked his head at her, as if to gage her reaction.

After a terrible half hour, it wasn't an unpleasant discussion. "I like horses. Things are simple with them."

"I agree. Take care of them and they're loyal to you. Loyalty is important to me."

"I imagine it is to everyone," she replied uncertainly.

"It's more important to some than others."

He looked out over the lawn, and it struck her how utterly sure of himself he was. He wasn't the type to change his mind easily or admit if he was wrong. Was he the curious sort? Was he curious about her? Was he fundamentally a good man? She didn't truly know, but she suspected he was not. She hoped she was wrong about that. He had said she had a choice regarding the marriage, so perhaps she was misjudging him.

He looked at her and smiled. "What are you thinking?"

"I was wondering who you are, deep down."

"I'm one of the privileged, and I don't apologize for it."

The response was off-putting, even somewhat offensive.

"Nor should you," he added. He finished "Would you care for another?"

She'd barely touched hers, which he could plainly see. "No, thank you."

A bell clanged, signaling dinner was about to be served, and Aaron stood. "We're seated together at dinner, as we will be from here on." His confidence was total, and it gave her a strange sensation, part dread and part thrill. She stood, he offered his arm, and so she also stood and they started inside.

As he escorted her in, she avoided her father's watchful gaze. She avoided everyone's. Caroline had always poked fun at how transparent her feelings were – but many were no less obvious. She saw envy in the gaze of some, curiosity in others, bewilderment in a few – and she was desperately trying not to notice. She flatly refused to look in Lance's direction.

As he'd forecasted, Aaron was seated next to her and was appropriately solicitous, but without seeming deeply caring. It was baffling. He wasn't in love with her, so why did he want to marry her?

The first course was split pea soup. It was offered alongside seared oysters and delicate sauteed mushrooms on silver skewers. Served with a Virginia white. As far as Sara Anne was concerned, they could have stopped there. The second course, served with Madeira, was a rich fricassee. A choice of lamb or venison was the third course, followed by desserts and either sweet wine or port.

"Our chefs are better," Aaron said discreetly.

Did he truly believe she was going to marry him? Surely, this was a bad dream. She didn't know him any more than he knew her. An engagement between them made no sense, but she couldn't voice that here and now. But why in the world would he have thought he wanted to marry her?

Dinner finally ended and the gentlemen were directed to the smoking rooms, the ladies to the salon for the hour before the ball began. Before he left her, Aaron bent to kiss her hand. She didn't know what to say, but it didn't seem to bother him. Had he even noticed?

She slipped upstairs to one of the rooms delegated for the ladies' use. Pressing her hands to her stomach, she breathed deeply. Unfortunately, she kept recalling snatches of things. People glancing at her, sizing her up, gossiping. *Mrs. Aaron Waldron.* Was that who she was to be? It didn't feel true.

She heard the room fill up next to her. Animated female voices talking and laughing, eager for the night ahead. She was as alone as she'd ever been. She went to a chair and sat. W*hat should I do?* She asked Caroline in her mind.

*Stay calm. Get through the night. What else can you do?*

"True," she whispered.

Minutes ticked by until strains of music were heard from below. An exodus began from other rooms along with peals of laughter and bits of conversation which held no meaning to her. What she wouldn't have given to be at home, dressed in her nightclothes, facing her sister. Together, they would have found a way out of this preposterous situation. But she was alone.

She stood with a sigh, imagining the moment the announcement would come about the engagement of Lance and Susan. She had to appear impassive. She would give nothing away. Show no emotion. None.

Aaron waited for her at the base of the stairs. He smiled and offered his arm. "I feel like dancing," he said.

She smiled as agreeably as she could. Keeping her gaze slightly down to avoid eye contact, she stayed by Aaron's side. It was cowardly, but she wasn't ready to face people or answer questions. Not when she still had so many herself. She didn't feel like herself, but that realization actually helped. She didn't have to be herself. This evening was about playacting. She would play the role of the oh-so-fortunate future Mrs. Aaron Waldron, even though that announcement was not being made yet. Thank Heaven! Of course, it didn't need to. Word had spread like wildfire.

It was merely playacting.

They joined in a contredance, danced the minute and then the allemande. It was great fun. It was playacting. She only paid attention to Aaron, her fellow actor. Even in the line dances, she paid little attention to the couple they danced with. She and Aaron were characters in a charade, each playing a part. Why, she did not know. Why was he engaging in this?

The announcement of the engagement of Susan Doreen Alvey to Lance Harriston came an hour later. The father of bride was pleased to announce it. He said so and he looked it. There was a lifting of glasses and a toast to the happy couple. Sara Anne lifted hers and avoided looking at anyone. If tears had sprung to her eyes, they would stay there. Damned if they wouldn't stay there. Not only that, but they would be gone – either returned to their source or blinked and discreetly wiped away by the time she looked at Aaron again.

Play. Acting.


A stroll around the grounds, several superficial conversations, three glasses of wine, and four dances later, a few guests began to leave. Her father had been drinking steadily and should have left some time ago. Sara Anne was more than ready. "If you'll excuse me a moment," she said to Aaron.

"I'll avail myself of the facilities, as well. I'll meet you back here."

"We should start home," she said apologetically. She sent a sideways glance at her father, and Aaron did same.

"Yes," he agreed with a slight curl to his lip. "I'll say something to them."

She turned to go upstairs to one of the rooms for ladies use. She found a room and used the chamber pot behind a privacy screen. On the way out, she glanced at herself in a mirror and was surprised to see how unruffled she appeared. How facades could and, in this case, deceive. Thank Heaven, the night was nearly over.

As she walked toward the staircase, Lance emerged from a darkened doorway. She stopped abruptly.

"You haven't been alone all evening," Lance complained.

She was momentarily overwhelmed by a feeling of betrayal, but as he took another step closer and into the flickering light of a sconce, the sadness and resignation in his eyes dissipated her hurt feelings. The truth, she suddenly realized, was that she'd been embarrassed and bewildered by his engagement, but only her expectations had been shattered, not her heart. He had never possessed that because she had never given it to him.

"Strange," he uttered. "Both of us engaged to other people. I had thought it would be to one other."

"So had I," she admitted.

"Ah, but you were spoken for," he said, bitterly. "As you've undoubtedly discovered for yourself."

The words surprised her, and her gaze roamed his face, searching for evidence of what he was holding back, that he'd cared more about her dowry than her person, but she didn't see any. No, it was her father who had been dishonest. It was her father who had seen an opportunity for financial advancement and was eager to leap at it. Unfortunately, as her aunt had stated, nothing that was done could be undone, and she was not a child any longer. "Yes. I learned it only a minute or so after learning of your engagement. Just before we arrived this evening. It was all quite … shocking."

"It was for me, as well. You saw me afterwards. I must have been pale as a ghost."

Confirmation. "You were not yourself," she replied carefully. She lowered her head, wanting to cry but refusing to give in to it. It was time to leave and she so wanted to go. This was senseless torture. She looked up at him with a wan smile. "Fortunately, you had Miss Alvey to turn to. "

"Indeed. All nicely arranged for me," he said bitterly. "Just as your future is arranged for you."

She was surprised and curious, but she heard ladies talking softly behind her from one of the rooms. "You should go. People shouldn't see us alone."

"I suppose you're right if … there's no changing things?"

He looked so hopeful than a painful a lump formed in her throat. "You know there's not," she whispered.

He nodded slowly and attempted a smile. "Then I suppose I'd best go find my bride-to-be." He stepped forward and pressed a soft kiss on her cheek. "Goodbye, Sara Anne."

Tears sprang to her eyes, and she realized it hadn't been merely her plans and expectations shattered, but the last vestige of her childhood naivety. How absurd that she and Caroline had imagined marrying a man they loved. They should have been forced to wear a sign reading 'available to the highest bidder.' Then it would have been clear to them that they were property, for sale to the highest bidder.

"We would have had a nice life together," he said quietly.

Before she could respond, he turned and practically careened into Aaron. It was likely the men glared at one another, but neither of them spoke. Lance stepped aside and walked on stiffly. Sara Anne's breath caught at the barely contained anger on Aaron's face as he stepped directly in front of her. "That was the last time anything remotely like that will occur," he uttered in a low voice.

She hated herself for trembling in the face of his anger. "He was saying goodbye," she replied, attempting to keep her voice calm and even.

"I saw the way he was saying goodbye, with his face pressed to yours!"

He grabbed hold of her arm and yanked her down the hall. His grip hurt. "Is sneaking around and eavesdropping a special talent of yours, Mr. Waldron?"

"Oh, call me Aaron, my darling. You're going to be my wife soon enough."

Panic welled inside of her, and she attempted to stop. "You said I had a choice."

"You do. Which Sunday would you prefer? If you wish, take a few days to think it over."

"Aaron, please. You are overreacting—"

"Your father and aunt are waiting," he interrupted.

"—to an insignificant moment you misunderstood."

They reached the stairwell and he stopped. "Take hold of my arm," he said, barely moving his mouth, "and do not let go until I give you permission."

It was humiliating, but she did it. By the time they reached the front hall, the playacting had begun again. People watched from all directions. The waiting footman opened the door to the carriage as they approached.

Aaron leaned in to speak to the occupants. "Apologies for keeping you waiting."

Del Aldridge waved his hand. "Zalright."

Aaron assisted Sara Anne in. "I'll be over tomorrow. Three o'clock. We'll go for a ride."

It was more a command than an invitation and she bristled, but refrained from remarking. She simply nodded once.

"Then you'll stay to supper," Delbert offered.

"Perhaps I will." His eyes flashed at Sara Anne. "After all, we have arrangements to make." He closed the door.

Sara Anne sat staring straight ahead without expression. She felt sick. She felt like she couldn't breathe deeply enough. It was a relief to hear the knock on the carriage and to have the carriage start in motion.

Delbert slurred, "Naughsobad, eh?"

Sara Anne trembled with rage.

~~~

Aaron downed another glass of brandy and slammed the glass down on the table. He could still picture her the moment she knew she'd been caught with Harriston. His eyes narrowed as he considered withdrawing his offer for her. The problem with that was he *wanted* her. She was beautiful, capable of humor, intelligent conversation and, best of all, passion. Furthermore, she was descended from nobility.

Her mother's father was Lord Leopold Shelly, an earl and one of the Lords Proprietors who King Charles II granted land to in 1663. Why her mother had chosen an oaf like Aldridge was beyond him, but Sara Anne transcended the Aldridge connection. She had too much spirit, which would require some breaking, but he could handle that. In fact, he would enjoy handling that.

Oh, yes. He wanted her and he would have her. If Harriston came near her again, he would have the man's throat torn out.

# Chapter Four

The sky, the next afternoon, was filled with fast-moving, heavy-looking blue-gray clouds. Rather like her mood, Sara Anne thought wryly. She paced the floor of her room, replaying the previous day's events over in her mind and her conclusion was always the same. Aaron Waldron was a tyrant. Unconsciously, she rubbed her arm where he'd bruised it.

Somehow, she needed to convince him that he didn't wish to marry her, because it didn't matter a whit what she wanted. She needed time. Which meant she had to ease his mind regarding any concern he had over Lance or over anything else for that matter. If she could do that, he'd grant her time, which she would use to change his mind about wanting to marry her at all. Perhaps it was possible that, given time, she wouldn't mind marrying him. Perhaps he wasn't as arrogant and bad-tempered as he seemed, but she didn't think that would prove to be the case.

By three fifteen, he still hadn't shown, and she found herself on pins and needles and expending entirely too much effort pretending that she wasn't. She decided to go riding without him, but as she stepped out the front door, he came striding toward her having just arrived. "You're late," she said lightly, forcing herself to don a pleasant, unperturbed expression.

"You will never tell me that I'm late or act impatient," he stated coolly. "Understood?"

She'd stiffened. He *was* every bit as insufferable as she had supposed him and more.

He slapped an envelope in the open palm of his free hand. "I'm going in to speak with your father and then we'll go."

Her eyes dropped to the envelope with a sense of dread. The writing on it was distinctive and loopy. Arrogant looking.

"I won't be long. Wait for me here."

42

The *nerve* of him, dictating what she was going to do and when she was going to do it. "I'll be in the stable," she replied, walking on before he had a chance to respond.

~~~

The tension in her body as she walked away was satisfying. He was making his position known and he would continue to do so. She'd learn. Besides, she was lovely when she was angry. Her teal blue riding habit was not new, but it fit her form well, and it was a nice form.

He found Aldridge in his study, bent over a ledger with a scowl on his face. He knocked and the man looked up, thoroughly annoyed until he saw it was him. "Ah, Waldron, come in. Have a seat."

Aaron walked in and handed the older man the envelope. "The official proposal."

Aldridge took it, his eyes gleaming.

"I'll need it signed by this evening if you find it acceptable," Aaron announced. "I'd like to set a wedding date as soon as possible."

"Naturally. Yes, I'll have it back to you. I feel certain it's all perfectly acceptable."

"I'm quite certain it is." Aaron turned and left, appraising the place as he went. This estate, once revamped, would be perfectly acceptable for one of the younger sons he would have. He enjoyed the trek down to the stable and entered to see Sara Anne leading a spirited stallion toward him. "Did you choose one for racing?" he asked.

"Is that a challenge?"

He grinned as he walked over to the whips and crops hanging on the wall. One was particularly vicious looking, with bits of bone sewn into the braided lashes. He ran his finger down it, wondering how it was made, and then selected a short leather crop and handed it to her. "Here you go."

Sara Anne took it with a sweet smile and then hung it back from the very place it had come from. "I don't use them," she explained before she continued out.

He lingered behind for a moment, a slight smile playing on his lips as he eyed her backside. *Oh, but I do.*

~~~

They rode hard for half an hour before they dismounted, tethered the horses, and walked along the riverbank. The sky was rumbling and spitting rain, but it was refreshing.

"Did you choose a date for our nuptials?" he asked.

"I wanted to speak with you about that, because, well, I need time to—"

"One of the Sunday afternoons in June," he interrupted.

"That is not enough time! It's already mid-May."

"Choose the last Sunday in June, if you wish. That's more than a month away. Plenty of time."

"I've always had my heart set on an autumn wedding," she said, switching approaches.

He leaned close and, for a minute, she thought he was going to kiss her. "June," he whispered.

"But I don't have a gown or—"

"June," he repeated stubbornly.

She frowned. Charm was obviously not going to work. "Why are you forcing me to do this?"

"It's simple really. I want you as my wife."

"Does it not matter what I want?"

"Not at this moment."

Her jaw dropped in astonishment, and he threw his head back and laughed. She felt utter fury.

He walked closer. "I apologize. It was … your expression that amused me. What I meant to say, was that marriage is frightening to a young woman, but I know you'll be happy once you adjust. We'll both be happy."

"You don't know me," she beseeched. "You don't know my mind or my heart. Truthfully, and I don't mean to be hurtful or to offend, but I think you are vain and arrogant, and I do not anticipate ever being happy with you."

Aaron blatantly looked her over, his dark eyes lingering last and longest on her shoulders and chest. "Well, you're finally breathing hard. The ride didn't much wind you, but talking back to your future husband does."

He looked calm, but his eyes flashed with a frightening intensity that did something strange to her stomach.

"As far as being happy is concerned," he continued, "that is up to you. But I'm going to be happy. You are going to make me very happy."

She was baffled. Had that been a compliment or a threat?

He walked on a few steps. "You'll come home with me now. My family wishes to spend some time with you, and you'll want to see your new home. We'll stop and inform your father."

"You might want to keep in mind that I am not your possession quite yet." He turned back to her slowly and she felt her heart hammering, the way it did when her father was brewing up one of his tempers. She tried to brace for it.

Surprisingly, though, his expression was conciliatory. "Marrying me is not exactly like facing a hanging, is it?"

"I've never actually been threatened with hanging."

He grinned. "Allow me to try this *invitation* one more time. If it please you, my dearest fiancée, I would very much like for you to join me for a few days at my home, which will soon be your home as well. My mother and father wish to spend some time with their future daughter-in-law."

She was suddenly curious. "What did they think of your wanting to marry me?"

"Did you think I would have asked for your hand if they did not approve?"

Grudgingly, she began walking and they fell into step. "You're saying they approve?"

"Why wouldn't they? Because of your father? It's you that I will wed, Sara Anne, not your father. And you are beautiful and of noble bloodline."

Was he mocking her?

He reached out and stopped her. "What part of that statement makes you frown so? There can be no question of your beauty to anyone with eyes, and you surely know of your mother's family?"

She lifted one shoulder. "Of course, I do. They're English."

"We're all English."

"We are *not* all English."

"Most of us. Certainly, all of us who have been here for a few generations."

It was an absurd contention. Charles Town had immigrants from France, Ireland, Scotland, Germany, the Netherlands, even the West Indies, but arguing held little appeal.

"Tell me about them," he asked.

"My mother's family?"

He nodded.

"My uncle, my mother's brother, and his wife and daughter live in northeast England."

"Are you close to them?"

"As close as one can be with an ocean between us. My cousin, Genevieve, and I write. We're nearly the same age. Caroline and I went for a visit once when I was twelve. My aunt and uncle are wonderful. They're all wonderful. I love them dearly."

"Your uncle is a Shelly, then."

She was surprised he knew this. "Yes."

"You do know that your grandfather was one of the original Lords Proprietors here. The king himself granted him land. My great-uncle was, as well."

Why had she never been told that? "My father doesn't discuss my mother. Or her family."

"Oh?"

"He … was so grief-stricken when she died." The explanation felt hollow and the reasoning she'd relied on for so long seemed lacking. It wasn't sadness her father felt for her mother, it was bitterness, perhaps even hatred. She'd seen it when the mere mention of her mother or the Shelly family came up. It made no sense that she knew of. Then again, she had no memory of her mother.

Aaron lifted her hand to his mouth and kissed it. "The last Sunday in June?"

She hesitated. "If it has to be June—"

"It does," he stated firmly.

"Then, yes, the last Sunday."

"It occurs to me that I've never kissed you."

There wasn't enough time to think or react before he leaned in, taking hold of the sides of her face. He kissed her lips softly, almost playfully, and it was surprisingly sweet. Then he pulled her closer and forced his tongue into her mouth. He plunged in as if exploring every depth and contour. She couldn't think. Her pulse was beating in an unnatural rhythm and her breath became strangled. Aaron had her pressed so tightly against himself that she could *feel* his arousal. His tongue was relentless, his hands caressed her buttocks, and powerful sensations pulsed through her faster than she could make sense of them. She twisted and pushed against him with all her might, feeling conflicted and ashamed of the feelings raging through her. He released her, and she took a few steps away. Her face was afire.

He came up behind her. "Never be embarrassed about sharing passion." He kissed the side of her neck and she shivered with pleasure at the feeling. "With me, that is." He bit her earlobe, playfully.

The nip took her by surprise more than it hurt. She tried to pull away and she would have succeeded had he not foreseen her reaction and held her firmly in place. "If you ever entertain a dalliance with anyone else, I will kill him and make you pay in ways you cannot even imagine."

He released his hold so suddenly, she nearly stumbled forward. She turned toward him, astounded they had gone from an incredibly sensual moment, unlike anything she had ever experienced, to an ugly one. To her astonishment, she found him smiling. He had offended utterly—and he was smiling. Had it been a jest of some sort?

"Come," he said, taking her hand and leading her onward.

It was bewildering. He was bewildering.

~~~

The grounds of the Waldron estate were manicured, and the home was an imposing three-story Georgian-Palladian design with an extended front porch and veranda. Sara Anne felt overwhelmed at the perfection of the place as she neared the front doors at Aaron's side.

In the grand front hall, marble sculptures stood in a semi-circle around the room, and the servants stood nearly as posed and unnatural.

"Where's my father?" Aaron asked one of them.

"I believe he is in his study, sir," a male servant replied.

"Tell him we'll be in the salon. And inform my mother, as well."

"Yes, sir."

Aaron made a gesture onward to Sara Anne and then led her onward. She had always found Aaron's parents, Robert and Nadine Waldron, to be rather cold and intimidating. Nadine was a dark-haired beauty with regal bearing. She was the silent, calculating sort. Everything she uttered seemed well calculated before the first syllable left her lips. Robert, on the other hand, exuded power and authority.

Aaron and Sara Anne entered the salon. "Bring lemonade," Aaron ordered. "Make yourself comfortable, my dear," he said to her. "I'll show you around more after we see my parents."

How was it possible this had come to pass so quickly? She was not prepared to become Mrs. Aaron Waldron. The thought of it made her stomach ache.

"Your mother has gone out," Robert Waldron announced from the door. "But I'm delighted to receive you, my dear." He started toward her.

*My dear* sounded as unnatural from him as it did from Aaron. She was vaguely surprised when he kissed her hand.

"We were surprised by my son's rather abrupt announcement, but ... not displeased." Robert's lips smiled, but his eyes were cold.

"Thank you," she replied. *You were not the only one surprised*, she thought. *And displeased. In fact, sickened by the thought.*

"Tomorrow evening we'll have a small gathering in your honor." His gaze flicked over her. "Have you something appropriate to wear?"

Her lips parted in surprise and her cheeks flamed. The question was rude beyond belief. She tried not to appear offended, which took a surprising amount of effort. "Of course."

"I thought we might go into town tomorrow and buy you something new," Aaron spoke up. "I've been looking forward to it, I've never been excruciatingly bored while waiting for my fiancée to get through a fitting."

"And you're looking forward to that?" Robert asked, dryly, with a lift of one bushy eyebrow. He walked over and sat.

Aaron's dark eyes sparkled mischievously, and Sara Anne felt a flush of surprise and appreciation. It felt as though he had declared himself her ally. How baffling. He'd obviously chosen her despite his parents' wishes. Why? Did he truly feel so much for her? How was that possible when they scarcely knew one another?

The red and gold bedchamber she was shown to was exceedingly formal and somewhat garish. She strolled around it, rubbing her arms and feeling utterly displaced. She'd never considered her family to be anything but fortunate, but the vast wealth of the Waldrons was foreign to her. The Youngs were of equal social stature with the Waldrons and Lucy and Aaron had seemed destined to become betrothed. What had altered that?

What sort of life would she have in such a stuffy, pompous environment? Of course, she had endured her father and aunt, and human beings didn't come any more joyless than they were. But perhaps it was time to stop complaining and begin concentrating on making the best of a situation. Aaron obviously had strong feelings for her. Was it not possible that she could grow to care about him, even to love him in time?

~~~

They were driven to town late the next morning in the most luxurious carriage Sara Anne had ever been in. "Pale pink," Aaron said.

She looked at him. "I beg your pardon?"

"You'd look splendid in a gown of pale pink. Or a medium shade of blue. Or bright blue, like the noonday sky." A slow smile spread over his face. "You're going to cost me a fortune. I won't be able to resist you in any color."

She was pleased and flattered. "That's kind of you to say."

His smile dimmed. "I doubt you'll think of me as kind for long."

Her stomach tightened. He was light one moment, brooding and disagreeable the next.

He looked out the carriage window. "Married people rarely appreciate one another like they should."

His parents *were* strange with one another. They were so formal. His mother had scarcely looked at her, much less spoken the previous evening. "Perhaps we can do better," she suggested.

He made a non-committal grunt.

She chewed on her bottom lip a moment before getting the nerve to ask. "May I ask you something that might be considered indelicate?"

He looked at her, his eyes suddenly dancing. "The more indelicate, the better."

"Why did you not ask for Miss Young's hand in marriage?"

The humor drained from his face. "Why me?" he asked, drolly. "Is that what you're wondering?"

She hesitated, disturbed by his expression and tone of voice. "Yes."

"The truth?"

"Of course."

"Lucy and a few others I've considered," he began. He paused to best frame his answer. "Their entire lives have been spent in preparation for marriage and to assume control of the social workings of a great house."

She cocked her head, wondering why that would not be a desirable thing.

"It bores me," he concluded. "Leaves too little challenge."

She blinked in surprise. "I, on the other hand, present a challenge?"

He smiled like a wolf. "You, I will mold and make, train and teach to be exactly what I want."

She was speechless. And insulted. And alarmed.

50

"Ah, that spirit of yours," he remarked, delighted. "That's what most attracts me. However, there is a time to display it and a time to stifle it."

She exhaled forcefully. He was insufferable!

"You will learn to be one person when we're in public or when I'm in a foul mood, and another when we're alone—"

"And not in a foul mood," she finished his statement for him, beginning to tremble with anger.

"Exactly."

She didn't trust herself to reply and she couldn't bear looking at his smug expression for one second longer. She turned her head and stared out the window. This arrangement would never work. She would never feel anything but off balance and miserable with him.

"And a wig," Aaron said abruptly. "We shall purchase you a fine wig for this evening."

"I detest wigs. They are hot and uncomfortable."

"They're also the fashion."

"This is how it's to be? You say what I am to wear—"

"And you wear it."

She felt dangerously close to exploding from frustration. "I fear you may have missed your natural calling, Mr. Waldron." She spoke low, trying to keep her voice even. "Are there no dictatorships available in the colonies at present?"

He laughed, gustily. "Only the one I've got."

# Chapter Five

I t's not so bad," Sara Anne whispered as she peered into mirror. Her silver-gray gown was beautifully made with large, hooped skirts. The powered wig was not too ridiculous looking, although she still detested it. She looked more like a china doll than herself.

Besides gowns, Aaron had purchased a sapphire betrothal ring and a strand of gray pearls, both of which she wore. They were exquisite pieces of jewelry, which was why he had purchased them. She was a reflection of him, and he would see that she shone brighter than all others around her. At least in terms of possessions.

It was time to go downstairs and face the Waldrons now and she dreaded it. She took as deep a breath as she could manage in the punishing corset. "Hope, where are you when I need you?" she whispered to the mirror.

She'd been informed that the invited guests were the elderly Colonel and Mrs. Hampton from Seven Groves, Mr. and Mrs. Humphrey and their grown son Reginald, the Waldrons' nearest neighbors, and Mr. and Mrs. Wilson from town along with their two, inexplicably beautiful daughters, Eloise, seventeen and Alexandra, fourteen.

A knock on the door signaled that Aaron had come to fetch her, as promised. She went to open the door. It was time for more playacting.

In the salon, she was received with perfectly appropriate manners and all the warmth of a firing squad. Only Mrs. Hampton showed any kindness. Mrs. Humphrey seemed smug, and Mrs. Wilson and her eldest daughter seemed almost hostile.

As far as the gentlemen went, the colonel was polite but distant, and Sara Anne got the impression that ladies made him uncomfortable. Mr. Humphrey couldn't seem to keep his eyes off her cleavage, and his son, Reginald, was even more brazen. These were members of the idle rich who lived beyond ordinary concerns and pursuits, and it was utterly inconceivable to picture herself among them.

She didn't belong here.

Dinner dragged on for an agonizing eight courses in which the gentlemen dominated the conversation.

"Have you heard from a man, an author, by the name of Barlow?" Mr. Humphrey asked when the final course, consisting of fruit and cheese, was served.

"I have," the colonel replied.

"Will you speak with him?" Humphrey asked.

"I'll meet with him."

"Who is he?" Robert asked, irritated by the clandestine tone at his own table.

"He is writing a book on Stono's rebellion."

"When all those runaway slaves were killed?" Alexandra Wilson asked, her blue eyes lighting up at the interesting turn in conversation.

"And twenty of us, as well," her father replied sharply. "Be silent until you're spoken to."

Alexandra pulled a face, but her parents either did not see or chose to ignore it.

"That was six or seven years ago," Robert exclaimed. "Why stir that up again?"

"I couldn't say," the colonel replied. "I have not yet spoken with the man."

"Is he local?" Wilson asked.

"No. From Pennsylvania, I understand."

"It was a local affair," Aaron spoke up. "And no one else's business. I wouldn't grant him an audience."

"I'll tell you one thing," Humphrey spoke up. "We don't need writers and agitators stirring up trouble amongst the niggers again."

Sara Anne felt the knot in her stomach harden.

Reginald scoffed. "How would they know? They can't read and who would tell them?"

Robert glared at him. "Word gets around. Why do you think *that* rebellion took place? Because they heard the Spaniards were promising freedom to any slave who made it to St. Augustine."

"Everyone knows it's illegal to teach them to read and write," Mrs. Humphrey said imperiously. "And we need to enforce it strictly. Burn out anyone who tries."

"Things are under control now," Aaron said coolly. "And we'll keep it that way."

"You never know about the darkies," Mr. Humphrey said, shaking his head. "They don't think like us. And there are a lot more of them than there are of us."

"It's up to each one of us to keep control of what's ours," Aaron stated. "You suspect a slave is making thinking about freedom, you watch him like a hawk. If they make any sort of move, stir any unrest, you make an example of them. Flay them alive in front of all of others."

Sara Anne stared into her plate and fisted her hands beneath the table. This would never work. Never, ever, ever. She could not be married to his man.

"This discussion is hardly appropriate for the dinner table," Robert stated, scooting his chair back with a screech. "Let's retire to the smoking room and allow the ladies some peace and quiet and more suitable dialogue."

Sara Anne didn't feel up to the next phase of the evening, but she had little choice. Mrs. Hampton took Sara Anne's arm as the women made their way to one of the withdrawing rooms. "How are, my dear?" she asked quietly.

"As well as can be expected. Thank you for asking."

"Who is at Riverbend now to keep an eye on things?" Mrs. Wilson asked.

"My father, of course, and my aunt has come from Beauford."

"Dora Leigh Aldridge," Mrs. Wilson said. "I knew her well."

"How do you flay someone?" Alexandra asked.

Her mother sent the girl a withering look.

Mrs. Wilson and Eloise turned into the drawing room behind their hostess. Mrs. Humphrey muttered, "Disgusting girl," before following.

Mrs. Hampton glanced at Sara Anne with a pained look and a sigh.

"Who would care for a glass of sherry?" Nadine Waldron asked.

They were the first words Sara Anne had heard her utter all evening.

"Please," Mrs. Wilson replied. She sounded put out, but Sara Anne had the suspicion she always sounded that way. A servant, a lovely young woman, was circulating with a tray of small glasses filled with sherry and everyone took one.

"When will you marry, Miss Aldridge?" Eloise Wilson asked.

Sara Anne turned to her but was too taken aback by the unveiled malevolence in the younger woman's eyes to speak for a moment. "The last Sunday in June," she finally managed.

"Eloise, dear," Mrs. Hampton said pleasantly. "How are your music lessons coming along?" She glanced at Sara Anne. "Eloise plays the harpsichord beautifully, although, I confess, I have not heard her play in quite some time."

"Very well, thank you, Mrs. Hampton," Eloise replied. "And how is Beatrice?"

"Very well. She's taking music and dance lessons from Mr. Unger in town." Once again, the older woman turned to Sara Anne to explain. "My granddaughter." She smiled proudly. "Our heart's delight."

Sara Anne felt herself responding with a sincere smile. It was heartwarming to see the affection Mrs. Hampton felt for her granddaughter. She and Caroline had never known their grandparents.

"Will she have her coming out this year?" Mrs. Humphrey asked.

"Yes. In December."

Sara Anne sensed someone staring. She glanced around and found Nadine's dark eyes trained on her.

"I don't recall *your* coming out, Miss Aldridge," Eloise said.

"I didn't have one," Sara Anne replied. "My sister was ill … and then she passed away."

"How sad," Eloise said, without a trace of feeling.

"I think if I died," Alexandra spoke up, "they would have packed me in ice, claimed I wasn't feeling well and gone right ahead with Ellie's coming out."

"Yes, we would have," Eloise agreed.

"You will desist at once," Mrs. Wilson snapped, directing it more to Alexandra than to Eloise.

Mrs. Humphrey sent a withering look at Alexandra. "Do you always blurt out whatever comes into your head, child?"

"That's hardly called for," Mrs. Wilson snapped.

"It's a singularly distasteful quality," Mrs. Humphrey said to Mrs. Wilson.

Eloise picked at some imaginary lint on her skirt. "And a dreadful habit of hers."

"Perhaps you're right," Alexandra replied. "Thank you for noticing and trying to correct my unseemly behavior."

Her voice was dripping with sarcasm and Mrs. Humphrey turned away, disgusted by her.

"Although I hope you won't mind my observing that your son couldn't keep his eyes in his head tonight," Alexandra said sweetly. "They were all over Miss Aldridge's bosom."

Mrs. Humphrey's jaw dropped, and her face turned bright red. Sara Anne also felt her face heat with mortification.

"Alexandra, leave this room until you can control your tongue," her mother hissed.

Eloise seemed on the verge of laughter. "I'll go, too, Mother. Lord only knows what trouble she'd get into."

"More sherry, I think," Nadine said calmly.

The Colonel and Mrs. Hampton were the first guests to leave, and Sara Anne excused herself shortly thereafter, explaining she had a headache, which was true. Her intention had been to return to her room but, when she saw an open back door, she slipped out for some fresh air.

The full moon provided ample light to make her way up to the overlook with its magnificent view of the sparkling black river below, where the sound of lapping water soothed her nerves. She pulled off her wig and unpinned her hair, sighing with relief. The breeze lifted her hair and caressed her skin and her headache eased. She leaned against the stone barrier and closed her eyes.

The evening had been miserable, She did not want to marry Aaron Waldron nor did she want to be part of this family. There had to be a way of extricating herself from the match. There simply had to be.

"I was hoping you'd be here."

Sara Anne jumped at the sound of Aaron's voice, and then turned to face him. "My head ached, and I thought the air might help."

Aaron slipped his jacket off and draped it over the wall next to her discarded wig. "And did it?"

"Yes, thank you."

"You don't have to be so polite with me." He stepped close enough that they were touching. "Nor do you have to make excuses."

She could smell the liquor on his breath. "Excuses?"

He reached out and ran his finger over the necklace he'd given her, eyeing it as he did. "Do you like it?"

"It's very beautiful," she replied honestly.

*But I don't want it. And I don't want you. And I don't want this,*

"Did you see them all? Ravaging you with their eyes."

The statement was shocking. Before she could think of an appropriate reply, he whirled her around and forced her back against him, one hand clamped on her breast. She felt a sharp tug on her shoulders as he attempted to force her gown down. "Stop it," she cried in a surprisingly small voice. It was because she couldn't breathe. She heard the dress rip. "Stop it!"

His mouth was on her neck as he kneaded her breast roughly. She drove her elbow against him, but, if anything, her struggling served to encourage him.

"I could take you right here," he said, his voice husky and deep. "I think I might."

He was too strong to fight off. "Stop! Please!"

He yanked her around to face him, keeping one arm pinned behind her back. He pressed his mouth to hers in an invasive kiss.

The twisted arm behind her back burned. He lowered his mouth to her neck as his fingers closed around a hardened nipple and squeezed. She drew breath to scream, but he suddenly backed off and the scream stayed trapped within her. She struggled to catch her breath and regain some control.

"Do you want to?" he asked breathily.

He was smiling. She wanted to claw it off his face. "No!"

"No?" He reached down quickly, as though he was catching something he had dropped, He brought his hand up beneath her skirts. "Are you certain?"

"Stop it!" she begged, pushing against him. It was useless. She couldn't stop him. "I'll scream. I'll—" she took a deep breath to scream.

He clamped a hand over her mouth and pressed her against the rock ledge. It sent pain through her lower back, but all she could concentrate on was his right hand, which was invading her most private self. His face was directly in front of hers, his black eyes boring into hers, and there was no tenderness in them. There was only a trace of sadistic victory as he explored where no one had before. He moved his finger inside her and she felt herself crying, not from pain but from humiliation. A sharp pain in the pit of her stomach warned that she was going to vomit. "I hate you!" she screamed into his hand.

Suddenly the pressure on her back eased and he withdrew his hands, first the hand from inside her skirts and then the one over her mouth. "I only wanted some of your scent to take with me," he said as he took a step backwards. He brought his fingers to his nose and inhaled with deep appreciation.

Her knees buckled and she crumpled to the ground. The pain in her stomach doubled her over.

She heard Aaron's words as if we were standing far away. "Too much to drink, my love?"

She felt his hand on her arm. "Get away from me," she bit out, hating him with a passion she hadn't known she was capable of. He was acting calm, as if nothing amiss had occurred at all, while she couldn't stop crying. She detested herself for it, but her hatred for him was all-consuming.

"Sara Anne, nothing that happens between us is shameful. We'll be man and wife soon."

*The bloody hell we will* she wanted to scream and yet she remained silent.

"Which means you're mine."

With that intolerable declaration, she looked up at him, full of loathing. He suddenly looked concerned. She was shaking all over and could not stop. A warm trickle of blood seeped from her lip.

"You're overwrought," he said. "Shall I go for now and you can take a minute to collect yourself? If you use the back stairs, no one will see you. Although I'd prefer to help you."

"Touch me again and I will scream," she swore in a low voice. "And I will keep screaming!"

"Collect yourself, Sara Anne."

Unable to bear the sight of him for one more moment, she looked away. After an agonizing few moments, he walked away. She managed to wait until he was out of earshot before she shuddered with revulsion and then broke into sobs.

Eventually, she went back inside per his instructions, and it took every ounce of energy she possessed to make her way to her room. Once there, she closed and locked her door before dissolving into fresh tears. It was the queer sensation of being watched that drew her attention to the corner of the room where Nadine sat observing her. Sara Anne gulped and wiped her face with both hands.

Nadine gaze was on Sara Anne's ripped bodice, "The Waldron men have a decidedly cruel streak." Her voice was without inflection and her expression was a well-trained, hard-earned blank. She rose and moved toward the door, as if to leave. "And they do enjoy their little cruelties. That's what makes it so unbearable."

"I w-will not m-marry him!" Sara Anne swore.

"You will do precisely what they want you to do. Had your mother lived, she would have told you so."

It was a monstrous thing Nadine Waldron had spoken, but the monstrosity lay in its brutal truth.

"If you believe in prayer," Nadine pronounced the word darkly, "then pray you have daughters." She reached down and unlocked the door. "Get a cool cloth on that lip or it will swell." She started to leave but paused for one last statement. "It will swell anyway, but don't fret. Everyone pretends they don't see."

And, with that, Nadine slipped out, quiet as the night's breeze.

Shaking, unable to stop shaking, Sara Anne locked the door again and then slid down it, crying.

# Chapter Six

Aaron walked into the breakfast room the following morning looking edgy. "You're late," his father commented without glancing up from the newspaper. "We have business to attend to."

"Have you seen Sara Anne this morning? She's not in her room."

Robert looked up sharply, surprised by this, and Aaron must have considered the implications. He drew a sharp breath, waving a hand in a dismissive gesture. "She mentioned leaving early, but we hadn't decided." He walked to the sideboard. "Wedding preparations," he murmured.

Nadine noticed the tension in his body with some satisfaction. When he sat back down, it was with a half-filled plate, and then, he only picked at it. "Not hungry, dear?" she asked coolly.

"Not particularly. No."

Robert leaned forward. "We need to meet with that Cary fellow this morning about terms and quantity."

"Last year's terms are sufficient," Aaron replied dismissively.

Robert's face grew slightly wider as he frowned. "Always go up by a percentage or two."

"In case you haven't noticed, Father, more and more of us are producing the same things. Do you not think we can be underbid?"

Robert glared at him. "By a percentage, maybe two."

"Then it's decided, isn't it? What do you need me for?" Aaron scooted his chair back, threw down his napkin, and left the room without another word.

Robert made a sound in his throat. "Too much to drink last night," he complained.

Nadine kept her gaze on the dregs of tea in her cup as she gently swirled them and said nothing.

~~~

Sara Anne had slept little and started her day early, anxious to be away from Waldron House. No matter how many times she told herself that nothing that had transpired was her fault, she still felt deeply ashamed, and she could not bear the thought of looking Aaron in the eye, or any of the Waldrons for that matter. Thank God they had ridden to Waldron House, otherwise she would be stuck there at their mercy.

She couldn't keep Nadine off her mind. *The Waldron men have a decidedly cruel streak.* She hadn't seemed a bit surprised to see her in such a frightful-looking state. Was it because she had endured a similar fate too many times not to expect it for her daughter-in-law?

Yes, that was it—and she would become just like Nadine if she stayed and allowed herself to be hurt and humiliated. Sara Anne swiped at her tears angrily. She couldn't stop them from falling, but she would not end up like Nadine because she refused to have a heartless bully for a husband. Refused! Her heart was in her throat as Riverbend came into sight. She would see her father right away and have her say quickly, preferably without looking at him.

She dismounted and dashed up the front steps. She sailed through the front doors and down the hall looking for her father. Sally, a pretty, fifteen-year-old mulatto, was walking toward her and growing more concerned with every step.

"You aw'right, Miz Sara Anne?"

"I need to speak with my father."

"He jes left to go—"

Sara Anne bolted past Sally, ran out the side door and kept running. Only when she caught a glimpse of her father in the stable, did she slow down to catch her breath. She had to appear calm and rational. She had to make him understand her point of view. He was saddling his horse as she walked in. "Father," she said shakily.

"I thought you were gone for a few days," he said without looking at her.

She clutched her hands in front of her. "I... need to speak with you."

He turned to her, irritated at first, but then his eyes dropped to her swollen lip and back up to her eyes. For a split second, his expression softened, then it hardened again. "What is it?"

Was that how it was to be? He saw and understood, but didn't care? "He attacked me."

Delbert's eyes narrowed. "To whom are you referring?"

He knew exactly to whom she referred. "Aaron Waldron."

"A husband can't attack his wife."

"I am not his wife," she cried, shaken to her core that he didn't care that she had been hurt.

"You will be," he said distinctly.

Her eyes filled and a painful lump made her throat ache. She turned and took a few steps to Ladyfair's stall and held on, struggling for control over her emotions. Her father detested the sight of tears. Any sign of them would only anger him further.

"You had a disagreement," he said, "and being a *woman*—" He spoke the word as if he hated the entire gender.

"I will not marry him," she interrupted, her voice stronger than before.

"Will not?" he repeated.

She couldn't face him, but she shook her head resolutely. His anger made her feel small and weak, but she had to be strong. There was no one to act as her advocate. It had been a horrible twenty-four hours but had *only* been twenty-four hours. If she weren't strong now, she would have a lifetime of misery and regret.

She could hear him stomping away. "I am sorry to disappoint you, but he's terrible. And—"

A burning pain knocked the breath from her. She had neither seen nor heard the whip coming, nor had she imagined such a thing was possible. Her knees buckled and only her grip on the rails of the stall kept her upright. Her brain barely had time to register the swish and hiss that signaled the whip coming again before a second slash ripped through her gown and the skin beneath.

She heard herself scream. She let go of the rail and collapsed to her knees, her body jerking spasmodically.

"You *dare* tell me what you will and will not do? Women are all traitors and Jezebels! You—"

A third lash drove her flat to the ground.

She heard a male voice calling to her father, pleading with him.

Footsteps.

More voices.

She thought of trying to crawl away, but her strength was gone. She was tensed for the next blow. There was a strange raspy, sick sounding noise. It was her.

"She bleedin' bad, masta. Please, sir!"

"Get out of my way!"

He was going to kill her. And she couldn't even draw breath to plead for her life.

No. He was leaving. He was riding off.

Time stopped and there was nothing but burning agony and the memory of her father's face contorted with rage. He hated her. How could he *hate* her? She wanted to die. She would do it. She would will herself to die.

"Oh, baby girl," Bet crooned.

She felt strong hands lifting her, and Sally was there, crying. Nothing felt real. She couldn't breathe and she wasn't able to speak to tell anyone so. But Bet was there.

Blackness descended.

~~~

Unconsciousness didn't last long enough. She came to in a sitting position, slumped against Bet as someone put salve on her back. She felt horribly, desperately sick.

"Oh, baby," Bet crooned. "Sweet girl."

Sara Anne moaned.

"Your Bet is right here. I got you. Nana, help me get some brandy down her."

"Alright," Nana Flo replied in her deep voice. She was their two-hundred-and-fifty-pound cook, whose real name was Florence.

No one was quite sure when she first started being called Nana, but the why was obvious. She'd had fifteen children and nine of them had survived to beget or bear their own children, sixty-eight of them. And they'd had children, who'd had children.

Bet eased Sara Anne upright while Nana Flo supported her. She was naked from the waist up, she realized dully. Things were filtering through her brain slowly. The searing pain was dominating all her senses and making her feel desperately ill. Bet held a glass of brandy to her lips. "Drink this, chile. It'll help dull the pain."

Sara Anne sipped and grimaced.

"*Drink*, I say. Those little ladylike sips won't do you no good a'tall."

Sara Anne held her breath and downed the glass in three burning gulps, then slumped back against Bet, who stroked her hair and breathed words of comfort in her ear. Nana Flo hummed a hymn she couldn't quite make out, although it sounded familiar.

"Tell me about my mother." Sara Anne's voice was almost guttural, spoken through waves of pain.

Flo grew silent, and Bet didn't respond for several moments. "She was a good woman. You her spittin' image, you know."

"Is that why my father hates me?"

"Oh, baby—"

"Is it?"

"What happened, make him go crazy like that?"

"I told him I wouldn't marry Aaron Waldron."

Bet let out a long sigh that expressed more than words.

"He attacked me," Sara Anne whispered.

"I know, baby. I see."

"Aaron Waldron, I mean."

"I know," Bet repeated softly. "I see."

"Lord, Lord," Nana Flo said behind her. "Cain't believe he done went and used that bone whip on his own flesh and blood."

Sara Anne felt a wave of nausea and she moaned.

Bet held her gently. "I know, sweet girl, I know."

~~~

65

Bet set the bowl of broth down, frustrated that Sara Anne refused to eat. "Now, you got to take some food in you. 'Specially now you took that medsun."

It was late, dark, and Sara Anne was lying on her side. The pain was dulled due to a dose of laudanum supplied by her aunt. "What happened to make my father hate my mother?"

Bet sat on the chair beside the bed. "Why you axin' that?" she whispered. "You know he don't abide us talking 'bout her."

All Sara Anne could do was to plead silently.

"Crazy thinkin' is what," Bet finally conceded. "Sometimes, when a woman has a baby, somethin' goes wrong wit the chile. Ain't nobody's fault. Jes' happen sometimes. And that's what happened wit' your mama. There was something wrong wit that baby boy. His head was too big, and it tore her apart."

Bet looked off and Sara Anne could tell she was revisiting the long-ago day.

"Your Aunt Dora Leigh was here. She made everything worse. I don't know who went and put it your papa's head that that couldn't be his chile your mama was havin', but I'd be surprised if it wan't her done it."

Sara Anne felt breathless. "He thought the baby had been fathered by someone else?"

"He convinced hisself of it."

Bile rose in Sara Anne's throat, and she fought the urge to vomit. She'd been sick earlier, and it had torn open the welts on her back. "Is it true?"

"God be my witness, girl—no, it ain't true." Bet spoke passionately. "Your mama was a good woman. She didn't do no lyin' around. But your father decided if that baby wan't right, it couldn't be of his line."

Sara Anne was suddenly picturing her mother in the throes of childbirth, her husband having turned against her. Had she known she was dying? "I don't remember her." It was a simple fact and lifelong condition of her existence, so why was the loneliness so wrenching, the missing so acute and painful?

A single tear rolled down Sara Anne's face and Bet wiped it away. "She's watchin' over you, though. "Tryin' her best to protect you."

Sara Anne squeezed her eyes shut, as a wave of pain shot through her. "She's not doing a very good job," she uttered through gritted teeth.

"Oh, baby."

"I don't believe in anything anymore."

"You listen to me now," Bet said, leaning close. "I want to tell you something I been wantin' to tell you for a long time."

The room grew silent. "What?"

"You know your mama's name?"

Sara Anne took a deep breath and let it out. The medicine was taking deeper effect, pulling her toward unconsciousness. "Opal Shelly Aldridge," she replied slowly. She closed her eyes, ready for unconsciousness.

"I reckon Opal was a hard name to say for a young'un, 'cuz your mama grew up with a nickname that almost everybody knew her called her by. She said it was your Uncle William come up wit it. He wan't but two or three when she come into the world, and he couldn't say Opal."

"What was it?" she murmured.

"Hope."

Sara Anne's eyes flew open.

Tears were pooled in Bet's luminous, dark eyes. "I always knowed it was her that was keeping you company and telling you sweet things when you was little. Things like you was special and how much she loved you."

"She was ... called Hope?"

Bet nodded.

"Did I know that? Had I ever been told that?"

Bet shook her head. "I don't see how. It was a childhood thing. Masta never called her that. William used to write her and call her that, but your papa burnt all those letters. Your mama, she looked like you, only she—"

"Had brown eyes?"

"That's right."

"Caroline tried to convince me I was making her up."

"Caroline din't know, and I couldn't tell neither of you or have you tellin' your papa 'bout it. That's why I tol' you not to speak of it."

"I thought you didn't believe me, either."

"No, baby, I always knowed. Now maybe you'll believe it when I tell you she's watchin' over you."

~~~

It took a long time for Sara Anne to get up and attend to the emptying of her bladder the next morning. She was dizzy and weak, but she needed to know how bad the wounds were. She used a hand mirror to reflect the image in the mirror back to her. There were three angry looking, raised, purple welts on her back dotted with dark brown scabs. Her eyes were quickly drawn to the worse area near the center of her back, where the whip had struck twice.

She fought back a wave of nausea. She tingled with lightheadedness and her vision wavered and went dark. Blindly, she felt her way toward the balcony for some desperately needed air. She made contact, slung the door wide open and collapsed in the doorway. It took several seconds before her vision came back and several more for the pricks of pain to stop jabbing and the lightheadedness to subside.

She had to think. She just had endured some of the worst days of her life, but her entire life was at stake. Her father had reacted violently to her proclamation not to marry Aaron, and there was no reason to believe he would feel any differently today or any other day. She would be forced into marriage if she remained here.

Genevieve's face flashed in her mind's eye. *Yes!* The idea had occurred to her in the night. She could go to her family in England. Her father and Aaron would be livid. Aaron would officially break their engagement and marry Lucy, and her father would despise and disown her. Unless … she could make a good match abroad. That was all he cared about.

She got to her feet, using the door jamb as support, and went back to bed. She carefully stretched out on her side and mulled over the challenge of booking passage. She had no money of her own, but Charles Town was an active port, and the *Gazette* would have advertisements about ships bound for England.

A knock at the door preceded its opening. Sara Anne knew it was Bet. She recognized the sound of her footsteps and smell of food coming from the tray she carried. Bet rounded the bed, her deep brown eyes full of compassion. "I'm still alive," Sara Anne said.

"We need to get some food in you."

"Is my father here?"

Bet set the tray down and sat next to Sara Anne with a plate in hand. "He is. Han't said a word to nobody. Can you sit up?"

Sara Anne managed it, and Bet handed a plate over.

"I 'magine he'll get hisself out the house after breakfast."

"And my aunt?"

"Why you axin'?"

"I want to avoid seeing her. I want to avoid them both."

"They know you not feelin' good. They won't say a word 'bout you takin' meals up here."

Sara Anne forced herself to take a bite. She thought of Aaron and wondered when he would show up, and what excuses would be made on her behalf. No matter what excuses were offered, he would believe she was avoiding him because of his behavior two nights ago. How he would behave from this point on was a mystery. He might react like her father—by avoiding her and then pretending nothing had happened. Or he might hover and watch every move she made. He might even apologize and beg her forgiveness. She didn't know him well enough to guess his reaction.

"Got to keep salve on your cuts. We got to keep it clean, doctored, and open to the air as much as possible. Nothin' tight against the skin."

She nodded.

"I'm glad to see you eat," Bet said. "You got to get strong again."

"I do," Sara Anne agreed.

It was the following afternoon before Sara Anne made it downstairs and into her father's study. The *South Carolina Gazette* was on her father's desk. Sara Anne picked it up and scanned the contents until the illustrations of ships caught her eye. '*For Barbados, directly,*' read the first advertisement. She scanned down and read, '*For London, directly.*'

"Yes," she whispered.

> '*The CAROL ADELE, William Davis, Commander, will sail with utmost expedition. For freight of passage, apply to said commander on board or to George Fields in Lodge Alley.*'

Her heart beat fast as she read on.

> '*For Liverpool/London, directly. The Ship, APHRODITE, Christopher Joseph, Commander, will sail with convenient speed,*" she read softly. "*For freight or passage, agree with said master, now lying at Charles Towne Harbor. She hath good accommodations for passengers.*"

Two choices, and this was likely the better choice. The *Aphrodite*. A sharp rap on the door startled her, and she dropped the paper. The door opened and Aaron stood there looking windblown and disheveled. "I was told you were in here."

She tightened her grip on her shawl. Bet had cut the back from an old gown well enough that it was not obvious from the front, and yet it still left her feeling uncomfortably exposed, even with a shawl draped around her.

Aaron closed the door behind him. "I regret that things got rather out of hand the other night," he said. "I had too much to drink. I hope you believe that I didn't intend to hurt or to frighten you."

She concentrated on breathing evenly. For her plan to work, everyone had to remain calm. When Aaron was alarmed, he overreacted. "I do." It sounded stiff and unnatural, but it was the best she could do.

Aaron came closer, close enough that he could have reached out and touched her. "I know I said you could choose any Sunday in June, but I'd like for us to marry at the first possible opportunity."

Her heart thudded harder.

"I've already spoken with the minister—"

"I cannot," she blurted.

For a moment, he didn't react at all, but then his expression darkened visibly. "You can and you will," he replied in a low voice.

"You don't understand," she replied futilely.

"No, you're the one who fails to understand," he challenged, his eyes flashing.

"My father and I had a … disagreement."

He drew back. "What are you talking about?"

There was no choice. She turned and lowered her shawl so that he would see her back. Other than the pronounced ticking of the mantle clock, there was no sound in the room. Her face was hot with mortification as she waited for him to say something. But he didn't. She turned back to see that he looked murderous with fury.

"What was this *disagreement* about?"

She couldn't tell him that.

"What did you quarrel over?" he repeated.

When she still didn't reply, he took her chin in hand and tipped her face up until she met his eyes. "Perhaps you decided you didn't wish to marry me after all?"

She held her gaze steady, neither confirming nor denying.

"It looks like quite a price to pay for a temper tantrum," he observed coldly. He let go of her and paced to the end of the room and back. "I have apologized for the other night. Is it behind us now?"

Her throat felt too tight to respond but she gave a stiff nod. He hadn't apologized, not really, but she had to focus on her goal, only on her goal.

"I will speak to your father about this."

"No! Please, don't."

"I will instruct him to be civil to you."

71

"It would be best if we act as though it never happened. Please, Aaron. I know my father."

"Fine, but we'll wed the first Sunday in June," he decided aloud as he retrieved the shawl from the floor and carefully draped it back around her. "It's *best* if I take you away from here."

She needed more time. She made her eyes pleading. "I won't be fully healed by then."

The door swung open, and Delbert jerked in surprise at seeing them. "I didn't realize anyone was in here," he said in a tone that revealed his displeasure.

Sara Anne raised her gaze back to Aaron's realizing whatever he said or did now would determine her future. It was obvious that it pleased him to see her deferring to him, which made defiance surge in her veins. It took all her strength to maintain eye contact without revealing any of her true feelings.

Aaron turned to Delbert. "I needed to discuss something with Sara Anne. I hope you don't mind."

"No, no. Quite alright," he replied stiffly.

"We were just leaving," Aaron said.

Sara Anne started toward the door. She did not look at her father as she passed him.

"Oh," Aaron said, almost as an afterthought. "We've decided the wedding will take place on the third Sunday in June. Isn't that what we decided, darling?"

She was forced to stop and turn halfway back. "Yes."

"Excellent," Del replied.

Sara Anne walked on. The third Sunday in June gave her four weeks to heal sufficiently, acquire a passage, and leave for Middlesbrough.

Aaron led her outside before speaking again. "Are you in pain?"

*In more ways than you could ever understand.* "Yes."

"I would never do that to you."

She flushed in humiliated recollection of what he had done to her. "What? Strike me?"

"Not with a whip on a bare back," he specified.

72

The clarification galled her. "It wasn't bare," she replied, almost as a challenge. "The whip tore through my clothing."

He made a sound of disgust.

A large part of her warned to leave well enough alone, but she couldn't help herself. "There are those who believe one person shouldn't have the right to strike another."

"Now you're being naïve. However, if one guards one's behavior and tries to please—"

She couldn't bear it. "I don't feel well," she said, turning away from him.

"Fine. Go lie down."

She started back inside, hoping that was the end of their time together, but he kept pace with her. "Invitations must be readied and sent soon," he said. "Your aunt can see to it."

Reluctantly, she turned to him.

He took hold of her hand and kissed it. "I'll be back in a few days."

# Chapter Seven

Sara Anne had never considered herself to be a sneaky person, but during the following days as she slowly healed, she proved she had the ability and cunningness to accomplish her undertakings.

Every necessary task was a challenge because she was watched all the time, but she managed them one by one. Sending a letter to the Shelly's. Obtaining a promissory note from her father for the printer and various nuptial related items. Everything required uttering a lie or trickery or some sleight of hand.

Acquiring her ticket for the voyage meant sneaking away from the house and getting to town unnoticed. As she dismounted near the harbor, hitched her horse, and walked along the waterfront, escaping her fate felt more real and possible than it had before.

From a distance, the ships were majestic looking but up close, they were massive and awe-inspiring. The billowing masts were so bright, they hurt her eyes. Everything about this place—the people, the sounds, the smells — marked it as foreign from her world. It abounded with sailors, merchants, and ladies of ill repute. It was fascinating that each person existed in a small world of their own.

A cloud mass passed overhead casting a shadow over the land. Sara Anne felt small and insignificant in it. It reminded her of God — enormous and far above the world. Could every person on earth matter to such a great entity? *Does he see that I am lost and struggling? Does he care?*

She stopped short when she spied the *Aphrodite,* simultaneously relieved and terrified. If she were seen boarding and that got back to her father or the Waldrons, all her plans would be ruined.

"May I be of assistance?" a deep voice said.

Sara Anne felt a sickening jolt at the sound of Aaron's voice directly behind her. She whirled about to face him, *she hadn't done anything wrong yet,* but it was a stranger who had spoken.

"I beg your pardon," he apologized. "I startled you.

"There's no need, sir," she stammered. "I was distracted by my thoughts."

"Are you looking for someone? Perhaps I can help."

She hesitated. "The captain of the *Aphrodite.*"

"Then I can be of help. Christopher Joseph, at your service." He gave a slight bow.

"Oh!" He looked to be no older than his late thirties and yet his hair had already turned silver-gray. The tanned, leathery skin on his face had been deeply scarred by the pox but, despite it, he was striking. She fumbled for her reticule and pulled out her father's letter with a trembling hand. "I wish to arrange for a passage to England."

He took it in hand and looked it over, before seeking out her eyes again. "Is the passage for you?"

"It is." It came out a little above a whisper.

"We leave on Saturday."

Saturday! Only three days away.

"If that's too soon, the *Carol Adele* leaves in a fortnight," he continued. "Of course, she only puts into London."

"Saturday is not too soon. However, my father is presently out of town."

He nodded slowly, waiting for her to continue.

"Would it be possible for you to collect payment for my passage on your return trip?" The more she spoke, the deeper she blushed. She could feel it. "As you can see, it's been approved by him."

"I could do that," he said, agreeably. "If I may hang onto this." He hefted the letter.

"Of course." She was tingling. "Then there are still accommodations available?"

"Yes, miss. We have quite acceptable accommodations. Would you care to come aboard and see for yourself? It might put your mind at ease."

"No, I'm sure they'll do perfectly."

"Well, weather permitting, we shall set sail between eight and half past on Saturday. So, I should reserve a cabin for you?"

"Yes, Captain. Please."

"A cabin for one?"

"Yes."

"Consider it done."

"Thank you, sir."

"It's my pleasure, Miss Aldridge." He tipped his hat to her. "I'll look forward to seeing you on Saturday. By eight o'clock," he reminded her.

She nodded and walked away first.

*Saturday!* She couldn't believe she would be leaving on Saturday. She suddenly imagined Captain Joseph showing up on their doorstep, unannounced, and revealing her intentions to her father. She shuddered, but she was being absurd when she had enough real concerns and complications to deal with.

~~~

By Friday evening, the muscles in her neck were so tight that her head ached, and her stomach was one huge knot. *Tomorrow.* The word whispered in her brain, over and over. Tomorrow, she would be leaving. She would be gone from here. God willing.

*God, please be willing.*

She could only hope and pray that Aunt Penelope and Uncle William would allow her to remain with them at Oakley, their estate in Middlesbrough. If they insisted that she return home, she would have nowhere else to turn and that was too terrible a plight to contemplate.

She had three important chores tonight. The first was to pack and that was done. She was taking one small trunk and keeping it as light as possible, as she would have to get it to and on the wagon herself. The next was writing letters. She had to write an explanation to both her father and Aaron. She had dreaded the chore but when she began, it proved to be easier than she had imagined.

*Father,*

*I have gone to stay with my mother's family.*
*Naturally, I realize this will anger you. While I have*
*regret for that, I feel I have been left little choice. I do*
*not love Aaron Waldron and cannot abide the thought*
*of a life with him. I wanted, I tried to discuss the*
*matter with you. I am quite sure that neither of us will*
*ever forget what occurred.*

*I do not know when or if we shall meet again.*
*Perhaps the opportunity may present itself. If and*
*when it does, I hope our hearts and prides will have*
*mended sufficiently for us to embrace in full and free*
*forgiveness.*

*Your daughter,*
*Sara Anne*

*P.S. The horse and wagon should be retrieved from*
*the stable yard near the harbor.*

She leaned back, satisfied with the letter. What was she to do about Bet? She certainly couldn't tell her what she planned. If her father even suspected she'd been given prior knowledge, he'd punish her for it.

She would leave Bet a letter as well. Her mother had begun to teach Bet to read and write before she died, and Caroline had later worked to improve her skills. Bet would be the most likely person to discover the letters but even if someone else discovered them, it would prove that Bet had no prior knowledge about her leaving.

*Dearest Bet,*

*I have gone to the Shellys. I hope you will*
*understand that I have to go, and you will not worry*
*too much. So much presses on my heart that I am*
*inadequate to put it into words. Know that I love you*
*and I will miss you as I do Caroline and the mother I*
*never knew.*

*Your girl,*

*Sara Anne*

A tear fell from her eye and blotted ink, obscuring half of a word. Sara Anne dried her eyes and fought for control. This was not the time to give into emotion. There was one last letter to go. "Finish," she whispered.

> *Dear Mr. Waldron,*
> *You urged me to call you by your given name, but it is no longer seemly to take that liberty as I am leaving with no intention of returning or remaining your betrothed. I have gone to England to be with my family. I ask that you <u>not</u> take this as a personal affront, instead to understand that we are not well suited. Withdraw your offer, sir, and choose a bride more suited to the life you offer.*
> *You have my sincere apology for any discomfort the situation may cause you and your family, however only the members of my immediate family are or will be aware of my departure. You may rest assured that it is not common knowledge.*
> *I wish you good fortune in your future choices and happiness in your life. I hope you will not begrudge me the same.*
> *Sincerely,*
> *Sara Anne Aldridge*

She took off her betrothal ring with a sigh of relief and stuck it into the envelope with his letter. It felt wonderful to be free of it. She had left the strand of pearls at Waldron House on top of the gown he had ruined. So, that was that. "I am done with Aaron Waldron," she murmured.

It was well past midnight. Fatigue pulled at her, but it helped allay the panic she'd been battling for days. She blew out her candles and waited for her eyes to adjust to the dark. When they did, she crept out of room to make sure the way was clear for hauling out her trunk. It was, although she was forced to take the chore one agonizing step at a time, dragging her trunk behind her. Step, drag. Step, drag. All the while with her eyes and ears straining for anyone who might be about.

It took a half hour to maneuver the trunk behind the carriage house and onto the wagon. Tomorrow morning, she would hitch the horse to the wagon and be gone before anyone was up and about. By the time the household was aware of her absence, it would be too late. She would be gone.

*God willing.*

It was nearly two when she crawled onto her bed to rest. She couldn't sleep. Either the fear of not waking in time or one of a thousand other fears kept her prickling with consciousness, but her eyes stung, and she closed them.

It seemed only a few moments had gone by when she heard the clock strike three. It wouldn't be long now, and she would get up and go. Sleep didn't matter. She had weeks to sleep on the ship. All that mattered was getting away.

She relaxed enough that she rolled onto her back without thinking about it. She moaned softly and shifted back to her side. The pain from the lashing had muted but she still couldn't lie flat on her back. For the first few days after the whipping, she'd been in agony, the pain biting and white-hot. It had dominated her senses and thought. To begin functioning again, she'd had to concentrate on something, anything, beyond the pain, which varied from a constant buzz-like sensation to sharp, piercing jabs.

Her father had inflicted three lashes on her. How did people who received forty, fifty, even a hundred lashes survive?

The clock struck four. In half an hour, she would get up and go. She needed only a small amount of predawn light, enough to hitch the horse and see the road. Fatigue was pressing her deeper into her pillow. Of course, it was *too late to sleep now.*

The clock began striking and she counted, although she already knew there would be five. Gong, gong, gong, gong, gong, gong.

*Six!*

She jerked her eyes open with a small gasp and sat straight up. With her heart hammering, she got up and put her shoes on as quickly as she could. *Stupid, stupid girl!* How could she have fallen asleep at the last moment?

She held her breath as she peeked out her bedroom door. All was quiet, but the servants would be up and at their labor already. Now, she would have to be especially careful not to be seen because even an innocent remark could alert her father or her aunt and ruin all her plans. She crept down the hall, toward the back staircase, cringing with every creak the heart-of-pine floorboards made. How could she have fallen asleep when she'd had so little time left to wait?

She'd made it down the stairs and all the way to the back door when she heard the faint strains of Nana Flo's deep voice from the kitchen. Bet's voice followed and then there was soft laughter. The pain in Sara Anne's chest took her by surprise and it took a concentrated effort not to break down. She didn't need to think about Bet or Nana Flo or Caroline or leaving the only home she'd ever known. If she stayed, she would be forced to marry Aaron and live in the fickle shadow of his mercy. That's what she had to think about. That's all she could afford to think about.

She slipped outside. The air was still and so humid that it felt heavy. Lifting her skirt, she hurried to the stable for Ladyfair, and then led her behind the carriage house to hitch her to the wagon. Fatigue made her clumsy, but she kept going, moving as fast as she was capable.

The back way was a quarter of a mile longer but because it was tree-lined, it offered the greatest chance for a successful escape. She couldn't risk being noticed leaving and there was far too much chance of that happening now. The ship was setting sail between eight and half after and it would take her better than an hour to get there if she didn't encounter any problems. *How could I have fallen asleep in the eleventh hour?*

"Come on, girl," she urged Ladyfair. "Come on!"

By the time she made it to the harbor, she had tortured herself with visions of her father catching up to her, of Aaron meeting her on the road and discovering what she was up to, and of the *Aphrodite* setting sail without her, so when she spotted the ship still in port, she went limp from relief.

She found a place to leave the wagon and climbed down, but then stopped, recognizing that this was the last chance she would have to change her mind and turn back. If she didn't, her life would never again be the same.

For a terrible few moments, she languished in indecision. What would Caroline have thought of her behaving this way? She'd no sooner formed the question in her mind than a calming reassurance washed over her. Caroline had always understood and supported her, and she still did. Death be damned. The bond of love survived it.

A boy approached and she fumbled for a coin she'd filched from her father's office. "Excuse me," she called. "Would you look after the horse until someone comes?"

"Yes, miss," he said eagerly as he took it.

"The owners are named Aldridge, and they'll be here sometime this afternoon or this evening."

He glanced her over and then nodded. "Can I get your trunk?" Without waiting for her to reply, he retrieved the trunk from the wagon.

"Thank you."

The morning sun came down in unmerciful brightness and reflected back on the water twice as strong. Sara Anne stopped in front of the ship with her hand shielding her eyes from the blinding glare.

The *Aphrodite* was abuzz with activity and all hands looked busy and focused with preparations to leave. A lone figure grabbed her attention from the main deck. He was dark because of the sun's position behind him, but it was clearly Captain Christopher Joseph who stuck up a hand in greeting and waved before he started toward her. "Morning, Miss Aldridge," he greeted as he approached.

"Good morning."

"Good voyage, miss," the boy said, darting off.

"I was wondering if you'd make it," the captain said. "I'll show you to your cabin."

"Thank you." It was difficult to keep her eyes on where she was going rather than spanning the harbor for signs of her father or anyone else who might have an interest in stopping her, but the captain walked at a brisk pace, and she kept up.

"Here we are," the captain said as he opened the door to a cabin. He allowed her to walk through first. The only furniture within was a narrow sleeping berth, a wooden table and chair, and a vanity stand. A pitcher, basin and pot – these were her amenities. A lantern hung from the ceiling and the cabin had a small porthole, for which she felt grateful. It was sparse but clean.

"Thank you, Captain."

"We should be off soon," Captain Joseph said, turning to leave. At the door, he hesitated. "Let me know if you need anything."

In the silence that followed she realized just how frayed her nerves were. She tried to calm herself with the fact that no one knew where she was, but of course, she'd left the letters. *What if they're discovered too soon? What if Father has found them and is on his way right now?*

Being dragged off the ship would be such humiliation, but worse was the inevitability of a life with Aaron. She sat on the cot and tried to breathe. She heard distant shouts and sprang back to her feet, her eyes wide. They'd found her! She was caught!

She felt a subtle jerk and then another there was a sudden sense of movement. She dashed to the porthole and saw that they were in motion. They had set sail. "Oh, thank God," she breathed.

She stepped back as a heady numbness enveloped her. How absurd. She'd been planning this for weeks. It had consumed her every waking thought. She went back to her cot, buried her face in her hands and sobbed. She'd done it. God help her, she'd done it.

Nearly an hour later, when she'd collected herself, she left her cabin, climbed to the deck above. With the salty breeze in her face, she watched the familiar walled city growing smaller and farther away.

~~~

Bet was cutting up potatoes for breakfast when Sally came into the kitchen and tugged on her sleeve.

"Girl," Bet scolded. "I got a sharp knife in my hand. What you tuggin' on me—"

"Miz Sara Anne ain't in her room," Sally whispered urgently. "I went to help dress her—"

There was fear in the girl's wide brown eyes that caused alarm to shoot through Bet's system. Sara Anne had been behaving oddly.

"Her bed ain't been slept in," Sally whispered.

Bet set down the knife, wiped her hands on her apron, and walked out of the kitchen with Sally on her heels. Nana Flo stopped her humming, which was as natural for her as breathing, and watched them go. Her hearing wasn't good anymore, so she hadn't heard a word that had passed between them, but she knew something was wrong. She issued up a silent prayer that all was well and went back to kneading batter.

Sara Anne's room felt unaccountably empty. It looked as though she'd lain atop the bed, but not slept in it. Bet walked to the bed and began smoothing the covers. She picked up a pillow to fluff it and discovered the letters stashed beneath. In an instant, she knew. She uttered a small cry and sat on the bed.

Sally was leaning against the closed door. She watched Bet tear open an envelope, then pull out and read the enclosed letter. "What is it?" she asked when she couldn't stand the suspense any longer.

"She's gone," Bet wailed softly.

"Gone? Where to?"

"Hafta think," Bet muttered to herself. Sara Anne had left that very morning, only hours ago. Would her ship have set sail by now? Her girl had gone this far; she *had* to able to get away. The master would be fit to be tied. "Tell you what do—"

Sally came and crouched down, and Bet took her hands. "Wait 'til Mr. Delbert and Miz Dora Leigh are eatin' breakfast, then peek in the room. You know Miz Dora. She be axin' what you lookin' at. Then you say you lookin' for Miz Sara Anne 'cuz she ain't in her room."

"Ise lookin' for Miz Sara Anne 'cuz she ain't in her room," Sally repeated solemnly.

"That's right."

"Where she go?"

"She done sailed off to England."

"Lawd have mercy!"

"That's why we don't know nothin'. You understand?"

Sally nodded.

"Nothin,'" Bet repeated.

~~~

"What is it?" Dora snapped.

"I'm sorry," Sally apologized. "I was lookin' to see if Miz Sara Anne was in here 'cuz I went to hep her dress—"

"No, she is not," Dora cut her off. "And do not poke your head in rooms you don't belong."

"Beggin' your pardon."

Delbert had looked over. "Not in her room?"

"No, sir."

Dora glared at the mulatto, and Sally backed off and shut the door.

"Off riding again, I imagine," Dora said bitterly. "You ought not allow her to ride astride. I have seen her do it and it is vulgar."

Del put off her suggestion with an irritated wave of his hand.

~~~

An hour later, Bet carried the letters, all but the one written to her, into Delbert's study, claiming to have just found them. His upper lip curled as he stared at the letters. "Where were they?"

"Inside her jewelry box, sir. They were hid good."

He snatched the letters from her. "Get out."

She did. He would be furious once he read his letter and she didn't want to be anywhere in the vicinity for the fallout.

~~~

Aaron cocked his head, slowly. "She what?"

84

Delbert Aldridge was flushed, sweating and he reeked of liquor. Instead of repeating the explanation, he held up a letter. "Here. This one's to you. Read it for yourself," he slurred.

Aaron yanked the letter out of his hand and ripped it open. The ring fell at his feet, and he stared at it, then narrowed his eyes at Aldridge before bending for it and slipping it into his pocket. He quickly read the letter and then wadded the paper into a tight ball. "This is your doing," he accused.

Delbert drew himself up. "Mine?"

"First you spoil her, and then you go mad and beat her. I saw it, Aldridge. I saw what you did."

Del turned a dull purplish red. "She wanted out of the marriage contract."

"And you overreacted!" Aaron stretched his neck from side to side and tried to clear his head. "I'll bring her back. In the meantime, no one is to know about this."

"The invitations haven't gone out, so we'll delay it and—"

Aaron narrowed his eyes. "I may have a better idea."

Delbert paled fearing Waldron was going to withdraw his offer.

"What if we moved it up?" Aaron said softly but quite distinctly. He took a few steps away, breathing easier now that he had thought of a solution. He stuck his hands in his pockets and toyed with the ring she'd left behind.

"I don't understand," Delbert slurred,

Aaron turned back to him, stern in his resolve. "You will."

# Chapter Eight

*Middlesbrough, England*
23 June, 1746

P enelope Shelly made a small cry as the invitations began scattering from a gust of wind. She tried unsuccessfully to stop them from blowing from their allotted piles, one for acceptance and the other for rejection after days, even weeks of neglect.

"Blast," she cursed under her breath. She leaned back in her chair as a long, protracted sigh escaped her. It was ridiculous, really, how a small setback could rob a person of their energy and resolve.

"Excuse the intrusion, my Lady," the butler, Anderson, said from the doorway. "But someone has called for you."

"At this hour? Who is it?"

"Your niece. Sara Anne."

Penelope bolted out of her seat as if she'd been yanked from an invisible string attached to the richly paneled ceiling and hurried past him. Sara Anne was standing in the entry hall, with her hands clasped in front of her. She was all grown up and quite lovely, but frail looking with dark circles beneath her eyes. "Oh, my dear," Penelope cried. As she closed the distance between them, the impression that Sara Anne was not well strengthened.

"Aunt Penelope," Sara Anne said in a strained voice.

Penelope embraced her niece and Sara Anne clung to her. When Penelope pulled away, she kept hold of Sara Anne's shoulders and studied her face. "Are you well?"

"I am. If I look dreadful, it's because of a long voyage and too many sleepless nights."

"You are lovely and a sight for sore eyes, though you do look peaked."

"Come," Penelope said as she led Sara Anne off. "Let's get you settled so you can have a good rest." She glanced behind to see the trunk being brought in by the driver. "Have it brought to the white room," she said to Anderson.

He tipped his head to her.

"Ginny's in town, but she should be on her way back home," Penelope said to Sara Anne. "What a wonderful surprise you will be for her and for your uncle. He's away another few days on business."

"I did write, but—"

"It takes so long to get a letter." They started up the long, winding staircase, and Penelope matched her pace to her niece's. Sara Anne's coloring was off. Perhaps she had been ill and was recovering but had not regained her full strength. Surely, grief had taken such a toll on her health.

"You must be wondering why I'm here," Sara Anne said haltingly when they reached the top.

Penelope turned to her. "A visit is long overdue," she in a gentle tone. "And if there is more to tell than that, you may do so or not, as you wish." Tears filled Sara Anne's remarkable green eyes, and Penelope felt it tug a maternal cord. She reached over and stroked Sara Anne's cheek. "We are your family. I was not wondering."

"You're so kind to say so," Sara Anne said in a thick voice.

"I'm not kind, I'm your aunt. And you are exhausted."

"Yes," Sara Anne admitted. "I am."

"Come." Penelope walked on and opened the door to a bedchamber decorated in varying shades of white. It was extremely bright in the late morning light, too bright for a young woman who desperately needed to sleep, so Penelope walked to the windows and began closing shutters and drawing the curtains. "That's better, isn't it?"

"'Ere's yer trunk, miss," the driver said, walking in and setting it down. He couldn't help but gawk at the room. It was the most resplendent bedchamber he had ever seen or even imagined.

Anderson cleared his throat and led the man back out, closing the door behind him.

Penelope went back to Sara Anne. "I can hardly believe you're truly here. And all grown up. We've thought of you and spoken of you so often."

Sara Anne was so fatigued that she was slow to respond, other than a smile and a nod.

"You must rest now," Penelope said firmly. "I'll send someone up to unpack and undress you, and we'll visit later."

"Thank you, Aunt Penelope."

"Are you hungry?"

"No, not really."

"I'll have something light sent up."

~~~

Being ordered to bed was a relief. In fact, the gratitude she felt at having made it there and having been received so warmly was overwhelming. She walked over to a chaise lounge and stretched out, knowing she could easily and gladly sleep there. She closed her eyes, still feeling the motion of the ship.

A maid, a young woman with carrot-colored hair by the name of Fern, showed up to unpack her trunk. She was a slight young woman but amazingly efficient and she finished with the unpacking and sorting of what got hung and what needed laundering. She excused herself, took the items to be laundered, and quickly returned with a peach-colored silk dressing gown. "You'll be more comfortable in this."

Sara Anne allowed herself to be undressed down to her shift, and into the robe.

Food came next, cucumber sandwiches, thin slices of veal, grapes, crispy biscuits, and a pot of tea. It was exquisite and she felt restored afterward. She rose and went to a window. Pulling back the curtain, she peered out on the sun striped lawn, remembering it from before. Oh, to be those carefree girls again, she and Ginny and Caroline. Her eyes filled and spilled over, and she shook her head as she wiped the tears away. If only headache could be so easily gotten rid of.

She crawled into bed and burrowed in, thinking of Ginny. Her letters were frequently about her ventures into society, fashion, her various governesses, and her lessons in French and music. As a girl, Ginny had been great fun and she'd not taken anything too seriously, least of all, herself, but that was six years ago. As a young woman, she might well be something entirely different.

Sara Anne, on the other hand, had never learned French and she had a strong feeling that Charles Town society was nothing at all like that of London. She had no talent for music or drawing or even sewing, for that matter.

What *was* she good at?

She closed her eyes and exhaustion took over and dragged her into a deep, dreamless sleep that she remained in all that day and night.

~~~

Penelope awoke with a feeling of expectation, and it stayed with her throughout breakfast and heightened in the hour thereafter. She tried to attend to correspondence, but it was an exercise in futility because she couldn't concentrate. She finally gave up the effort and meandered outside enjoying the late morning air.

When she reached the carriage house, she saw that William's coach had returned. She clasped her hands together and rushed back inside to find her husband.

~

William Shelly walked into the morning room and squinted at the sunshine streaming through the open doors that led to the gardens. His wife was there, staring out. "That sun will blind you, my dear," he said.

She turned and it became instantly apparent that it was not Penelope. William reeled with the shock of seeing his sister. "Hope!"

"William?" Penelope called behind him.

"Uncle William," the apparition before him said.

William couldn't tear his stare away from her. She looked so like Hope.

"It's Sara Anne, dear," Penelope said.

He shook his head in wonder. "Of course, it is! Sara Anne!" He held open his arms.

She came to him, and they embraced.

"You look so like my sister," he breathed into her hair. When they parted, he continued to stare with an expression of awe. "My goodness, you are all grown up."

Penelope could scarcely take her eyes off Sara Anne. The long sleep had restored her color. "You look much better after your sleep," she commented.

"I feel better," Sara Anne admitted.

"What a homecoming," William burst. "Has Genevieve returned home, as well?"

"No, not yet," Penelope replied.

"We should send word that Sara Anne is here."

"I wouldn't want her to change her plans," Sara Anne spoke up.

"They were to have started back by now," Penelope said to her husband. She looked at Sara Anne with a wry expression. "She would stay for the entire season if we allowed it, but we feel she's too young. We consent to a handful of events under the supervision of my sister or a trusted friend."

"Well," William said, reaching out and grasping Sara Anne's hands. "Perhaps this is a better arrangement, anyway. Give your aunt and me a chance to spend time with you. I want to hear everything. How is your father?" he asked stiffly.

She felt stymied for a moment. "Caroline's passing changed him, hardened him. He—" Her voice faded off. "The truth is I left home without his knowledge or consent."

Her aunt and uncle were clearly disturbed by her announcement, and so she rushed to explain the events of the past few months, leaving out only the humiliation and punishment she had suffered at the hands of Aaron and her father. When she finished, Penelope murmured a sympathetic, "Oh, my dear."

"You left your father a letter," William confirmed.

90

"I did."

"How do you think he'll react?"

"He'll detest me, at least for a time. But I rather think he did anyway."

"Sara Anne," Penelope objected. "You mustn't say—"

William looked at his wife. "She should say as she feels, dearest."

"But no father detests their own child."

"Aunt Penelope, you don't know him. He detested my mother in the end—"

"Why is that?" William asked in an intense voice. "Do you know?"

"William, please," Penelope said, frowning. "We must not encourage—"

"I know the reaction I got from the man," he interrupted. "What Sara Anne says is true. I felt it and yet I couldn't get an explanation from him. I couldn't even get a civil reply." He looked back to Sara Anne. "Do you understand it?"

"I didn't until recently," she replied reluctantly. "You know my mother died in childbirth."

"As did the child. A son, I believe."

"Yes." She hesitated because it was difficult to say. "His head was ... too large."

Penelope sucked in a sharp breath.

"Because of its ... deformity, my father chose to believe it was not his child."

William fumed. "My sister would never—"

"I know," Sara Anne spoke up quickly. "And no one has ever spoken an ill word of her. Even my father kept his suspicions to himself, so far as I know."

"Then how do you know?"

"Bet told me. Servants see more than anyone."

William turned and walked to the large hearth in the room. He fingered the ivory figurines on the mantle for no particular reason other than having something to do. "Poor Hope."

"And what of Mr. Waldron?" Penelope asked her, gently. "You said he was arrogant, but that describes a good many men. Does he have no positive qualities you hold in esteem?"

"There was a time or two I thought he might. Times I thought he was defending me."

William turned to her.

"Something changed your mind?" Penelope prodded.

Sara Anne drew a breath to reply but no words would come. How could she possibly explain having her trust violated? How could she explain fearing someone because she sensed the cruelty in him? How could she explain what Aaron's own mother had intimated? She couldn't. "He changed my mind."

William and Penelope exchanged a look before William came back to her. "You are welcome here for as long as you wish to remain. I hope you know that."

"Thank you," Sara Anne whispered.

"We know you have a good heart and a good head on your shoulders," Penelope said.

Sara Anne was unable to speak for the lump in her throat.

"A woman should have some say in whom she marries," Penelope continued. "I wish it were always the case."

Sara Anne sighed. "I know that love may be too great a thing to hope for, but I do wish for tenderness and compassion and decency."

"Oh, my dear girl," Penelope said. "Love is not too great a thing to wish for. Aspire for it! Life is a brief, wonderful gift, but only when you're content with your lot."

"Last time you were here, your beverage of choice was chocolate," William said, cheerfully. "Remember?"

She smiled. "Of course, I do."

"Would you care for one now? I seem to have a sudden craving."

"I'll have some made," Penelope said, starting from the room.

"Did you ever learn to play chess?" William asked Sara Anne.

"You tried to teach me."

"You didn't have the patience for it then."

"I couldn't understand it, and Ginny kept laughing at me."

Penelope turned back from the door. "There is a bit of the devil in her," she remarked with a smirk. "I can't for the life of me fathom where it came from."

William chuckled. "Perhaps we should try again, before my devilish girl returns."

# Chapter Nine

T he letter Sara Anne had written was delivered to Oakley on the same day Genevieve arrived home from London. She arrived in the afternoon to discover both her father and mother were away. "Where is mama?" she asked Anderson as she looked through the post that had been delivered.

"Having tea at Langston House."

Genevieve came to Sara Anne's letter and smiled. "My cousin!"

"She's upstairs being fitted—"

Genevieve jerked her head up at him so violently that he stopped speaking.

"Oh," he exclaimed, reddening in his embarrassment. "Oh, you didn't realize—"

"My cousin," Genevieve repeated.

"Yes."

"Sara Anne from the colonies." She held up the letter, as if to prove her facts.

"Yes, Miss Ginny. She has come."

"Here?"

"Yes."

"Sara Anne is here?"

"She is. She is installed in the room next to yours."

Ginny shook her head. "When? When did she arrive?"

"Five days ago. On Tuesday."

Ginny rushed off. She dashed upstairs and heard voices behind the door to Sara Anne's room. She knocked, barely stifling a giggle.

"Come," was the curt, arrogant response.

Ginny recognized the voice of Madam Adele, the dressmaker, and she opened the door slowly, smiling with anticipation.

Sara Anne was standing on a stool, arms slightly out, while Madam Adele pinned the bottom of an elegant gown. Sara Anne's beauty was astonishing, but the best moment of all was when she

94

saw Ginny standing in the doorway. The sheer joy on Sara Anne's face made Ginny laugh out loud and clap like a child.

"Miss Shelly, really," Madam Adele exclaimed.

Ginny hurried in. "I cannot believe you're here!"

Sara Anne started to step down, but then stopped. "Oh!"

Madam Adele clucked her tongue in disgust. "Pins," she reminded the girl.

Sara Anne looked pained but close to laughter as she looked to Ginny. "Pins," she repeated.

"What a surprise this is! What a brilliant, wonderful surprise. I just arrived home and was thrilled to bits by a letter from you, and then here you are!" She grasped Sara Anne's hands.

Madam Adele huffed. "Could you possibly do this later?" she demanded in her clipped, French accent.

"Madame Adele, I haven't seen my cousin in years," Ginny complained.

"And I will through in half an hour," Madame Adele came back at her.

"Oh, alright." Ginny squeezed her cousin's hand. "I shall retire to my room and read your letter and send for refreshments. But come the very second you're finished."

"I will."

Ginny backed up a few steps, waiting for Madame Adele to go back to work on the hem before she made a face at the older woman.

"She can be such a child," Madam Adele commented as if she had seen it plainly.

Ginny burst into laughter. "Madam Adele, doesn't my cousin have the most wonderful accent?" she asked. "Have you ever heard anything like it?

"I have not," Madam Adele replied, disapprovingly. "Which colony are you from?"

"South Carolina."

"I have heard they are all savages there."

"Not all," Sara Anne replied. "Although I have known one or two."

"I think it sounds wonderfully exotic, myself," Genevieve spoke up.

"You would," Madame Adele retorted.

~~~

With her honey-colored hair, blue eyes and slightly turned up nose, Genevieve strongly favored her mother. It was strange to see a lovely young woman where a mischievous girl had been, but a great relief that Ginny was still Ginny. She still had the same warmth and the same irresistible vivaciousness. In that way, she reminded Sara Anne of Caroline. "I would have come the instant I knew you were on your way," she said when they were together.

"And missed all those gay events in the city?"

"I wouldn't call the mood gay, exactly. Victorious, I suppose, but not gay. It's all talk of the quashed rebellion and—"

"Rebellion?" Sara Anne asked.

"Scotland tried for independence again."

"I didn't know."

"This time they came closer than ever before so, naturally, the punishment will be all the harsher."

Sara Anne felt a shiver pass through her. The description struck too close to home.

"It took more than a week to get back home," Ginny continued. "It's so far to London, you know. Two hundred and fifty *interminably* long miles." She got up and poured them each a glass of wine from the carafe she'd had sent up.

"Last year," Ginny said, "we all went for most of season, but now Papa has some business keeping him here and Mama doesn't want to go without him. Nor do they want me gone for much more than a fortnight at a time, even thought my aunt is there and perfectly willing to chaperone me." She handed Sara Anne a glass. "I don't know how they'll manage when I'm grown and married." She sat and sipped her wine. "Tell me exactly what happened in Charles Town. I want to hear everything."

"I'd rather hear all about your adventures."

"You first."

Sara Anne sighed and sat back. "This past spring, I knew I'd be expected to become involved with social activities again."

Sympathy filled Ginny's face. "More than a year. I can't believe it. Has it gotten easier?" Ginny asked softly.

"I never stop missing her, but acceptance does finally settle in."

"Were you at all looking forward to getting out and about again?"

"There were days, I suppose. And then Aunt Dora came to escort me."

Ginny grimaced.

"Exactly," Sara Anne said.

"Well, I want details. Tell me of each party."

Sara Anne explained the spring season in Charles Town and about her association with Lance Harriston before segueing into the story about discovering Lance's engagement and the fact that Aaron Waldron had offered a proposal of marriage for her.

"Good gracious," Ginny said, frowning. "Go on."

Sara Anne relayed details about the Alvey's party and the next few times she had seen Aaron. The wine was taking effect, making her more emotional and candid than usual as she began to divulge what had taken place at Waldron House.

Ginny set her glass down and leaned forward in her chair, mesmerized as the story spilled out in a torrent of tears, choppy sentences and hiccups. She took hold of Sara Anne's hand, her blue eyes full of compassion. "That horrid, vile creature!"

"And then, I t-tried to t-talk to my f-father."

"Slow down and catch your breath."

"In the s-stable. I t-turned—"

Ginny crossed over to her and perched on the side of her chair to hold her. "It's alright. You're here and everything is going to be fine."

"He'll h-hate me."

"Who, darling? Your father?"

Sara Anne nodded miserably. "I na-know I shouldn't care."

"He won't hate you. He may be angry for a while—"

Sara Anne shook her head.

Ginny rose and crossed to her washstand. She poured some water from the pitcher to the bowl and dipped a washing cloth in it. "You must stop crying this moment." She crossed back to hand Sara Anne the cloth. "Put this on your face."

The cool rag was soothing. A second later, she felt Ginny's hand on her arm. "For the most beautiful girl I know, you look quite atrocious," Ginny teased.

That drew a smile from Sara Anne.

"You did the absolute right thing in coming here, you know," Ginny spoke soothingly. "It was very courageous."

"I left because I was t-terrified of being a p-prisoner for the rest of my life."

"It still would have been easier to stay and accept the situation, as unfair as it was. You took a tremendous risk, you know. If you'd been caught—"

Sara Anne shuddered at the thought. Somehow, it was more frightening now to think of what could have gone wrong.

"I'm so terribly proud of you."

Sara Anne rose and walked to the washstand. The attached looking glass reflected a dreadful image. "I do look atrocious."

Ginny walked up behind her and squeezed her shoulders. "But when you've collected yourself and face is back to normal, you'll still be the most beautiful young woman I know, and no will ever know you looked quite so frightening except you and I." She leaned closer. "And I will never tell," she promised in a whisper.

Sara Anne turned to her, and the girls embraced.

"It will be alright," Ginny soothed.

She wasn't looking quite normal again by dinner, but no one behaved as though they noticed.

"Are the Stafford girls still visiting next week?" Penelope inquired of her daughter.

"They are, but they'll only stay a day or two. Oh, and Glennis Augsberger, as well." Ginny looked at Sara Anne. "They're friends of mine. You'll like them, except Cynthia perhaps. She can be so dreadfully snobbish. Cynthia and Felicity Stafford. Their father is the highly esteemed General Cornelius Stafford." The last few words were spoken with a stiff neck and highly exaggerated diction.

Sara Anne grinned.

"Cynthia is newly engaged to Mister George Howell the fourth. Felicity and Glennis are my age. Glennis had her coming out a few months ago."

"She tippled too much champagne, turned green and was violently ill," William added. "No one will ever forget it."

"Oh, I hope that's not true," Penelope said. "The not forgetting it part, I mean. Perhaps in time." She quirked an eyebrow at her husband. "You will not mention anything of it when they're here."

William smirked.

Ginny grinned. "He wouldn't. My father is cursed with being a perfect gentleman."

William chuckled. "Cursed, am I?"

Servers removed the soup bowls and presented platters of roast pheasant, vegetables, bread, and more wine.

"How did it go today with Madame Adele?" Penelope asked Sara Anne.

"She's so rude," Ginny remarked before Sara Anne could reply.

"Of course, she's rude. She's French," William replied.

"She is one of us, now, dear," Penelope disagreed.

One side of William's mouth turned up. "She married an Englishman, lives in here and speaks our language ... most of the time, but she *is* French."

"Isn't it odd that the colonists developed an accent that's so different from ours?" Ginny posed.

"America is a long way from here," William said. "Another world, really. Sara Anne can attest to that."

"Yes," Sara Anne agreed.

"I wonder if it would disappoint, if I was to travel there," Ginny mused.

"That is not likely to happen, my dear," Penelope spoke up, her tone a bit sharper than she had intended. "You said the girls will only stay a day or two?"

"Yes. Their brothers will be taking them on to Scotland."

William cocked his head at her, a pained expression on his face. "Good God, whatever for?"

Ginny put down her fork. "The general has been offered his choice of estates there." She turned to her cousin. "The Scots tried another unsuccessful rebellion—oh, but I told you that already."

Sara Anne gave a quick nod to affirm.

"The rebel leaders all had their lands and money and possessions taken away."

Sara Anne felt a strong pang of pity. It was bad enough to lose a war, but to lose everything one owned on top of that?

"It's certainly not an appropriate place for young ladies," William stated.

Penelope watched her daughter respond, already sensing her desire to go with the Stafford family.

"Oh, Papa, it's *perfectly* safe," Genevieve argued. "The rebellion is all over and done with and there's martial law in Scotland. The English are everywhere."

William looked from his daughter to the knowing eyes of his wife, then back to his dinner, finally understanding what was happening.

"I have always wanted to see it, you know."

"Why?" William asked conversationally.

"Why?" she repeated. "To *see* it. To see their culture and—"

"Then this is the wrong time," William said, cutting her off. "Their culture will not be their own. It will be one of fear and defeat."

"I also would like to see the architecture and the countryside," Ginny continued stubbornly.

"All battered by war, my dear."

Sara Anne watched the family dynamics, fascinated by it. Genevieve was trying to get her way, she wished to go to Scotland with the Staffords, which her parents were both aware of and trying to avoid by debunking her arguments for going before she had even asked.

"They asked me to go along, and I would like to. On the condition, of course, that Sara Anne may go, too." She rushed on even though both her parents had drawn breath to speak. "If she wants to, that is," she said, looking directly at Sara Anne with pleading eyes. "Otherwise," she dropped her eyes. "I would stay, of course."

Sara Anne swallowed, but luckily, she didn't have to respond because Ginny had continued her argument.

"It will be a great opportunity. One, I imagine, I will only get offered once in my lifetime."

"Genevieve—" Penelope admonished. "You are being positively theatrical."

"Ginny," her father started in.

"You have yet to hear the plan. There is a rather large party going in two of the Stafford's' best coaches."

"Who is going?" he asked.

"Errol and Jamison Stafford, John Michael Price and his mother, who will act as chaperone." She turned to Sara Anne. "She's ever so kind. You'll love her. We all do."

"You were saying," Penelope prodded.

"Cynthia and Felicity, of course, Glennis, hopefully us, and two family servants."

Penelope frowned. "Not the general?"

"He's already there. We're going...I mean to say *they're* going to join him. Mrs. Stafford is there, as well." She looked from her mother to her father. "It would be perfectly safe, and I so want to go."

Silence.

"I'll think about it," her father finally said.

Ginny beamed a pleased smile and Sara Anne saw it have an immediate and profound effect on her uncle. She discreetly glanced at her aunt in time to see Penelope sigh and shake her head. Sara Anne was torn between excitement and dread since she was only just recovering from her voyage. "How far is it?" she asked.

"Yes," William spoke up. "Precisely where are they going?"

"To Jedburgh, which is just over the Scottish border." Ginny smiled sweetly with a little shrug.

Her father was somewhat placated.

"And?" Penelope asked.

"The second estate, a castle actually, is in Edinburgh or just outside of."

"Edinburgh!" William exclaimed. "That's entirely too far."

"Not for a once in a lifetime trip," Ginny begged. "Oh, please. Edinburgh is a great city and—"

"Ginny, it would take weeks," Penelope interrupted.

"But it will be broken up with interesting stops along the way."

"I don't wish for it to be discussed anymore this evening," Penelope said.

*Nor is it necessary,* Sara Anne thought wryly. They would give in to her request and all four of them knew it.

# Chapter Ten

The company, consisting of Cynthia and Felicity Stafford, Glennis Augsberger and another young woman by the name of Margaret Lambert, arrived a week and a half later in time for afternoon tea.

Sara Anne wore a new, dusky-rose afternoon gown and took pains with her appearance. These young women were from the most privileged class of arguably the greatest city in the world. Every facet of their wardrobe was the latest style, cut and color.

With her raven-black hair, striking deep blue eyes and delicate features, Cynthia Stafford was quite possibly the most beautiful girl Sara Anne had ever laid eyes upon. Of course, one did not have to observe her for long before noting the haughty lift to her chin and the cool, cutting way in which she looked at others. This was a young woman who had an exceedingly high opinion of herself.

Felicity Stafford, Cynthia's younger sister, was different. She had less dramatic coloring than her sister and less remarkable blue eyes, but Sara Anne did not doubt for a moment that it would be far more pleasant in her company. She seemed unpretentious, cheerful, and Sara Anne liked her on instinct.

Glennis Augsberger had the palest hair Sara Anne had ever seen. It was nearly white. Her pale skin was flawless except for some faint frown lines at the corners of her mouth which seemed out of place in one so young. She was willowy with light eyes that appeared frail and watery. As the afternoon wore on, it became obvious that she took cues solely from Cynthia and seemed highly concerned with impressing her.

The only pleasing feature Margaret Lambert possessed was lustrous, auburn hair. Otherwise, Margaret, Margie they called her, was thick looking. Her skin was rather mottled, her eyes were a

103

colorless gray and Sara Anne suspected she had a personality to match.

Sara Anne was introduced, received perfectly correctly, and eventually asked the standard questions about the colonies everyone wanted to know. What was it like? Did she still consider herself British? Had she seen many red Indians?

"Your accent is so interesting," Glennis said. Her expression read more like she smelled something suspect but was too polite to comment on it.

Sara Anne was spared having to come up with a suitable response by Felicity, who remarked, "Isn't it astounding how many different accents there are to the English language? In Scotland—"

"They butcher the language," Cynthia spoke up. "They might as well be speaking a foreign language as the Welsh do, for all one can understand them."

The conversation continued dominated by Cynthia's views on all non-British things and people, until it was time to change for dinner. As they rose to leave the salon, Sara Anne became aware of Cynthia's cold blue-eyed gaze on her.

"*Quelle agréable robe*," the dark haired beauty uttered. "*Peux je supposer que la Madame Adele l'a conçu?*"

Ginny had prepared her for Cynthia's penchant for embarrassing others by exposing what she perceived as their weaknesses. Cynthia had used the tactic on other young women whose French was either poor or nonexistent and Ginny had suspected she might try it on Sara Anne. Thus, she had gone so far as to develop an elaborate scheme to fool Cynthia and to prevent embarrassment to her cousin.

She'd thought of four all-purpose responses and taught them to Sara Anne along with a signal that would indicate which response to use, depending on what Cynthia chose to say or to ask. A discreet touch to her hair meant Sara Anne should recite, '*Merci. Comment gentil de votre dire ainsi.*' Meaning, Thank you. How can of you to say so.

If Ginny she scratched her nose, '*Je ne pense pas ainsi, non.*' Or, I don't think so. No.

Nose, no. *Non,*" Ginny had instructed, thoroughly enjoying the exercise of outwitting Cynthia. There was logic behind each gesture and phrase and, fortunately, Sara Anne was a quick learner with a remarkable ear, and an almost uncanny ability to mimic with perfect inflection.

If she brushed her skirt, Sara Anne was to say, '*Oui, je suis tout à fait d'accord*'—yes, I quite agree, and a subtle shake of her head indicated the use of '*Avec respect, je suis en désaccord,* for respectfully, I disagree.

Once Sara Anne uttered the phrase, Ginny would take over and basically shame Cynthia for having put her cousin on the spot. That was the plan. Out of the corner of her eye, Sara Anne could see that Ginny smoothing her hair, her cue to utter the first phrase. However, the expression on Cynthia's face was too much. "I don't speak French, Miss Stafford," she replied without a trace of embarrassment. "I don't speak Spanish or Portuguese either, in case you were going to try asking in those languages next."

It occurred to her how much Caroline would have enjoyed her response and a corner of her mouth twitched.

Cynthia flushed. "We'll stick to our language, then," she replied coolly. "Unless, of course, in the interest of fairness, you would prefer yours."

"Either works perfectly well for me," Sara Anne said in a perfect British accent she'd mastered years ago.

Cynthia turned abruptly and walked away before anyone else. Glennis rushed after her and Margie went after Glennis. Sara Anne turned to see Ginny and Felicity shaking with silent mirth.

"She admired your dress," Felicity said.

"And asked if Madame Adelle designed it," Ginny added. "We had a perfect response worked out."

"I know we did," Sara Anne conceded. "But I don't wish to put on a performance for anyone."

"What a perfect answer," Felicity said, walking toward Sara Anne with a gleam in her eye. "I'm so glad you're coming along with us."

~~~

Sara Anne looked up from her book as Ginny came into her room that night.

"I can't believe they brought Margie," Ginny complained. "I have never liked her. I saw her trip a servant once at a party." Ginny sat on the bed, then scooted back and got comfortable. "The poor man had a tray full of drinks and they went," she waved her hand in a grand, sweeping motion, "everywhere and then he was berated in front of everyone."

"That's terrible," Sara Anne replied.

"I know. What are you reading?"

Sara Anne lowered the book so she could see. "*Pamela*."

"'O soften him! Or harden me!'" Ginny quoted. She stretched out. "I can't believe we leave tomorrow. What an adventure it will be!" She rolled over on her side. "So, tell me, what did you think of everyone?"

"Cynthia has very strong views," Sara Anne replied tactfully.

"Oh, yes."

"Felicity is kind. I like her."

Ginny nodded.

"And Glennis," Sara Anne continued, "has very light hair," she said haltingly.

Ginny laughed. "She's better when she's not around Cynthia. I don't know why she cares so much about what Cynthia thinks and does ... and eats and wears and—"

Sara Anne chuckled.

"We'll just have to make do," Ginny concluded. Excitement suddenly overwhelmed her. Her eyes widened and she shivered with excitement. "We're really going. It's my first real adventure."

"You've been to London so many times."

"Mere distance does not make an adventure make," Ginny waned philosophic. "I've been to London several times a year for as long as I can remember. Perhaps it was an adventure in the beginning. But I've never been to Scotland. I don't suppose it will be the same as it usually is, all war torn and tragic and such, but still."

Sara Anne couldn't bring herself to respond to her cousin's romanticizing. She had seen the results of a rebellion. There was nothing romantic about it.

"I suppose we should go to sleep," Ginny said. "But I don't think I shall be able to." She considered. "I might have cook make me a cup of hot milk with brandy or perhaps a cup of chamomile tea. Do you want one?"

"No, thank you. I shall sleep fine," Sara Anne replied, sinking down deeper into the covers.

"Alright, then," Ginny said, popping up. "Until tomorrow."


As always, Sara Anne was up, washed and waiting in her shift and a dressing gown when Fern came in the next morning to help her dress. She was self-conscious about the marks on her back and didn't want anyone to see them. They had faded to raised white marks and Sara Anne suspected she would bear them for life.

"The post came," Fern reported cheerfully, producing a letter from her pocket. "You have a letter. Just think, miss, if it had come just one day later, you would have missed it."

Sara Anne took the letter and stared at the childlike writing. She felt a heady flush of warmth as she recognized it had come from Bet's hand.

Sara Anne pulled off her dressing gown as Fern went for the corset. "Are you looking forward to the journey?"

Sara Anne braced herself against a bedpost as Fern began drawing and tying her laces. "Perhaps not compared to Ginny."

"Have you seen the carriages yet?"

"No."

"They are something, miss. There's two of them, each drawn by four fine horses. Cleveland Bays, they're called," she said, proud of her newly acquired knowledge. "Enormous animals. Seventeen hands high."

Sara Anne smiled at Fern's enthusiasm, despite being tugged this way and that.

"The carriages are silver and they have the family crest on the doors. Smart looking, they are. Never ridden in anything like that before."

When Sara Anne was dressed and ready and Fern had gone, she tore into Bet's letter. She felt an initially let down by the few lines written, but then reminded herself that would have taken a good while to compose. Writing was not Bet's strong suit.

> *My sweet girl,*
> *Mister Arin Waldron be comin to fetch you. Thers a*
> *plan afoot tho I don no wat. I git a bad feelin bout it an*
> *I figered you best be tol. You take care. Yor Bet luvs*
> *you.*

Sara Anne's eyes were round and unblinking. Aaron was coming to fetch her? She had never considered the possibility. She sank onto the bed. What did he think—that he could drag her back? Her head suddenly throbbed and she pressed her fingers to her temple. She needed to see her uncle to get his stance on the matter.

She didn't pass anyone as she made her way to her uncle's study, which was a relief since she was in no frame of mind to engage in idle chitchat. She had just raised her hand to knock on the door when it opened. A man with frizzy gray hair and a ruddy completion was standing before her and he seemed startled by her presence, although he quickly collected himself and bowed slightly.

"Miss." His voice was high-pitched with a nasal quality.

The door opened wider, and William stepped around the man. "Good morning, my dear."

"Good morning, Uncle William."

"Dalton, allow me to introduce my niece, Miss Sara Anne Aldridge from Charles Town in the colony of South Carolina."

The man cocked his head slowly as her uncle spoke, to such a degree it looked as though it must have strained his neck.

"Sara Anne, dear, may I present Sir Dalton Fox."

Sara Anne curtsied. "Sir Dalton."

Dalton bent to kiss her hand and she felt a cold prickle of disgust. It was something about the way his gaze lingered on her bodice.

"You are a long way from home," he observed.

His voice was comical and her inclination to giggle was fierce. She clinched her fists together, digging her fingernails into her palms to keep from it. "I am."

"Are you prepared for your adventure?" William spoke up.

"Yes, but I was hoping we could speak for a moment."

"Of course. Let me just see Sir Dalton out first."

Anderson rounded the corner and almost collided with the small group. "I beg your pardon." He held up a stack of letters in hand. "The post came."

"Set it inside."

William gestured the way out to Sir Dalton. "Shall we?"

"A pleasure to have met you, my dear," Dalton Fox gushed, lingering a moment longer.

William patted Sara Anne's arm as he passed. "I'll be back shortly. Make yourself comfortable."

Anderson walked past her and put the letters in a tray on the desk, then turned and tipped his head to her. "Good morning, Miss Aldridge."

"Good morning, Anderson."

When he was gone, Sara Anne looked around the wood-paneled study. She hadn't been in here since her last visit. The paintings that lined the walls were of hunting scenes or of dogs. She walked to the large, circular window and looked out at an overcast morning wondering how to broach the topic she needed to.

Her fear was that her father had either written or would soon, conveying his wish that she be returned to Charles Town. Otherwise, Aaron would have no hope of forcing her back. Only her uncle could say whether she could stay, given that circumstance.

She went to sit in a chair in front of the desk, but her shirt brushed against the letter tray, and she knocked it and the letters to the floor. She bent to retrieve them, but her hand froze midair when saw the familiar *W* seal on the back of an envelope. She had seen that seal before. She picked up the letter and turned it over. Even through tears that had sprung to her eyes, she recognized the penmanship. Aaron had written to her uncle.

*Why?*

There was a plan afoot as Bet had warned and this was part of it. She could feel it! Her heart was beating wildly as she stood and put the letters back as they were with the exception of Aaron's, which she slipped up her sleeve.

"Sara Anne," Ginny said from the doorway.

Sara Anne jumped, startled by her voice.

Ginny's hand flew to her mouth to stifle a grin. "I beg your pardon. I didn't mean to frighten you."

Sara Anne shook her head quickly, her face heating with the guilt she felt. "I was waiting for your father."

"Is he coming back?"

"Yes." She felt breathless and slightly sick. "He's walking Sir Dalton out."

"I'm so glad I missed *him*. I always feel as if I need a wash after he slobbers over my hand. 'Oh, my dear girl,'" she mocked in a high-pitched, nasal voice. "It's so very wonderful to see you again and looking so well.'"

Sara Anne walked toward the door, feeling the need for escape. "I was going to say goodbye."

"Are you ready?" Ginny was positively glowing with excitement.

"Nearly. I'd better see to it."

By the time Sara Anne got back to her room, she was nearly frantic. What had she done, taking the letter? But what had Aaron Waldron done, writing to her uncle in the first place? She pulled the envelope out of her pocket and stared at it. Her hands were shaking as she broke the seal and withdrew the letter.

*Waldron House*
*28 May, 1746*

*Dear Lord Shelly,*

*Permit me to introduce myself as best I can on mere paper. I am your nephew-in-law—*

Sara Anne gasped and shook her head as she reread the sentence. She felt strange and tingly as she read on, with astonishment and mounting tension.

*As you may or may not be aware, I married Sara Anne. She is now Mrs. Waldron, although she somehow managed to disappear from Waldron House and sail to England before we could consummate our vows.*

*Understand, sir, I could have chosen to annul the marriage, but I did not. I did not and do not wish to humiliate the Aldridge's, most especially my Sara Anne who must be terribly frightened and confused. I attribute this fear to having been denied her mother while growing up. She is my wife and I want no other. I forgive her fully and wish only to reassure her of my continuing devotion.*

*I am coming to Middlesbrough for her. Please, hold her there for me. You are bound by duty, law, and morality to do so. Together, we can reassure her that all is and will be well. I look forward to meeting you and your family, which is now, I am pleased and honored to say, an extension of my own.*

*Warm Regards,*
*Aaron Waldron*

Sara Anne moved unsteadily to a chair and sat heavily. She couldn't think for the shock of the lies. She shook her head, trying to think. Good Lord! Aaron was coming. He would try and convince her aunt and uncle that they were married. But how could he? His claims couldn't be substantiated because they weren't true. And yet he was no idiot. He was an intelligent, calculating man, a gambler who played to win. But what game was he playing that was based on such a blatant untruth?

She stared down at the incriminating letter. Uncle William could never discover that she had opened it. She got up and walked to her fireplace, struck a match and set the letter ablaze. She set it on the grate and watched it disappear before going back for Bet's to do the same.

She had thought she would feel better when they were gone but new worries came flooding to her mind. What if someone had paid close attention to the stack of letters and realized one was missing? She had been in Uncle William's office, and they would suspect her. No, she was being foolish. Besides which, the letter was gone now. There was no undoing what was done. She needed to concentrate on what was important. Aaron had made an outrageous claim, knowing full well she would contest it.

*Proof.* He would have some kind of manufactured proof. But what? And, more importantly, how could she go about proving an event had *not* taken place?

A knock on the door startled her. "Yes?" she called.

Penelope opened the door. "Are you ready?"

Sara Anne tried to appear calm. "I believe so. My trunk was already taken down." She stood on weakened knees and walked out, anxious to be clear of the room and the guilty scent of burnt warnings and lies.

As goodbyes were said, Sara Anne grew more and more conflicted. She was beginning to feel that she should stay to deal with whatever trouble Aaron seemed determined to bring her way, but if she did, Ginny might not go, and she would be disappointed, and everyone would ultimately resent her.

Uncle William was relaxed and jovial as he kissed Sara Anne on both checks. "I'm sorry I was so long with Fox. The man doesn't know when to stop blathering on."

Sara Anne was unable to speak for a moment due to the lump in her throat. She never wanted to disappoint him. "I wanted to thank you," she finally managed.

A look of tenderness filled his face. "Oakley was your mother's home, and it is yours as well."

Aunt Penelope approached from behind. "Have a wonderful journey. The two of you watch out for one another."

The occupants of the coach sat three per each side. Sara Anne was sandwiched between Ginny and Margie Lambert, who took up double what her space should have been. Not all of it was bulk. Some of it was that Margie was supremely inconsiderate. The Staffords' female servant, Mrs. Buckley, John Michael Price, and Glennis Augsberger rode across from them.

John Michael Price was Jamison Stafford's closest friend. He had ash-blond hair, an easy smile, and excellent manners. His nose was a bit too sharp and would have marred his looks more except for the magnetism of his personality. It occurred to Sara Anne that, if one had to choose a brother, he would be an ideal candidate.

Glennis, sitting next to him, obviously thought him an ideal candidate as well, though not for a brother. She flirted more aggressively than anyone Sara Anne had ever witnessed. It was fascinating in an acutely embarrassing sort of way. It should have been Glennis who was embarrassed. As for John Michael, he seemed polite but dismissive of her and exerted most of his effort trying to engage the others in conversation.

The lead coach was carrying all the Stafford siblings, plus Mrs. Price and a male family servant. Errol Stafford, the eldest Stafford brother, was only in his late twenties but his dark hair was already receding and thinning noticeably. Although she hadn't spent but a few minutes in his company, he struck Sara Anne as every bit as arrogant as Cynthia. Jamison was a year younger than Errol and resembled his brother, although there was more to him— more humor, more hair, more warmth. The Staffords were all attractive, but none of them as striking as Cynthia.

It was sunny and breezy when they stopped for luncheon just beyond Newcastle upon Tyne. Errol announced they'd made excellent time, that they were traveling ten miles per hour and would be over the Scottish border by nightfall. And so they were.

The party stopped at a roadside inn. Their first destination, one of the estates General Stafford had been offered, was only fifteen

113

miles further, but no one thought it wise to venture any further in the gathering darkness.

The Inn, a stone lodge with exposed wood-beams darkened by age, had small rooms dominated by large hearths. It was small enough that the group was forced to sleep either two or three to a room. It didn't bother Sara Anne. She fell into a deep sleep and didn't wake until Genevieve shook her awake the following morning. It was already light, and Ginny was fully dressed. "I've overslept—" Sara Anne realized in a hoarse voice. "I'm sorry."

"Don't fret. Come down when you're ready. I'll order you some breakfast."

Sara Anne dressed as quickly as she could, choosing the traveling garment Aunt Penelope had made for her since it was boned and required no corset. She felt pressured to rush. She was not only a guest of the Staffords, she was the guest of a guest. It would certainly not do to keep the others waiting.

She entered the tavern, nearly tripping over a small girl playing in the doorway. The child couldn't have been more than four. She was a frail little thing with large, solemn brown eyes, a runny nose and a filthy dress. Sara Anne squatted down to make sure she was all right. "Did I frighten you?" she asked softly.

The girl shook her head.

"I didn't knock into you, did I?"

The girl shook her head again.

"Then you cannot knock me back," Sara Anne teased to the delight of the small girl.

Distracted by an eerie feeling, Sara Anne stood and looked around at several occupants of the small room watching her with what she only term malevolence. It was a new experience to be despised by strangers. She smiled down at the girl before forcing herself to move on to the table where Ginny, Glennis, Cynthia, and Margie sat. Sara Anne sat next to Ginny.

"Isn't it disgusting?" Glennis hissed at her. "I will not touch the food, myself."

Glennis looked even more bloodless than usual. Sara Anne thought food and drink would do her a world of good, she wouldn't say so.

"The others are outside, getting ready to go," Ginny said. She seemed stiff and uncomfortable, and Sara Anne understood the feeling perfectly. Ginny leaned closer to whisper, "Do you think they hate us because of the rebellion?"

Sara Anne nodded. It seemed a logical assumption.

"I didn't expect to feel it so profoundly," Ginny commented.

Cynthia was sitting very upright, staring straight ahead, but at no one in particular. She was neither eating nor drinking.

"I ordered you tea and bread," Ginny said, nibbling at her own. "It's quite good and there is some delicious jam."

Margie pushed her empty plate away. "Your taste astounds me. It was perfectly vile."

"How do you know they didn't poison it?" Glennis asked, directing her question to Margie. "They hate us, you know." She folded her arms tightly against herself and glared around the room.

It was suddenly, blindingly obvious to Sara Anne that some occupants of the room enjoyed the mutual animosity. Glennis and Cynthia and Margie, for example—for all their frowning and complaint of being hated, this experience provided a spark of adventure in their lives. Funny, the way something could become so clear in a mere instant. These young women lived lives of great privilege, but also of great restraint, so much more than she'd ever endured.

Sara Anne had always known there was something different about Caroline and herself, and not just because of Aunt Dora's criticism. There were condescending stares and whispered comments behind beautifully spread fans from some of the ladies of Charles Town, particularly regarding their choice of dress.

"It's pity over being motherless," Caroline would say with a roll of her eyes. "Poor us." And that would usually be followed with a comment over something the offending party should be extending their pity on.

A coarse-looking woman set a hunk of brown bread and a mug of tea in front of Sara Anne, jarring her back to reality. The woman glanced up at the girl in the corner and sloshed a bit of tea in the process.

Glennis and Margie both gave a disgusted harrumph.

"Il fetchahdag," the woman said, narrowing her eyes at Glennis.

Glennis looked at Cynthia. "What did she say?"

*I'll fetch a rag.* Sara Anne had understood perfectly. She had gotten used to concentrating on the spoken word to understand it and respond promptly. "Please don't bother," she replied to the woman. "Not much spilled and we're not staying long."

The woman raised her chin as she studied Sara Anne through slitted eyes. "Ere yeh fromthin?"

Admittedly, her thick Scottish brogue took more discerning than the British accent. Sara Anne started to reply but Cynthia spoke over her in distinct, clipped words. "From the British colonies in America."

Sara Anne noticed Cynthia still did not deem it necessary to look at the woman.

The woman made a sort of grunt. "Glad I dinna spit in yers, then," she said. "I saw yeh were kind tae the gerl." She jerked her head over to the small girl playing in the corner. Then, with a satisfied grin, she walked off, brushing her hands on her apron as she went.

Ginny looked horror-stricken.

"I told you," Glennis declared, victoriously.

"She didn't mean it," Sara Anne told her cousin, although her meal didn't have as much appeal as it had a minute ago and there wasn't enough gold in all the British empire to have made her finish Ginny's.

"I feel sick," Margie complained, clutching her stomach.

"After all you consumed, I would think so," Cynthia replied, disgust evident in her voice.

Ginny looked pale as she rose to leave. That seemed to work as a cue and the others followed.

"I'll be right there," Sara Anne said. She took a sip of tea. It was strong, hot and fresh. She took another sip, wishing she had time to finish it. The small girl was suddenly back, brave enough to approach now that the others were gone. "Do you live here?" Sara Anne asked.

The little girl shook her head. "My sister cleans rooms." The child's voice was breathy, young, and sweet.

"What is your name?"

"Malie."

"I'm Sara Anne. Have you eaten yet this morning, Malie?"

The child looked at the bread in Sara Anne's hand, then shook her head slowly.

Sara Anne tore off a third of the hunk and handed the larger part to the child. "We'll share."

Malie's eyes lit up. *"Tapadh leibh!"*

Sara Anne was taken by surprise by the foreign words, and she couldn't help smiling at the child. "You're welcome."

It was only a short ride today to the first estate and Sara Anne had agreeable riding companions. Somehow, recounting the morning's experience was far more amusing than the experience itself had been. Even Ginny laughed as Sara Anne shared it with the others.

The coach slowed and then stopped, and they all peered out to find out why. They had been riding for less than half an hour so too soon to be at the estate. The driver called something out, but Sara Anne couldn't make the words.

"What did he say?" Felicity asked.

"I'll find out," John Michael said, scooting forward on his seat.

Jamison climbed out behind John Michael.

Errol appeared outside the coach door. "There's felled trees in the road," he said huffily.

"Well, we didn't put them there," John Michael quipped.

Felicity laughed.

"Let's not waste our effort trying to be amusing. Shall we?" Errol snapped, rolling up his shirtsleeves. "This will take all of us. Looks to me as if the damned things have been placed there on purpose."

Jamison and John Michael removed their jackets and tossed them back in the coach.

"Let's get out and see," Felicity suggested.

Sara Anne and Ginny followed her out.

117

"The Hall shouldn't be far," Felicity said. "Father said it was just over an hour's ride past town."

One small tree laid atop another and the men—gentlemen, servant, and drivers alike—were positioned, three per side, bracing themselves to lift the first.

"On three," Errol called. "One, two—"

A din of rumbling thunder alarmed everyone. The ground shook, the men stood upright, and everyone looked around, fear rising as the noise and sense of impending danger escalated. Horses suddenly broke though the surrounding woods transporting masked men who were brandishing pistols.

"Footpads," Jamison cried.

"Don't shoot," Errol cried, sticking his hands high in the air.

The bandits encircled the group. "Don't plan on shootin' les' yeh make it impossible not tae," one called out. "Be a bloody shame if there were a few less English in the world." His voice was clear and understandable despite its distinct Scottish accent. "Fact is, we'll only be requirin' the young ladies at present."

Sara Anne felt a stab of cold fear.

"No! Absolutely not!" Errol puffed up.

"You can't," John Michael cried. "Please! We'll give you anything we have."

Four men were off their horses and approaching, pistols at the ready.

"We can an we will," the leader spoke clearly. "An' I advise yeh not tae be foolish if yeh wan' tae live."

Cynthia was jerked out of the lead coach and was hustled forward to a man on horseback. "Get your hands off me," she cried, plucking at the man's arm to no avail. "My father will—"

The horseman pulled her up and over the saddle and took off at a dead run.

Sara Anne didn't realize that Felicity had grabbed hold of her hand, until a man walked toward them and began pulling Felicity away. *Was this a vendetta against the Staffords?*

"Wait, please!" John Michael begged. "If this is about money—"

One of the bandits hit him with the butt of a pistol and knocked him down.

Jamison bent over him, holding out an arm to protect him from any more blows.

"Of course, it's about money," the leader replied. "What else is there?"

John Michael's head was bleeding profusely, and Felicity stared back at him with grief-filled eyes as she was pulled away and spirited off.

Sara Anne felt rough hands grab her and she saw Ginny being pulled away at the same time.

"Please," Jamison begged. "We'll pay you whatever you want, just stop this."

"We know yel pay," the leader spoke. "An' their families will pay. Now, remain calm an no one has tae die."

Abduction for the purpose of ransom. Sara Anne's mind reeled as her hands were tied behind her back. She was grabbed up and lifted to a rider, who clamped his arms around her and took off. Within minutes, she neither heard nor saw anyone else. Had they all taken different paths?

They rode for what felt like a long time, but it was hard to judge. In a dense wood, they were forced to slow. "Where are you taking me?" she asked, not able to stand the suspense any longer. "Where are the others?"

"Yer no English?" the man asked.

She clamped her mouth shut.

They finally passed into a clearing and a cold, misty rain. She could see decaying structures ahead of her and a group of men assembled there, perhaps fifteen or twenty of them. She didn't see Ginny or any of the other women. She noticed that none of the men were bothering with masks anymore. Was that a good sign or a bad sign? The men were more human looking without the faceless masks, but they risked exposure by shedding them. If they had true intentions of letting them go, why not stay masked?

Her rider dismounted. He'd already removed his mask, revealing that he was young with fair hair and a strangely innocent look about him. He helped her down and then unbound her wrists.

Another man, this one well in his fifties, with wild looking gray hair and a grizzled face, walked over and took hold of her arm and led her toward an old barn that looked as if it was about to collapse in on itself.

"I'll tell yeh, wha' I told the others," he warned in a menacing tone. "If yeh run, we'll catch you an make yeh sorry yeh made us go tae the trouble." He gave her a shove into the barn, where she saw Ginny, Cynthia, Glennis and Margie hovered in one corner. Ginny got to her feet rushed to her.

"Are you alright?" they both asked at once.

"I am," Ginny was the first to reply. "But one of them bit Margie and beat her with a stick. Two other men had to pull him off her."

Sara Anne glanced over at the young women who were sitting on a dirt-covered floor for the first time in their lives. "He bit her?"

There was a streak of dried blood under Margie's nose and it was apparent she'd been crying. Sara Anne hadn't particularly cared for Margie but she felt pity for her now.

"I said too much, apparently," Margie replied. She was both furious and upset. "And that scum screamed in my ear for me to shut up and then he bit me." She pulled her hand away from the side of her face, revealing an angry looking bruise. "I hope he gets hung and beaten and burned!"

"He hit her with a stick," Glennis spoke up.

"Over and over," Margie embellished.

"Where is Felicity?" Sara Anne asked, noticing she was missing.

"They're *interviewing* her," Cynthia replied, her blue eyes dark with suppressed rage.

Sara Anne blinked in astonishment. Their captors had her only sister, and she was insulted by their choice of words?

"I hope they hang every last one of these bastards," Margie said. "I want to see it. I want to light the fire that burns them while they are still alive."

Sara Anne swallowed convulsively, shaken by her virulence.

"Shut up," Cynthia snapped. "Do you want them to come in here and start beating us all?"

120

Margie closed her mouth and breathed nosily through her nostrils.

Sara Anne walked close to the open doorway of the barn and peered out. Two men were posted outside the barn door, but their attention was on the group assembled under the crude wooden structure. A pale but composed Felicity was being walked back, although the man beside her didn't have a hand on her. She looked unharmed, and Sara Anne breathed a sigh of relief.

Felicity entered the barn went to Sara Anne and took hold of her hands.

"Are you alright?" Sara Anne asked. She could feel her trembling.

Felicity nodded.

One of the men continued forward and gestured to Glennis. "Gerl wi' white hair."

Glennis looked utterly panicked and Ginny moved to help her up. "Don't worry, Glennis. See? Felicity is fine."

The man led Glennis out, and Felicity and Sara Anne crossed back to the others. "What did they say?" Cynthia demanded of her sister.

"They know who we are. They said Father described us well."

"Father?"

"Apparently, he left instructions in Jedburgh for us to be taken care of when we came through and they've been planning this ever since."

"What do they want with us?"

"Money. They will trade us back to our families."

"That's what they say now," Margie said ominously.

Cynthia glowered at her, and Margie dropped her gaze.

"Just tell them what they want to know," Felicity said.

"They didn't hurt you?" Ginny asked.

"No. Actually, they were very polite."

"Oh," Cynthia remarked scathingly. "We have polite abductors. Isn't that something like charming vermin?"

Sara Anne couldn't remain still. She walked back to the doors to watch the proceedings. She heard Margie ask, "What does she think she's doing?" behind her back but ignored it.

Staring out the doors, she heard light footsteps behind her and felt someone take her arm, knowing it was Ginny without looking.

"What are you thinking?" Ginny whispered.

*Aaron—arriving at Oakley in time to learn of this, buy my freedom and doom me forever.* Sara Anne shook her head, her thoughts too jumbled to relay.

"What is it?" Ginny pressed.

"Don't tell them who I am," Sara Anne said quietly.

"What? Why?"

"Aaron Waldron is coming for me."

"He is? How do you know?"

"Bet wrote me. I received her letter yesterday, just before we left. I can't go back with him, Ginny."

"No, of course not. Nor can he make you."

"What if my father has sent a letter stating that is his wish?"

Ginny blinked. "Would he do that?"

"Yes."

"My father will protect you. You can remain at Oakley with us. They cannot force you."

"What if he claims we're already married or that I'm a wanted criminal or—"

"You're talking foolishness."

"I'm not. You don't know him. He has a plan. He plays to win."

"Are you suggesting this is a game?"

Sara Anne nodded. "One he's determined to win."

"But what does any of that have to do with telling them who you are?"

Sara Anne looked back out and saw Glennis being led back toward them. Her normally white skin was red and blotchy from crying.

"You don't know me well," Sara Anne spoke quickly. "I am merely an acquaintance from the colonies. That's so far away. Perhaps they'll just let me go."

Ginny frowned, not liking the sound of it.

"Just say nothing about me," Sara Anne begged. "I doubt if they'll ask you, anyway."

"If you're only an acquaintance, how did we meet?"

"In London, when you were last there. It was there that you invited me to go with you."

Glennis was let off at the door and the man waved Ginny forward.

"You'll be fine," Sara Anne whispered, squeezing her suddenly cold hand.

Glennis was sobbing and the rest of the group moved in to soothe her and to find out what had been said, all but Sara Anne who stayed at the door watching Ginny being led off. She strained to listen to what Glennis recounted, but it was impossible to make sense out of anything she was saying.

# Chapter Eleven

Adrian McGoldrick leaned against one of the back posts of the lean-to. On second thought, he straightened back up since he didn't want to be responsible for sending the whole place crashing down around them. He was uncomfortable being here, and he loathed this scheme. None of the women would be hurt, but if the English rode in now, it wouldn't matter. They had committed a crime by taking the females and they would be executed without exception or delay.

Even if they got away with it, someone, some poor Scot, would pay somewhere down the line. Of course, they'd pay, anyway. As long as they were under English rule, they would pay whenever and however the English felt like it.

He was only halfway listening to Robert Kinnaird, the mastermind behind the operation, as he questioned another young woman. "*Lord* William Shelly," Robert repeated. "An' you are his only daughter?"

"I am," the young woman replied softly.

The fair-haired girl was innocent looking. Adrian detested English Lords, English Generals, and English rule as much as anyone, but this young woman didn't deserve to be frightened out of her wits. None of them did.

"Thank you, Miss Shelly," Robert said. "That will be all."

Adrian wanted to be done with it. He wanted his assignment. He would complete it and then return home with the promised reward to aid his sisters and their children. Nearly all of his clansmen had been wiped out at Culloden. Whoever was still left at home would be suffering in more ways than one and they needed him. Without question, he was involved in a bad thing, but it was for a good reason.

He had been badly wounded at Culloden and these men, strangers at the time, had rescued him, brought him back to their home in Jedburgh and seen him nursed back to health. He owed allegiance to them. He owed his life to them. Plus, he needed the money they were offering in exchange for his assistance with this venture. This *criminal* venture that would get every one of them hung and disemboweled if they were caught.

The fourth young woman was led in. She was the large redhead Fitzpatrick had laid into for some reason. He didn't know which female would become his responsibility, but he hoped it wouldn't be this one. Their best hope was for this to go fast and easy. Collect the money, make the exchange, and then go their separate ways. One thing was for sure and certain, if this were to become an ongoing operation, he would have no future part to play.

"Yer name?" Robert asked.

The redhead started to cry, and Adrian almost moaned. *Why did they all have to start crying?*

"M-Margaret L-Lambert."

"Try an' calm yourself, Margaret Lambert. I've only a few questions tae ask yeh." He paused and gave her a moment to collect herself. "Who is yer father?"

"George L-Lambert of St. J-James Square in London."

"Do yeh have brothers an' sisters?"

She nodded and sniffed. "A s-sister. An older sister."

"That is nice, isn't it? Is she married?"

She swiped her nose with her sleeve and nodded.

"So, yer the only Lambert child at home?"

She swallowed and nodded.

"An' yer mother an' father are both alive?"

"Y-yes."

"Anyone else live wi' you, other than servants, a' course. I'm sure yeh have a mess of those."

She shook her head.

"Good enough. See? Tha' wasna so hard." He waved a hand. "Take her back."

Adrian shifted from foot to foot. Ten thousand guineas would be his to take back home with him, and it would go a long way. Still, he wished they would hurry up and move onto the next phase.

He was better on his own and with his charge than he was waiting here. If the English swept in now, they'd all be swinging in the wind in no time.

~~~

Sara Anne was the last to be interviewed. As in the inn that morning, *only that morning*, the air seemed to seethe with hostility as she was led through the lean-to. It made her afraid in some deep place within herself. Any of these men could easily kill her, could kill all of them. Perhaps that was the plan, anyway.

She was brought to the front of the group, to where three men seem to be holding court at a crude wooden table. "An' you are?" one of them asked. She recognized his voice. He was the leader, who had done the talking earlier. Only then, he'd worn a mask.

"My name is ... Hope." She hadn't planned to say it; she'd simply panicked at the thought of uttering her own name.

There was a brief stunned silence. Then, "I told yeh," a man spoke up. It was the young man she had ridden to camp with. "I told yeh she wasna English."

The leader considered her as he leaned back. "Where are yeh from, lass?"

"South Carolina."

"What's yer surname? Who's yer father?"

She spoke slowly to avoid stammering in her nervousness. "He's in America."

He cocked his head waiting for her to go on. "We assumed as much."

"I would prefer not to say," she answered in a small voice.

The leader smiled, but without even a trace of humor. "Yer with these rich English," he snarled the last two words. "Dressed as they," he continued, flicking his eyes over her. "Which means yeh come from money, which means yeh *will* say."

The man who led her in grabbed a hand full of her hair and shook her head, to help make the leader's point. "Or do yeh need convincin'?" he growled in her ear.

A man seated to the side of the leader leaned in to confer in hushed tones. "It would take months tae deal wi' someone in the colonies. Mayhaps even longer."

The leader waved the man off Sara Anne.

"It's no wha' we planned," the man continued.

The leader squinted at her. "Why are you with the English? Are they friends? Is one of them family?"

She shook her head. "No. I only just met them in London."

"Why were yeh in London?"

"I'd never been," she stammered.

A general snickering erupted, although she hadn't meant to make light of his question. She had no wish to infuriate him or any of the others any more than she already had.

"Who were yeh stayin with?" he fired back quickly.

"I was with a companion."

"Who?" he demanded.

"I ... I am a paid companion."

This started a clamor and allowed her a few precious moments to think. She hadn't thought out the lie before she blurted it out, it had simply occurred to her, and she had said it.

The leader was holding up a hand and a few others were calling for quiet. "A paid companion?" he repeated, his tone full of disbelief.

"Yes. My employer is a lady I met through an advertisement in the paper back home. She hired me to come to London with her for the summer as she had no other family nor friends to travel with."

Now that she had a story, it flowed fluidly. This wasn't unlike a game she and Caroline had frequently played as children where one of them would start a story and the other would have to take over convincingly. Only this time, she alone had begun it and she alone would finish. "The lady, Mrs. Huggins is her name, was somewhat embarrassed about the arrangement so she passed me off as a cousin." She paused. "She who bought me these clothes."

She saw the looks exchanged between men. They were disappointed in her station, but their hostility had diminished, given that she wasn't wealthy or English.

"She'd never pay a farthing for me," Sara Anne finished. "No one would. I took the position because my family, my four younger brothers and sisters, needed the money."

~

In the back of the room, Adrian crossed his arms and pursed his lips, fascinated by the girl's performance. She was lying, of course. She definitely came from money, but it was interesting to see her weave her tale. And she was breathtakingly beautiful.

Robert was scowling with displeasure. "Take her back," he snapped with a violent swatting motion.

Adrian glanced around at the others, shocked they were buying this cock and bull story. She was playing them for fools. How could they not see that? He hadn't paid much attention when she'd been led in, so he studied her as she was led toward him. A tingle of strange recognition took him by surprise, and he frowned, trying to place where he could have seen her before. But, no, he couldn't have seen her before, or he would have remembered. She was too beautiful to forget.

The other young woman, the dark-haired general's daughter had beauty as well, but she was filled with a superiority that left him cold. This girl was different, vibrant and unique. He would have recalled having met her or even having just seen her. So, what was this odd, nagging feeling that he knew her?

On instinct, he turned and fell into step beside her, subconsciously noting her walk and the tension in her body. He realized she hadn't cried. No, she had a sense of control. She glanced at him, and he saw her eyes were pale green. He would have liked to have turned her around and stared into them until he got his fill.

~

Sara Anne tried to remain calm, but there was something about the man walking beside her that shook her composure. Between his deep brown eyes and the longest, darkest lashes she had ever seen, he would have been considered almost pretty, except for a strong jaw line, a small cleft in his chin and the aura of maleness that emanated from his every pore.

His clothes were ragged, and his brown hair desperately needed to be cut, but it wasn't his appearance that was so disconcerting; it was the way he looked at her, as if he could see through her ruse. As if he knew her.

When they were nearly to the barn, he uttered a curt, "I'll take her."

The man who had been escorting her grunted something indiscernible and allowed her to be led away by this new man who guided her to the cover of trees between the barn and the lean-to. The rain was light, but she was getting wet despite the cover of trees.

He took hold of her hand and brought it close to his face to inspect it, nodding as if he had confirmed something to himself. "That was quite a tale yeh came up with," he accused quietly.

She looked away from him because the last thing in the world she wanted to do was to gawk at his handsome face. He was the enemy as much as Aaron Waldron. "I don't know what you mean, sir."

He moved suddenly, taking her chin in hand, and forcing her to look at him. "Consider this a warnin' an' a service, lass. It's only money we're after. No one has tae get hert; no one should an' no one will unless yeh get foolish."

She felt herself quiver. "Only money," she repeated disgustedly. She *hated* money! It poisoned men, including her own father. "Was it worth selling your honor for?"

He jerked back as if he'd been struck. "What would yeh know of honor?" he asked quietly, his brown eyes lit from an inner passion that burned deep within.

"Oh, it is recognizable. If anyone comes around who possesses it while you're in my presence, I'll be sure to point it out."

He grabbed her arms and gave her a shake. "Yer goin' tae tell me who you are an' who yer family is or I'm goin' tae march yeh back an' tell them you lied."

Clearly, she had infuriated him by questioning his honor.

129

"All tae prevent a little money from goin' from yer wealthy family—"

It was unbelievable. *He* was disgusted with *her*. "I am from America," she defended herself. "And I do not come from the wealth you imagine."

"Yeh dinna ken what I imagine."

His intensity rattled her composure. "It is too far to send for ransom," she reasoned. It was absurd, this desire for him to believe her. It was because he was handsome, which was childish, girlish, and stupid. It was not like her at all. She was not Glennis flirting shamelessly with John Michael.

"I want the truth," he demanded.

She withdrew a step. "You want the truth? Fine! My father would never pay," she admitted in a hoarse voice, blushing from the shame of it.

The raw pain in her was undeniable and it must have resonated with him. "They'll use you in some other way," he warned. "They willna let yeh go, if that's wha' yer thinkin'."

She seemed to shrink within herself. She hadn't considered what else they might do with her, nor had she considered that his warning was truly a service to her.

"It's not too late," he said softly. "Tell me who yeh are an' ye'll get back where yeh came from. I swear it on my life."

As inconceivable as it was, she did believe him, but the thought of Aaron waiting of her in a cold rage suddenly filled her mind and she shivered.

"Yer name?" he pressed.

For a terrible instant, her mind went blank. Then, "Hope," she blurted.

It had come a split second too late, and his instincts were too good to not recognize she was not being truthful. "It's all a lie," he accused. "Everythin yev said."

She felt a flush of shame at being caught in a lie and then a torrent of anger. After all, she was the victim; he was the aggressor.

He shook his head, disgusted with himself. "Understand this, *Hope,* someone will come up wi' some money for yeh. By no bein' honest wi' us, yer makin' a choice. We only wanted money, but it seems yer prepared tae give flesh an' blood instead."

She tried to control her breathing and pretend she hadn't been shaken by his words. "You and your friends planned on us all being from wealthy, English families," she said in a voice that gave away her nerves. "I'm not and you detest the fact you made a mistake," she challenged.

"Oh, yer from a wealthy family. Deny that."

She started to, but then refrained. His expression was too intense, and, again, she had that feeling that he somehow knew her.

"I could take yeh back there," he jerked his thumb toward the lean-to. "They would be happy tae beat the truth out of yeh. Yeh may be stubborn, but ye'd talk. Eventually."

Angered by the bullying tactic, she looked him straight in the eye and did not flinch. She was trembling, which could not be helped, but she did not and would not flinch, nor would she tell them the truth. Whatever beating they would subject her to, it would be nothing in comparison to what she'd receive in the custody of her father and Aaron Waldron.

"Huh," he muttered. "So, it's not just stubbornness. What is it?"

She looked away, fighting a foolish inclination to cry. He was too close to the truth. It felt as if he was reading her mind.

"Look at me," he said.

She drew in a shaky breath and looked into his eyes. They were the most beautiful eyes she'd ever seen. Why did he feel like someone she could trust? He was one of them. He was the enemy.

"Yer makin' a foolish choice," he said angrily, fixing her with a hard stare.

"It's my choice," she said weakly.

"Rethink it, lass."

She stood there stubbornly although her heart was pounding a sickening rhythm. He took hold of her arm and led her away again. For an instant, she feared he was leading her back to the men, but he returned her to the barn. She wanted to say something — but what? *Thank you for not having me beaten? Thank you for trying to help, despite the fact you're one of our captors?* It was absurd! Preposterous! Even the feeling he had been trying to help her.

He released his grip on her arm. "Go."

It took all her will to keep moving and not to look back at him. She still felt a lingering warmth where his hand had held her arm.

Ginny ran to her. "Why were you so long? What did you say?"

~

Adrian craned his neck from side to side as he went back to the meeting. He was shaken that he'd lost control with her. It wasn't like him. The men of Jedburgh called him Iceman because of his detachment from everything and everyone. Not that *that* was like him, either. At least, not the man he used to be. It was the rebellion that had changed him. Hardened him. It was the defeat and death and the mindless, senseless incalculable loss that had deadened him.

"I know wha' tae do with her," a man named McKiever spoke up from the center of the structure. "Lord Carmichael of Stonehaven."

"What about him?" Robert Kinnaird asked.

"He'd pay tae acquire her."

Adrian felt a knot form in his belly.

Slowly, Robert smiled. He had counted on every one of the women being worth a hefty sum. Granted, there were ladies than they'd thought there would be, but from the moment he saw them, he'd been tallying. "What would he pay?"

"He's a rich man. I've heard him say he'd pay a king's ransom fer a beautiful wife."

That brought a hoot of laughter that aggravated Adrian. He'd warned her. He'd told her they wouldn't let her go. "She wasna tellin' the truth," he spoke up. "She comes from wealth. I can get her tae talk."

"She may have been lying about that, but she comes from the colonies, Iceman," Conner Boyd spoke up, shaking his head. "That accent—"

"Aye," Adrian agreed. "But—"

132

"Which is too far," Robert decided. "Takin' her tae Carmichael is a far swifter resolution."

Adrian tried to shake off the frustration he felt. After all, what was she to him? Just a beautiful woman who had made a bad decision. He'd warned her.

"Alright then," Robert said. "As planned, we take the women into hiding, except for," he waved his hand, having forgotten the last girl's name, "the one from America."

Regret flooded through Adrian and that infuriated him. He should have gotten her to speak the truth.

"Two men fer each gerl," Robert was saying. "Keep yer hands off them, unless it becomes absolutely necessary tae do otherwise. Understood? I'll speak wi' each of yeh one at a time regardin' yer assignment. Dinna speak of yer assignment tae anyone. That way, if yer captured, ye'll no be able tae say much."

Agonizingly long minutes passed before "McGoldrick!" was called, summoning him to the barn to receive his assignment. Several men had been called ahead of him and he'd caught glimpses of an occasional exodus through the woods. They were already leaving with the women.

Adrian's chest felt tight as he walked through the rain. He would be glad to have this over with. Glad to go back home and forget the English and everything that had happened in the past year. In the Highlands, he would once again don his kilt and listen to the haunting music of a bagpipe, outlawed or not. One thing was certain, once he was home again, he would stay.

He walked into the barn and shook off all the wet he could and then looked over at the young women standing in the far side of the barn. Only three of them were still left, including her. He wasn't prepared for the way his heart lurched at the sight of her. Perhaps, he would be assigned her. Not that it would give him great pleasure to deliver her to Carmichael.

Robert Kinnaird and his younger brother, Leith, were conferring in whispers as he walked up to them. Only the Kinnaird brothers would know all the players and all the parts played.

Robert turned to him. "Do yeh know Stonehaven?"

He *was* being assigned her. He nodded. "Fishin' village near Aberdeen."

"There's a castle southeast of there, called Abermire. Take our pretty friend there, an' offer her tae Lord Duncan Carmichael. Ask for fifty thousand guineas, but if he balks an' offers less, take it. Try tae get as much as yeh can, a' course."

"How do yeh think ye'll go?" Leith asked.

"Best tae stay away from towns," Adrian replied. Cities and towns were heavily occupied by the Crown's troops. "North tae the coast—"

"Agreed. Then take a boat tae Stonehaven."

"I'll need money."

Robert nodded at Leith, who tossed Adrian a bag of coins. Adrian caught it with one hand and slipped it into the pocket of his breeches without counting it.

"Afterwards, meet me in Dunblane at the house of John MacAdam," Robert added.

"MacAdam," Adrian repeated. It was a relief he wouldn't have to travel all the way back here. Dunblane would be on his way back home. Of course, Robert knew that. He was no idiot. He wouldn't let anyone walk around with guineas that belonged to him.

"Take her round back an' I'll send someone tae join yeh."

Adrian turned and found the girl's eyes fully on his. She was hoping it would be him, just as he had hoped he would get assigned her. Heart pounding, he gestured to her, then watched as she spoke to the fair-haired Shelly heir. The two of them embraced. The Shelly girl was crying. *Queer behavior for a mere acquaintance,* he thought wryly.

"Keep her bound," Leith warned behind him. "She's got spirit an' if she tries tae get away, she'll get hert."

"That reminds me," Robert said as he stood. He bent his head to say something discreetly in Adrian's ear. "Find out if she's pure. A virgin should cost Carmichael a bit extra."

Adrian pulled away, disturbed by the thought, but he nodded dutifully before leading his charge away.

Outside, away from Robert and Leith and the others, he breathed a bit easier.

"Where are we going?" she asked.

He didn't answer her until they reached his horse. "Yer goin' tae be—" He swallowed, frustrated it was so difficult to voice. "Offered tae a wealthy nobleman." She flinched, apparently shocked, and it made him unaccountably angry. "I told yeh they would not let yeh go," he reminded her.

"What do you mean offered?"

"He'll have tae pay tae keep yeh," he replied. "As his wife, most likely." *Lucky, rich bastard.*

A long silent moment passed before she snorted and then burst into laughter.

He couldn't believe his eyes. "Why do yeh laugh?"

She shook her head, unable to answer. Her laughter had grown into hysterics and would not stop. "It's...it's—" Finally she was able to sputter. She took a few breaths and held her side. "It's the same, no matter where I go. I'll never be free unless I ... I don't know. Unless I kill all of you or run to the end of the earth." She breathed hard, regaining a small fraction of control. "Where is the end of the earth exactly?"

He shook his head, stymied by her strange reaction. "Wherever yeh stop, I suppose." He frowned, not understanding her, and looked around again, keeping her in his peripheral vision. "It's not too late tae change yer mind," he tried one last time. "Yeh cou' be back from where yeh came from in only a matter of days." He turned to her for a reply, but she stood there, stubborn as a mule, not speaking. At least, she had finally sobered. In fact, all hilarity from the moment before had vanished. "Is there a reason yeh dinna want tae go back?"

She averted her eyes and blushed. That was exactly it, he realized, but she was making such a mistake. "Perhaps yer makin' somethin' werse than it is. Think, woman. Do you want tae be trapped forever?" A strange look crossed her face and he frowned, wishing he understood what she was thinking.

"I don't want to be trapped forever, no," she finally said. "Believe it or not, that's why I'm here."

Her words were bewildering. She was bewildering. She struck him as bold, almost brazen, one moment — after all, this was the very young woman who had weaved a tale of lies and deception in front of scores of men who could have killed her for it — and yet vulnerable the next. He watched as she reached up and stroked his horse.

"May I ask your name?" she asked.

Adrian hesitated. They weren't supposed to divulge their names or anyone else's, but that was really for the women who were going back home. This one wasn't going back. Furthermore, Aberdeen was a good way off. It would take weeks to get there since they would have to lie low and avoid the Crown's troops, which were everywhere. "McGoldrick."

She looked puzzled. "Is that your first name?"

Adrian saw Edmund Tully approaching. He shouldn't tell her. She didn't need to know. "Adrian," he replied anyway.

"Goin' tae tie her?" Edmund asked, reaching them.

Adrian took his horse's reigns in hand. "Isna' necessary."

"Does she need help up?"

"No," she spoke up for herself. "Thank you," she added with a touch of sarcasm.

"Ye'll sit in front," Adrian explained. "I can mount ferst an' pull yeh up—"

"I'm told I was riding before I was walking."

She mounted in a smooth practiced move, seating herself astride the horse and the sight sent blood surging to Adrian's loins. Edmund made a gesture to Adrian expressing the need to keep a good eye on her. As if he needed to be told. Adrian mounted behind her, and he felt her stiffen when their bodies made contact. He prompted the horse forward regretful that his erection couldn't be helped. Sorry, too, that he was delivering her to another man. Sorry in general.

"What route are yeh thinkin'?" Edmund asked, as they rode, side by side.

"Due north."

"No tae Edinburgh an' around?"

136

"No." They would stick as much as possible to the unpopulated countryside and when they made it to North Berwick, they'd catch a ship to Aberdeen or to Stonehaven. There were always coal shipments going that way.

"I suppose that is better," Edmund conceded. "Less risk."

# Chapter Twelve

H
our after hour, they rode at a steady pace and without a word being exchanged. After a while, Sara Anne relaxed against Adrian, *her guard*. That's how she would think of him. Not as her captor, but as a man who would guard and protect her until it was time to break away from him. She'd been told that English troops were everywhere, so how difficult could it possibly be to get the attention of someone in authority?

She was beginning to see it all quite clearly. Word of their capture would be sent to Uncle William with the abductors demands, and Ginny's ransom would be paid immediately. Her aunt and uncle would wonder and worry why there was no ransom demand for her, but there would be choice except to wait for Ginny to return home to get any information. Eventually, Uncle William would have to inform his brother-in-law what had happened, and Aaron would learn of it when he arrived at Oakley.

They wouldn't give up hope right away, but surely in a matter of weeks they would have to suspect that she was gone one way or another. Aaron Waldron would loathe coming up short but, eventually, he would have to return home. Then she would be free to return to Middlesbrough.

How long she would have to remain a captive was the real question. If Aaron was already at Oakley, which was a possibility, he would know of their capture within a few days. How long would it be before he gave up and returned back home? A week? Two weeks? A month? "How long will it take to get where we're going?" she asked, breaking the long silence.

"Depends."

She rolled her eyes and huffed. "Might you please elaborate on that very terse answer?"

"Terse," he scoffed. "There's a word fer you."

138

"Would you like me to define it?"

"If it means something other than abrupt tae fine ladies such as yourself, aye, do please define it. I'm only a poor, ignorant wretch of a Scot."

"Not to mention testy," she complained.

"Why do yeh ask how long it will take? It's no' like yeh have somewhere else tae be, is it? Yeh saw tae that."

His warm breath on her ear sent little shockwaves through her that did strange things to her body. With his body pressed to hers and his arms pinioning her, she was experiencing reactions like never before. It was due to their unnaturally close proximity, of course, and nothing more.

*Alright*, his too-handsome face and his too-perfect physique *and* their unnaturally close proximity. And nothing more. "Why don't we pretend I have somewhere else to be?" she tried again. "How long is it supposed to take to get to where we're going?"

The older man, riding slightly apart from them, glanced their way with a scowl of disapproval. He was a lean, balding man in his fifties without a great deal of personality. In short, a grump.

"Depends on wha' we encounter."

She gave a dramatic sigh. "Approximately?"

"I dinna' play pretend."

"You also don't answer straightforward questions very well."

"Tell me why yeh ask, an' perhaps I'll give yeh an answer." When she hesitated, he grunted. "Yeh see? Yeh want answers, but yeh willna' give them."

"That is not true," she objected. "It was just such an obvious question to ask, I was trying to think of how to answer it that wouldn't make you touchy again."

"If yel answer a question truthfully, wha' is yer real name?"

She twisted around to look at him. "Sara Anne Aldridge." She faced front again and noticed his strong hands on the reins. She forced herself to look away at the landscape. She didn't need to forget that he was her enemy; no matter what strange reactions her body was experiencing due to his unnaturally close proximity.

"Why did yeh call yerself by another name, Sara Anne Aldridge?"

She shook her head, wondering at it herself. "Fear, I suppose."

"You were afraid ... so yeh made up a name an' a tall tale," he said drolly. "*Huh.* Perhaps it's just me, but I would think that was the time fer tellin' the truth."

"It felt I needed to protect myself. It wasn't all thought out, I just said it."

"It was a good story. I dinna' think I could have come up with names an' details so quickly."

"I didn't make them all up. Hope was my ... sometimes companion when I was young. At least, I thought she was. It's a long story."

*Hope.* A flash of recognition filled his consciousness. His angel of hope — the vision, presence or hallucination who had come to him on the bloody field of Culloden. It was *she* that Sara Anne had reminded him of. How bizarre that he would experience a near-death vision that would resemble a young woman he would later meet in this way. Gooseflesh covered his arms. "We have time," he said. "Fer yer story."

"Hope lived in my looking glass at home."

"Ah."

"Yes. My sister insisted I made her up. That'd I'd dreamt her and then made her into my imaginary friend."

"Yeh have a sister?" He immediately felt a pang of regret about asking the personal question.

She shook her head and sighed. "She died. A year and four months ago."

Why had he asked? He wouldn't make the mistake again. "I'm sorry."

"She was wrong about Hope, though. She was not an imaginary friend."

"What did this ... sometimes companion look like?"

"Oh, very like me. Almost exactly like me, only she had a bit of red to her hair and—"

Another painful shiver passed through him.

"Is something wrong?"

"No," he replied brusquely.

"And she also had brown eyes," she finished. "But, otherwise, she looked just like me."

"Yeh must know now that yer sister was right."

"She was *not* right. I know it for a fact, but it's a long story that I really don't care to get into."

"Fine. Except there's no way someone can live in a looking glass."

"Not a living, breathing person, no," Sara Anne replied with some exasperation.

"So, she was an imaginary friend. Like yer sister said. Perhaps yeh just didn't want tae admit she was right."

"She was not right, but I'm not discussing it anymore."

Riding alongside, Edmund had strong disapproval evident in his gaze, but Adrian ignored him. "Perhaps yer one of those that canna' admit when they're wrong?"

"I most certainly can admit when I'm wrong. Can you? Because you could not possibly be more wrong in what you're doing."

"Yer right," he said lightly. Moments of silence lapsed before added, "We won't talk anymore."

She huffed. "Convenient time to give up the conversation."

"Yeh will tell me if she shows up? I wouldn't mind seeing her."

She refused to answer.

"In fact, if she shows up, I'll take her an' leave yeh tae find yer way home. How would that be?"

Edmund glowered. "We get near town an' she gets gagged," he stated.

Sara Anne looked at him, insulted. "You might notice I'm not the one talking."

He turned his glower on her and then rode ahead.

"By the way," Sara Anne said. "You didn't answer my question about how long this will take."

"Weeks."

"Thank you. That wasn't that so terribly difficult, was it?" She paused, giving him a chance to say something further, but he didn't. "How many weeks?"

"Three. Four. Ten. I don't ken. It depends—"

Four or five weeks, she thought. That length of time missing ought to be perfectly adequate.

~~~

"Let's break," the older man called at mid-day.

*Thank Goodness.*

Adrian followed the man into a copse and dismounted first. When Sara Anne dismounted, he gave her a warning look. "Yeh may have a bit of privacy fer yer needs, but if yeh try an' run—"

"I realize that would be futile," she interjected.

"I hope so. Because if yeh try it, we will catch you an' it will be yer last bit of privacy, an' yeh willna' like that."

"You're right. May I go now?"

He nodded and she went. When she returned, both men were watching her. "Ye'll ride with me, now," the older man said sternly.

She tried to conceal the dismay she felt. He offered a strip of dried meat, and she took it.

"Let's go."

"Can we not break for longer?" she complained.

"No."

The one positive aspect about riding with the older man, is that she was able to discreetly study Adrian McGoldrick who rode just ahead of them. He was the one with the pulse and the personality. He would be the key to escape when it was time.

What was he doing risking his life by becoming involved with these men and this scheme? She flashed back on his face, on his fury, when she'd questioned his honor. He did have honor; she felt sure of it, although this was a dishonorable venture. His involvement was a mystery that she'd need to unravel in order to persuade him to release her. It was either that or she'd have to slip away.

Adrian glanced over and saw her watching him, which made her flinch. She looked away and spoke to the man behind her. "I don't suppose you'd share your name?"

"Yed be right," he replied cryptically.

142

It was a relief when they stopped at day's end. Sara Anne was sore from the long ride. "I don't suppose we could just walk tomorrow?" she asked wryly.

No one replied.

The older man left to scout the area while Adrian set up camp.

"I'm curious," she said as he went about his task. "What do you tell yourself about why you're here and … doing what you're doing?"

He looked at her. "I tell myself, we're goin' tae need sleep." He pointed at the bedroll.

The older man was already back, which she resented.

"And we're goin' tae need tae eat," Adrian added.

"Hunt us up some fresh meat," the older man said. "Will yeh?"

"Aye." Adrian squatted and withdrew a knife from his knapsack. He sheathed it as he stood.

He walked away and it was odd how she felt his absence. It was as if a protective cloak was suddenly missing, leaving her exposed. It was absurd when he was one of her captors. "I need to, uh … take a moment," she said to the older man.

He was unsaddling his horse. "Yeh have two minutes," he warned. "I can track, gerl. Dinna' test me."

She held up her hands in concession and walked away. When she returned, apparently within the time limit provided, he was building a campfire. "May I help?"

"No."

She rolled her eyes, although he wasn't looking at her. "I suppose if you won't tell me your name, I'll make one up."

He ignored her.

"I think I'll call you The Shadow."

Silence.

"Because you're silent as a shadow. Where I'm concerned."

"An' perhaps I'll call you she who never stops talking," he returned without looking up.

"When people do talk back and forth, it's called conversation. It can make the day go faster."

143

Flames took hold and he stood watching it. "Some days are naugh supposed tae go fast," he returned gloomily.

The statement silenced her. When Adrian arrived back in camp, it was with skinned squirrels. He roasted them, and she watched in silence. They also ate in silence. Which was fine, she no longer wanted to chat. The Shadow's last words had cured her of the desire for the moment.

When Adrian opened his bedroll and gestured her to it, it was a relief. "Lie just in from the middle," he said.

She sat, took off her shoes and then lay back, feeling highly conspicuous. He sat and removed his boots. She rolled onto her side, facing the bigger half of the cover. She'd felt tired earlier, but she was wide awake and on full alert. He reached around and tugged the cover over them. She was in the crook of the bedroll, trapped, for all practical purposes. He was behind her, not touching her but close enough that she felt him.

Seconds passed.

Minutes.

She would never be able to sleep lying so close to him. She closed her eyes and began to isolate the sounds of the night. They were not so different from home. But she was attempting to sleep on the ground, which she'd never done before. Next to a man, which she'd never done before. A man whose body she could *sense,* whose absence she could feel. A man she'd ridden next to for hours until she knew the feel of his arms around her, and the feel of his body pressed to hers. She'd felt the surprising hardness of his male part. She'd been glad her face was turned away from him at the time.

The Shadow began snoring.

"Why would yeh no' admit who yeh were?" Adrian asked quietly.

She shivered because lying next to him and conversing was so sensual. "I have a reason," she replied just as softly.

"Are yeh cold?"

"A little."

"It's naugh cold," he said.

"It feels cold. My home is far warmer."

144

"Wha' is it yer hidin' from? Or is it a who?"

Seconds of silence elapsed and then she turned to face him, but it was no less strange or seductive lying face to face, especially given the troubled frown on his face. Was it the concern or his physical beauty that made her want to admit the truth? But she could not risk it. "It's someone and something worth hiding from. That's all I can say."

"Yer bein' sold because yeh willna' say. How can that be better?"

"I'm being offered, you mean. This other man may not want me."

"Dinna' be daft, woman. He'll want yeh, alright." His scowl darkened. "Did I mention he's a homely man whose eyes go in different directions? That's why he canna' find a wife of his own."

Her eyes narrowed. "You're only saying that to be mean."

He shook his head. "It's wha' I was told."

"And that's the reason he'll want me? Because he's homely and his eyes go in different directions?"

"He'll want yeh because he's a red-blooded man."

She wondered how to begin planting a seed in his mind. "What if someone could offer more?"

Distrust flashed in his face. "Who?"

"I asked you first. What if someone could offer more? Would you change course?"

"Is this someone in America?"

She shook her head.

"England?"

She nodded.

He glared furiously. "An' how would we get werd tae them? Yer time fer tellin' the truth has passed!"

The old man's snoring stopped for a moment, and they grew silent until it started again. The frowns on their faces were no less intense, but neither wanted the older man woken. "I told yeh this," he accused in a whisper.

"I know that and I'm sorry, but I have to protect myself."

"From who?"

"I cannot say. But I don't want to be sold."

"No more than I want tae sell yeh, but nor am I seein' a choice."

"But *if* someone could offer more money than the man you intended to—"

"Intend," he corrected harshly. "Yeh speak as if I had a choice, but isna' one."

She glared furiously, as frustrated as he was.

"I dinna' care if yeh make that face or no. I gave yeh a chance tae speak the truth."

She huffed in frustration, and he gave her a righteous nod, which made her mad enough to spit.

Something changed in his expression. "Yeh tell me right now or—"

She rolled back over, because she couldn't think straight, but he wasn't having it. He reached around and pulled her back against him. "I can't breathe," she complained through clenched teeth.

"Too bad! Yeh should have thought of that. Now, go tae sleep."

She huffed again and shifted toward him. "I have been taken against my will and you behave as if I'm at fault!"

"I said *sleep*."

She seethed because he was far too close and so stubborn. "*You* are the criminal," she stated.

He lifted his head and brought his lips against her ear. "An' yeh might want tae remember that," he threatened in a husky whisper.

Her breath caught and her nipples stiffened. She huffed even more furiously but turned back around knowing she would never be able to sleep.

# Chapter Thirteen

S ara Anne woke to a gray, early morning aware that she was alone in the bedroll. She lifted her head and saw the men across camp conversing in hushed tones. It seemed strained between them, although she couldn't make out their words. They suddenly turned to look at her. The older man strode toward her, his expression dour, and she sat up, blinking sleepily.

"Do yeh want tae tell us who yeh really are?" he demanded.

She shook her head, although she felt anything but defiant.

"Then we're goin' north tae present yeh tae Lord Carmichael, an' we'll hear no more about it. Do yeh understand?"

She nodded miserably.

"Ye'll ride with me, an' yel' stop tryin' tae charm Iceman."

She glanced at Adrian, who didn't look any happier about the arrangement than she felt. "Why do you call him Iceman?"

"Yeh dinna get tae ask questions," the older man snapped loudly.

"Yeh dinna' need tae shout at her," Adrian retorted.

The older man gave him a disgusted harrumph and walked away.

Adrian looked at her. "Yev one last chance tae say," he stated. "I willna' keep warnin' you."

She considered, but it was too soon. She couldn't go back to Middlesbrough this soon. Not with Aaron waiting to get his hands on her.

"I mean it," he warned.

"I know," she said quietly and regretfully. "I understand."

He shook his head and flexed his hands. "I could throttle you."

"I still wouldn't say," she replied with a shake of her head.

He turned and stalked away. "Get ready tae go," he called over his shoulder.

They rode hard all day, stopping only once, and not a dozen words were spoken the entire day. It was perfectly wretched. That night, she had hopes of sleeping with Adrian, especially when he came toward her once bedrolls were readied, but he merely handed her a wool blanket.

"If yeh get cold," he said.

All of four words. She was about to utter her thanks, but he'd already turned and walked away. In the morning she returned it with a coolly spoken, "Thank you."

He accepted it without reply.

The pattern was the same the next day and the next. On the fifth day, she rode with Adrian again, but there was still no conversing. She tried a few times only to be met with a wall of silent stoicism or curt one-word answers.

That evening, The Shadow rode on to scout the territory, and she was glad of it. Until Adrian bound her hands and tied her to a tree so that he could go hunt. "This isn't necessary," she complained. "Where do you think I'm going to go?" He gave her a look and then extracted his knife. It caused a moment of uneasiness, even knowing he wouldn't hurt her. He bent and lifted an edge of her skirt. "What do you think you're doing?" she demanded.

He cut a long strip before standing back up and coming at her. "Oh, no! You cannot be—"

Her words were cut off as he forced the gag between her lips.

She continued to complain even though her words were mostly indiscernible.

He tied the gag behind her head and stepped back, ignoring the daggers she shot with her eyes. "I willna' be long," he said calmly. He walked away, but after only a dozen paces, he turned back to her. "Do yeh remember when I told yeh how yeh cou' say who ye were an' go right back home again?"

She narrowed her eyes at him in the most virulent manner she could, which was not virulent enough, given the smug look he returned before walking off. It did not take him long to return with a string of fat rabbits, but it felt like it since she had been feasted on by cursed midges. When he released her, she removed the gag and began scratching the bites. "I hate you!"

"Yeh dinna' have tae be here, now did you?"

"Ye dinna' have tae go and snatch women, now did you?" she mocked.

He looked at her sternly until he gave in to a half grin, despite his best effort not to. "Yer a funny one," he muttered as he bent to start a fire.

"I was practically eaten alive." He drew breath to speak – to remind her again that it was her fault for being there, so she held up her hands. She frowned miserably and scratched at her legs.

"Yeh can make a mud paste fer the bites. Helps."

"As if I'm not dirty enough? No thank you."

"Suit yourself."

She watched in dread fascination as he skinned the rabbits and put them on a spit to cook. "What I wouldn't give for a bath," she complained as she scratched at her arms.

"I imagine yer maid cou' be drawin' one up fer yeh right now, if yeh were back home," he commented without looking at her.

As aggravated as the statement made her, she was still glad they were talking again. The meat had started to sizzle when the older man returned to camp. Given the agitated expression on his face, he'd encountered something. He dismounted and gestured for Adrian. They moved out of earshot, but close enough to keep an eye on her, and spoke in whispers. When they returned, it was with long faces, but no words of explanation.

Adrian pulled the rabbits off the fire and doused the fire. She drew breath to ask what had happened, but the older man's expression kept her silent. It wouldn't tell her, anyway. They ate in strained silence, then took the horses deeper into the woods until they found a clear enough area to sleep for the night.

Preparing their bedrolls, the old man finally spoke. "She can sleep with me tonight."

"No," Adrian rejoined. "I'm naugh a boy tae be protected from myself."

Even in the scarce moonlight, Sara could see the wry look the older man gave Adrian. "Let's hope naugh fer yer sake. I'll be the ferst tae admit she'd got beauty an' wit, but it's no' worth yer life."

Sara Anne was appalled by the sentiment. "You have a very low opinion of me," she exclaimed. "I would not purposely cost him his life. I wouldn't even purposely cost you yours."

The older man's troubled gaze found her in the darkness. "My *opinion* is that yeh were taken against yer will which was neither right nor honorable, an' if I hang fer it, I've got no one but myself tae blame. But I willna' hang if I can help it," he added grimly. He turned and walked away, leaving an uncomfortable silence in his wake.

It was late, the Shadow had long since fallen asleep, and Sara Anne knew Adrian wasn't sleeping. She turned over to face him and found him watching her. "What was he upset about when he came back?"

"Nothin' yeh need tae know about."

She glowered at him.

"I dinna' ken why yeh think I care about that frown. Yer nearly as pretty with it on yer face."

She huffed and turned back over, then turned her head to say, "I desperately need a bath. As do both of you. Not to be rude."

"Oh, no. Not tae be rude. Go to sleep."

# Chapter Fourteen

Penelope's hands were clutched together and pressed to her chest as she watched Mr. Waldron pace. It had been a horrible two days. Yesterday, they had received word that Genevieve had been taken and was being held in lieu of a thousand pounds. Today, Mr. Aaron Waldron had shown up on their doorstep to collect *his wife*, Sara Anne.

The ransom was a fortune but that was irrelevant. They had gathered and sent the funds exactly as they had been directed to do. The puzzling thing was that Sara Anne had not been mentioned in the missive. They did not understand why, or what exactly had happened.

Before telling Mr. Waldron what had occurred in Scotland, they listened as he spoke of Sara Anne. He talked of their lifelong friendship, their betrothal that was all the talk of Charles Town, and their wedding. Lastly, he spoke of Sara Anne's shocking departure.

Lord and Lady Shelly were stunned.

William finally began sharing what they had learned. At first, Mr. Waldron was silent and motionless, but then he'd begun pacing, filling the room with more tension that it could hold. "I will go," he announced. "I've come this far, and I will have her back."

Penelope drew back at the statement and its tone.

"But surely," William said, "it's best to wait until Genevieve has returned and can tell us—"

"I will not wait!"

The room grew silent.

Aaron sank into a chair. "I apologize for raising my voice. But I've come too far—"

"I understand your frustration," William said.

151

Penelope turned to stare out the window, confused and conflicted. The waiting was horrible, nearly unbearable.

"Tell me where they were headed," Aaron said. "Please. Tell me everything you know."

When they were alone again, Penelope turned to her husband. She was exhausted from worry and sleepless nights. "How could she have lied to us?"

"She was frightened, I suppose."

"Do you think he loves her?"

Seconds ticked by. "I hope so, my dear. I do hope so."

"They will come back to us."

Her statement sounded more like a question. William looked at his wife. She was pale and deeply shaken. "Of course, they will."

"They will not … hurt them—"

He closed the distance between them and took hold of her arms. "This is a desperate ploy by beaten men. It is about money, as their message stated. They will not hurt our girls."

"They aren't really girls anymore," Penelope murmured. "I sometimes wish they were."

"I know."

"I sometimes miss—"

Her voice broke and William pulled her to him, battling his own urge to break down. "I know."

~~~

Aaron found Felter Hall without difficulty and was received graciously, if somewhat warily. General Stafford and his men were standing around debating logistics and strategy in one salon, while in an adjoining, Errol Stafford was slouched on a deep-blue velvet settee, drinking and conferring with his mother in whispers and squeaks. The sight of him was an embarrassment to every man present other than Aaron who neither knew nor cared to know the man.

Jamison Stafford and John Michael Price stood slightly apart from the general and his men, listening to the discussion and occasionally adding a comment.

"We've three hundred men out there scouring this godforsaken land," the general thundered. "We'll find these scoundrels and they'll pay with their lives!"

The man's face was red, and Aaron thought he might well give himself a heart seizure. Hysterics bored him, so he turned his attention to Jamison Stafford. "Exactly how long has it been?"

"They were taken five days ago. In the morning."

"And the first thing you did after the women were taken?"

"Well, the bandits stole our horses, which forced us to walk the rest of the way here. Once we were here, we sought help, of course."

"How soon did help arrive?"

"Three hours or so, I'd say."

"They arrived just after four," John Michael interjected.

"We returned to the site it happened, but the tracks scattered out in every direction."

"And it had been raining," John Michael added sourly.

"We've sent out search parties in every direction, but no one has—"

"Did anyone go back to the inn and ask questions?" Aaron asked.

Jamison nodded. "Yes, of course. No one knew anything."

Aaron pursed his lips. "Is that so?"

John Michael Price looked at him sharply.

"It's the obvious starting point," Aaron stated.

"Is it?" John Michael asked coolly.

"Of course. The ambush didn't formulate out of thin air. It was planned, timed and well executed, by the sound of it. If they weren't at the inn, they were nearby."

"The place had a rather menacing atmosphere," Jamison commented, looking to John Michael for confirmation.

"It was uncomfortable," John Michael concurred.

Aaron nodded. "We'll begin there."

~~~

153

Three hours later, John Michael braced himself against a wall fighting the urge to regurgitate his stomach contents. He had just witnessed the interrogation of the woman who ran the inn. Waldron had demanded the names of the men who were at the inn the morning of the abduction, the ones who had left shortly after the party in question. The woman had feigned ignorance, so Waldron had ordered her to be held down.

John Michael shook his head slowly. He should have left then. Instead, he'd watched as Waldron stuck the tip of a knife into the palm of her hand and twisted it until she came out with names amidst a lot of blood and screaming.

Jamison joined him and clapped his friend on the shoulder. John Michael glared at him.

"At least he got names," Jamison said quietly.

Waldron strode out of the inn with three 'peacekeeping' soldiers behind him. "We're off to find some of the men they mentioned," he said casually. "Care to come along?"

"Yes," Jamison replied.

"No," John Michael said, shifting his glare to Waldron.

"As you wish," Aaron said. He started off. "We'll let you know what we find out."

Jamison looked at John Michael with a worried, almost apologetic expression on his face and then hurried to catch up with the others.

# Chapter Fifteen

ost of the time, Adrian had Sara Anne riding in front of him, but today she was behind him. Her hands rested on his sides, the rest of her was wrapped around him, which was probably exactly what he wanted. Not that he had ever let on. He did not ever reveal his thoughts and feelings. Meanwhile, being pressed against him for days on end had altered something within her. He'd unleashed a fierce yearning. She only hoped a similar desire was gnawing at him, too.

"Up ahead," Adrian said to the Shadow. "We'll make camp."

"I'll ride on a bit," the older man.

It wasn't necessary to establish that fact, since he scouted the area every evening when they stopped. Adrian dismounted and helped Sara Anne down. She knew his touch so well now. She'd never known any man's touch or smell so well. She'd also developed a sense of him. She knew when he was alarmed or amused or irritated. Did he also have a sense of her?

She walked away and stretched, trying to clear her mind. She was dwelling on him because he was her constant companion. Once that was no longer the case—

Her stomach tightened at the thought of not ever seeing him again.

He strode past her with a sharp stick that he used to spear fish. "Come," he said.

She followed him to the bank of a river, aware of his walk and his movements and his physicality. For goodness sake, she *had* to get control of her thoughts.

"Yeh said yeh were wantin' a bath."

"That's right. And five minutes alone to take it."

He gave her a look. "I was teasing. This current is far too strong."

She shrugged. "I could swim in this."

155

He cocked his head at her, his expression pained. "Dinna be ridiculous."

"For your information, Charles Town is built on a peninsula and my home was on the bank of one of the two rivers that empty into the ocean."

He grunted. "That so? I dinna realize great ladies swam."

She shrugged. "As far as I know, great ladies do not. But I do and my sister did."

As he waded a few steps in, she stepped out along large rocks that jutted from the river's surface, balancing with both arms out.

"Be careful," he warned.

"I'm not afraid of water."

"Sara Anne—"

"I'll be careful! I won't fall."

"I mean it. No further than that," he insisted.

"Fine." The water swirled and foamed along the sides of the rocks and occasionally sprayed her. Admittedly, it was fast flowing. The bottom of her skirt got wet and dampened her stockings with each step, and it was cold. She stopped on the flattest rock, the one Adrian referred to, and turned back. She squatted and hugged her legs to watch him fish.

His body was tensed, his concentration complete. What would it feel like to have that much of his attention focused solely on her? His attention toward her was as complete, simply not as direct. He watched her all the time, although he attempted to be discreet. Even when she had to relieve herself, he only allowed her a short distance for privacy's sake.

With a sudden stab, he speared a fish and held it up, beaming a brilliant smile. He rarely smiled or even reacted strongly, so when he did, she felt an immediate reaction. He tossed the fish onto the bank and went back to watching the water.

One thing had become very clear to her. She needed him to get to know and to care about her. She needed it because she had to able to break away when it was time. At some point in time, an opportunity for escape would arise and when it did, he had to be willing to let her go.

She tried to swallow the painful lump that rose in her throat. What was wrong with her anyway? This was a journey that would end one way or another and relatively soon. It wasn't as if they could just keep riding forever. It wasn't as if he was falling hopelessly in love with her, so much so that he'd never be able to deliver her to another man. So much so that he'd be willing to follow her back to England and take up residence at Oakley. As if he would be welcome given what had transpired.

She rose. The river was wide, and the surroundings beautiful. In different circumstances, she might have enjoyed being there.

"That's enough," he said, finally satisfied with his catch. "We've a good supper ahead."

She started back to the bank as he strung the fish together. "Yeh can bathe if yeh want, if yeh can stand the cold water, but ye'll have tae stay right on the bank. This water is too fast fer a swim. Agreed?"

"Agreed!" She was surprised and glad. She desperately needed to wash.

"Alright. I'll go just over the ridge tae build a fire and allow yeh a bit of privacy. Dinna' abuse the freedom."

"I won't," she said with a roll of her eyes.

"Yeh felt how cold the water is," he said wryly.

"Yes, I did, but it's better than smelling bad."

He shrugged. "Suit yerself."

She watched him go before turning back and scanning the riverbank. She walked several yards downriver to the cover of trees where she undid the buttons of her shirtwaist, pulled it off and sighed with relief. She slipped her skirt off and glanced at the ridge before slipping out of her chemise, pantaloons, and stockings. He wasn't the type to spy, but the Shadow would not like that she'd been given any privacy. He might have come charging forth to get her back, the old grouch.

She'd hurried to the water's edge. She'd planned to dash into the water quickly, but the chill changed her mind. Instead, she crossed her arms and hugged herself as she took baby steps in. She made a pantherlike sound as she drew air through her clenched jaw. Covered in gooseflesh, she began shivering and her teeth began to chatter. She forced herself under. It was painful, almost a burning sensation, so she pushed off, kicked and moved her arms to get the blood flowing.

She wasn't going out far, no farther out than she could stand up, but an immediate tug of current caught her by surprise. She tried to touch bottom but couldn't get her footing. She turned to swim back to the bank and felt panic. The current was powerful, and she was caught in it and being carried along at a frightening rate of speed. Adrian had warned her, and she had ignored him. A cross current spun her around and she knew how wrong she'd been. This river was vastly different than back home.

God above! She was almost to the row of rocks she had walked atop earlier. She had to make it to one or she was lost. She stroked with all her strength to control her direction. She'd been pulled out a good way and if she missed the last rock, she'd be irretrievably lost.

The rocks were coming at her, fast. *There!* She grabbed hold and hugged the rock ferociously. She was too shaken to attempt scrambling to the top, so she just clung, but the water kept pushing and pulling, loosening her grip. She would never make it. She thought she heard Adrian calling and a wild stab of hope pierced her. She strained to listen and heard it again. It was definite and closer. He was coming but, little by little, she was slipping. She closed her eyes and prayed for strength and was answered by two strong hands that gripped her arms.

She looked into his terror-filled brown eyes. How familiar that face was to her now. He pulled her up and against him and wrapped his arms around her badly shaking body.

"Damn yeh, Sara Anne! told yeh tae stay on the bank! I told yeh the water was too fast!"

It was too much. She was exhausted, she'd nearly drowned, she was naked and, worst of all, she'd been wrong.

~

He'd seen her hysterical with laughter. Now she sobbed with the same abandon.

"Yer alright," he breathed into her ear. "Stop cryin'. It's alright." He held her tighter realizing how shaken he was, as well. He'd nearly lost her. "Come. We've got tae get off these rocks an' yev got tae get some clothes back on."

"You g-go f-first and don't look b-back."

"No. I have tae make sure yeh get across." She was shaking violently. Not only had she been terrified, she had overextended her reserves of strength. "Yer not so strong right now."

"You can t-take my hand and I'll fah-follow—"

"Damn it, woman. I've seen naked flesh before."

"Please!"

He knew she was humiliated, but this was her life at risk. Still, he turned his head, then his body from her. "Put yer hand in mine."

She did. He stepped sideways to the next rock balancing on the far edge. He was extended as far as possible to keep hold of her hand. She followed quickly.

He breathed a sigh of relief, but this was shredding his nerves. If she slipped back in, she would be gone and there would be no getting her back. The river was a tributary to the North Sea and the flow of water was treacherous. He'd thought she'd understood that. "Try an' step right behind me. With me."

They managed it, stepping more as one than two, and her hand ended up pulled in front of him, her body pressed against his back. He would not let her go. He couldn't.

When they reached the bank, he felt weakened from the delayed shock. "Fetch yer clothes," he ordered gruffly. He kept his face averted for more than one reason. Naturally, she desired privacy in her exposed state but, also, he was feeling too much. If he even revealed a small part of what he was feeling, it would be too much. She should never know how shaken he was.

~

Sara Anne picked up her shift with a badly shaking hand, but a gust of wind snatched it from her and sent it into the water. She was crying as she scrambled to get it. She glanced back at where Adrian had been, but he was gone. She picked up the dripping wet shift and carried it back to her pile of clothes, dropping it before she dressed again.

She wiped her face and then wrung out her soaking wet undergarment, hiccupping from her cry. She'd managed to stop blubbering, but she burned with shame as she trudged back to camp. What excuse was there? She'd given her word and gone back on it. Not only that, not only might *she* have drowned, but she could have pulled him in, as well.

Adrian had busied himself roasting the fish, but there was no doubt as to how furious he was. His face was dark with it. She felt a new and deeper fear than before, not of him, but of the damage that had been done between them. She hung her shift onto a branch and came closer. "I am so sorry," she said slowly. She didn't want to stammer, but she was so cold, her jaw wanted to lock. "I didn't mean to go out—"

He scowled at her so blazingly, she halted mid-sentence.

"I thought I could wade in just a bit." she added weakly.

"Despite wha' I said! Despite wha' yeh promised!"

"I'm sorry! It was foolish and reckless, and I am sorry!"

"Wha' yeh are is a spoiled brat. A hand's never been laid on yeh, has it? Yev never had tae be accountable for yer actions, have you? What I ought tae do is take yeh over my knee and teach yeh a lesson yed never forget!"

He'd come closer as he ranted, probably with every intention of forcing her over his knee, which she did deserve. But the last words spoken had struck a nerve and so she took a step back from him and began to unbutton her shirtwaist again, which stopped him in his tracks.

He blinked in incomprehension. "Wha' are yeh doin'?"

Rather than answer, she turned away from him, unfastened the last buttons and lowered her shirtwaist allowing him to see the scars on her back. In the silent moments that followed, the mortification of what he was seeing washed over her, making her feel even more ill than before. As she put back on the shirt and began buttoning it, she saw the blanket, his plaid, he called it, had been pulled from his pack for her. He'd known how cold and upset she was and, despite the rage he felt, he'd gotten it for her.

160

Tears blurred in her eyes, but she blinked them away as best she could and turned to face him. Forcing herself to look at him had never been so difficult, but she did it. He was watching her with an unfathomable expression, not knowing what to make of her. Whatever his preconceptions had been, she'd just shattered them. Again. "I said I would go no farther in than what you were," she said quietly. "And then I did, thinking it would do no harm." A tear escaped her frail control, and she hurriedly brushed it away. "I am more sorry for that than I can say."

He exhaled through his nostrils and looked down at the fire. His fury may have dimmed, but his mind still raged.

"I will never go back on my word with you again, not that I expect you to trust me."

His jaw jutted forward.

"But do not presume that you know me," she added with a shake of her head.

He looked at her sharply, having picked up on the change of tone.

"You don't really know anything about me." He was still angry with her, but now she could sense wary confusion, as well.

"I know a thing or two, Sara Anne. I know yeh refuse tae listen even when I'm tryin' tae protect yeh!" His voice had risen until he'd all but yelled the last of it, startling birds from trees.

"I was wrong, and you were right," she cried. "If you want to take me over your knee, as you put it, I won't fight you. I do deserve it."

"Aye, yeh do!"

"Then do it! If it'll make you feel better, do it!"

He leaned in. "It would have made me feel better," he said with a firm nod. "At least once my palm stopped stingin', which might have been tomorrow. But now—"

The moment was so intense, she stopped breathing. Then he turned and walked back to the fire and to tending to their meal. She managed a breath and then turned and walked woodenly to the bedroll he'd laid out. She opened the plaid and wrapped it around herself, suddenly so tired that she could have curled up and gone to right to sleep. She sat, drew her knees up, hugged them.

161

"Who did that tae you?"

She didn't want to think of what had happened, much less tell the story, but she owed him whatever he wanted to know. "My father."

"Why?"

"I defied his wishes. Or, rather, I said I would."

"About?"

"About marrying a man I didn't love," she said tiredly.

"Is that why yeh wouldn't say who yeh were? Fear of your father?"

"It's ... more complicated than that."

"How is it more complicated?"

"It just is. It wasn't fear so much, not of him. Or not fear of physical reprisal." She felt a surge of agitation. "Why am I always answering your questions? I have a few of my own, you know."

"So, ask."

His reply surprised her. She studied him for a moment and saw that his anger had diminished to almost nothing.

Almost.

"I'm wondering what your life was like before."

"It was good," he replied quietly. "Simple. Although I dinna' appreciate it like I will if I ever get back."

The longing in his words made her ache for him.

"We call our village *Ceann-a-Ghuibhsaich*." He paused. "Head of the pinewood. It's surrounded by forest so lush an' vast."

"It sounds beautiful."

"Aye. It is. An' we've the River Spey, an' a great castle nearby called Ruthven Barracks, an' we make the best whiskey yev ever tasted."

"What of your family?"

"I've three sisters an' they have families." The words had been spoken haltingly and then he grew quiet before adding "A good many of my clan were wiped out at Culloden."

She bit on her bottom lip. "I'm sorry."

"So am I."

He'd been her sole focus for days, so it was strange to imagine him part of a family and a clan. It made her feel more isolated than before. "What did you do for a living?"

"I'm a cooper, by trade, an' there is always demand fer my casks. Our whiskey is well known an' highly sought."

He squatted to reposition the fish away from a hungry flame, she tried to picture him in his former life. "What will you tell your family about this business when you see them again? Or will you tell them anything at all?"

"I'll tell them the truth," he replied without looking up at her. "They willna' like hearing it anymore than I'll like tellin' it, but I will own up to it."

She hugged the blanket tighter imagining the day he was there, and she was only a fading memory to him. Her stomach tightened and then she felt a familiar aching hollowness. It expanded upwards into her chest until drawing breath became difficult.

He pulled the fish off the spit and brought it to her on a tin plate. "Is it my turn tae ask a question?"

She took the plate, which gave her something to look at. "Go ahead."

"This man yer father wished yeh tae marry. What was he like?"

She frowned at the fish. "Aaron Waldron is his name. He's tall, considered to be handsome. His family is very wealthy, which is the reason my father wished for the match."

"Handsome and verra wealthy," he repeated. "I can see why ye ran."

Her chin shot up. "He's also arrogant and without compassion. I couldn't *bear* the thought of being married to him. He's cruel. He's without mercy. And I said he was *thought* to be handsome. I never found him so."

"An' so yeh ran away, sailed away, an' got caught up in this mess," he said as he squatted to pull off his fish.

"I assume you can see the irony of it?"

"Aye."

She took a bite and chewed slowly. "My mother's family is in the north of England. I went to them."

He looked at her with flashing eyes. "So yeh do have family there," he said accusingly. "Yeh could have gone tae them."

She glared right back. "I could have if I wanted to end up in the exact same boat I was in."

"What?"

"Right before we left for Scotland, I discovered that Aaron Waldron was coming for me. To bring me back. I couldn't *stand* the thought of being handed over to him! You have no idea how terrible he is."

"The Shelly heiress—" he said.

"She's my cousin."

"Yer cousin," he repeated. He flushed. "Of course, she is."

"When you said something about me about going back to where I came from … that's what I thought about. Returning to Oakley, my aunt and uncle's home, to find him there, demanding that I come home with him. You don't know him. He would have found a way to make me."

Adrian sat and studied his food with far more intensity than it merited, which meant he needed time. She ate most of her food and set the plate aside.

"Finish that," he said.

She picked it back up and finished it. She wasn't about to argue with him again if she could help it.

"Was it worth it?" he finally asked.

"Leaving? Running? Ending up here? Yes." She saw that her answer surprised him. "Believe it or not, I'm not a naturally defiant person. I wouldn't have chosen any of what happened. But I was left no acceptable choice. None. I learned, I *experienced*, how terrible he was, but my father wouldn't listen. You saw how he listened."

He cringed.

"He didn't care," she said quietly. "I could have told you and the others who I was, and been returned with Ginny, but he may be there waiting for me. If not, he'll be there soon. Going back with him to Charles Town would be a prison sentence. I would be at his mercy, and I already mentioned he is without mercy," she added ominously.

164

He gave a frustrated shake of his head. "How do yeh see this playing out?"

"I don't know, but why are you so angry at me?"

He started to speak before stopping himself.

"No, please, tell me!"

"Yev been playin' with fire, Sara Anne. An' yer goin' tae get badly burned. That's why!"

"That may be, but I didn't choose this situation, Adrian McGoldrick. You did. You chose to go off to a rebellion and you chose—"

His eyes narrowed. "Yeh canna' begin to understand my life!"

"Nor you, mine!"

He drew breath to say something but shut his mouth when the older man rode back into camp. "What's this, then? Goin' at each other like an old married couple. I canna' leave yeh alone fer five minutes."

Adrian sent one last withering look at Sara Anne before he rose and walked away.

That night, Sara Anne was the first to lie down. She'd hoped to fall asleep quickly given the strain of the day, but she hadn't. She pretended to be asleep when Adrian lay next to her and settled in. The Shadow began snoring softly. How funny that she knew his snore. She would have recognized it anywhere.

"Yer not sleeping," Adrian said quietly.

"No," she admitted. She rolled onto her back and looked at him. "Are you still angry at me?"

"Aye."

"That's hardly fair."

"You could have died."

"I know. I really am sorry."

"I'm sorry, as well. I'm sorry I have tae bring yeh tae Carmichael."

She grimaced. "May we change the subject?"

"Depends."

"Of course, it depends."

"I'll make an exchange with yeh."

"An exchange?"

"I'll answer a question fer yeh. Then yeh answer mine."

"Alright. What is it you want to know?"

He suddenly looked uncomfortable. "It's not wha' I want tae know, it's wha' I was supposed tae find out."

"What is it?"

"I'm supposed tae find out if yer … pure. Untouched."

Such heat surged to her face that she was glad for the darkness. "Why?" It came out breathy and small sounding.

"For Carmichael. A lady possessing her maidenhead—"

*How were you supposed to find out?* she wondered. She thought of Aaron invading her and shuddered. Had Aaron been able to tell? Was that what he had been trying to discover? A possible route of escape suddenly dawned on her. "Would he not want me if—"

Adrian blinked in surprise. "It's only a matter of establishin' a price. He'll want yeh no matter what. The man's no an idiot."

A price! Money! Again! Her every source of humiliation began with greed. "Why are you involved in this?" she asked angrily.

"The men behind it saved my life."

The reply robbed her of speech for a moment. "In the rebellion?"

"Aye." He shifted onto his back and raised his shirt to reveal a scar that ran breast to hip. "I thought I was dead." His eyes looked distant, his face haunted. "Perhaps I am, anyway."

She looked up at the stars. There were so many, and they were so beautiful. "What was the rebellion over?"

"I suppose like all war, it's one thing tae one man, and another tae another. Fer me, I was expected tae go, pledged by the laird. But I thought of it as a fight against tyranny."

She turned her head to look at him.

"We want tae rule ourselves. We want freedom tae live the way we see fit. Now we canna even dress the way we like. Our kilts and tartans have been banned; our music has been banned. We canna' carry weapons."

"And yet you carry a knife and a pistol."

"An' if I'm caught with them, I'll be hung."

"It's quite a risk," she replied coolly, in complete contradiction to how she felt.

"Yeh could say that. If I'm caught with yeh, I'll be executed, an' if I fail to deliver yeh, the other side will find me."

She sighed. Everything was so backwards, somehow.

"Perhaps yed like tae see me hang fer my crime."

She came up on an elbow and glared at him, furious at the statement. "I would not care to see anyone hang! And, no, it would not bring me satisfaction if you were caught. I don't even think you really believe that."

"I dinna' ken what I believe anymore," he said quietly.

Tears sprang to her eyes. He was in a terrible position. Perhaps it was all how own fault, but she couldn't help caring about him. It wasn't just that he'd saved her life earlier; it was that he was truly decent, even noble, in his own way. He had lain next to her for seven nights and never once touched her. He had longed to. She had seen it in his face before he averted his gaze. But he hadn't. Aaron Waldron, on the other hand, had been offered her on a silver platter and still had refused to behave decently in the few short weeks before becoming her lord and master.

"*Tha mi sgith agus tha thu sgith,*" he uttered softly.

She was curious about the strange language and touched by his gentle tone. "What did you say?"

"Yer tired, an' so am I." He paused. "Rest."

He had said more than that, she was sure. She lay back and turned on her side away from him. "You may tell Lord Carmichael that I am not," she spoke clearly and slowly. There it was. She'd said it. She'd told the tale, diminished her *value,* and disappointed the handsome abductor she'd foolishly grown to care about. Tears pricked the backs of her eyes, but she fought against breaking down. She might have managed it except for the protective arm that closed around her.

Emotions surged and the tears flowed. She tried to be quiet and still, but it was impossible. He shushed and held her so gently that a sob escaped her. She pressed a hand to her mouth to muffle the sound and, the next thing she knew, he was turning her around and pulling her into his arms. She clutched his shirtfront and waited for the grief to subside. When it finally did, she felt leaden with exhaustion. As she drifted toward sleep, she thought, *How ironic. I love him.*

# Chapter Sixteen

Sara Anne woke and was surprised by the light of mid-morning and the fact that no one seemed to be around. She rose, stretched, and walked until she found a secluded spot to relieve herself. As she meandered back, mulling over the words spoken the night before, she knew it was time she established a few rules for herself, beginning with she could not and would not go falling in love with her abductor.

She stepped back into camp to see Adrian repacking. "Eat an' we go," he said, with barely even a glance in her direction.

After the intimacy of the night before, it felt particularly cold. It wasn't reasonable to feel hurt, especially given the resolution she'd just made, but she couldn't help it. "And I wish you a fine morning, as well," she said. He didn't react. Of course. Mister Stoic Stoneface that he was.

She picked up the plate of dried meat and freshly picked berries that he'd set out for her and ate it with her back to him so she wouldn't have to guard her expression. "Where's our friend?" she asked impassively when she'd finished.

"He'll be back. He knows where we're goin'."

"I don't suppose I might be let in on that?"

He gave her a look of exasperation. "We're staying tae the river fer a few days. Any other questions, yer highness?"

"My guess is that English troops are nearby. Am I right?"

He narrowed his eyes at her warningly.

She gave a mock shiver. "Ooh, what a frightening look. Please stop," she said so dryly, his look really did darken.

He took hold of her arm and started her walking.

"I'm coming," she complained, pulling her arm from his grasp. "You needn't pull on me."

"Except fer that you're my captive. Remember?"

"Would I forget that? If you thought I had this confused with a holiday, you're wrong."

"Walk!"

"You see this movement my feet are making? And the fact that we started back there but are now here and moving ever forward?"

He scowled at her. "I'll have no more of your lip."

She shrugged. "Except I have two."

He stopped, his body rigid, and then continued on without turning to look at her.

Needling him was strangely enjoyable. All that tension in his shoulders, she'd put it there. Which served him right. "Besides which, I didn't offer you my lip."

He stopped again, dropped the reins, grabbed her and kissed her. Soundly. Just short of roughly. When he released her, she took a step back, stunned, and unbalanced.

"I warned yeh about giving me lip. I'm quite aware yeh have two."

She loathed herself for the reaction her body was having, especially the part of it he could see and would likely take credit for. The flushed face, the trembling, the labored breathing.

"Anything else ye want tae say?" he challenged.

She glared fiercely but refrained from comment.

"Ooh, that look yeh give me," he mocked. "Please stop."

She folded her arms angrily. "Has it occurred to you that I could start screaming right now and bring the English down on your head?"

"Has it occurred tae you that I'd have yer scream cut off before ye so much as alert the berds in the trees? An' that yed' be gagged fer the duration. Which yeh would no' enjoy, since yeh like talking so much."

It took real restraint, but she kept her lips pressed tightly together.

"Excellent," he said calmly. "Now, walk!"

~~~

They rode alone all day, not speaking. Not speaking because too many thoughts and feelings had been shared and too much was felt. They were colossal mistakes Adrian resented making. They had made camp and eaten before Edmund returned. "English," he spat before he dismounted.

Adrian tensed. "Where?"

"Camped a mile away perhaps. They're goin' north, but we need tae get tae better cover in case they scout the area."

"Food's prepared. Go eat."

"We should gag her," Edmund said quietly.

"No."

Edmund huffed in frustration but strode to the food and ate. When he finished, they rode upriver until they were able to cross to the other side. "They were ridin' hard, headin' north," Edmund said.

"How many?"

"Ten or twelve. Headin' north right on our tails. I dinna' like it."

"Might be nothing," Adrian muttered. But it wasn't. He could feel it.

~~~

When they finally stopped for the night, Sara Anne was exhausted enough to fall asleep standing. Adrian laid out the bedroll for her and she climbed in. The men went a short distance away to talk.

"I didn't see anythin' at ferst," the Shadow was saying to Adrian. "Then I saw 'em comin'. Ridin' hard, kickin' up dust. I found a place tae hide and stayed there until they were past. I followed, keepin' a good distance, an' I saw them stop an' make camp."

It had taken a few minutes for the warmth of the bedroll to penetrate, but it was, and it felt good. The men were conferring more quietly. She was so tired, but she tried to listen.

"—fear we're ridin' into a trap," the older man said.

"Yer jumpin' tae conclusions," Adrian replied.

She couldn't make out the next words until, "—turn back."

Adrian made a sound of disgust and said something she couldn't make out.

"Wha' if it's over?" the Shadow fretted.

"Then it's over. We go our separate ways."

"An' wha' of the gerl?"

"I'll see she gets home," Adrian said.

Sara Anne's eyes filled. He wasn't going to just leave her. Of course, he wasn't. He cared about her.

"She knows your name, Iceman,"

More silence. Sara Anne felt her heart pounding. What was Adrian thinking during that silence?

"It'll be alright," he finally said.

She exhaled.

"Yeh shouldna' trust her."

Adrian sighed heavily, and the sound made her want to weep. It wasn't true. He could trust her. She did not want to see him hurt.

"I'm tired," Adrian said. "Let's sleep."

She pretended to be asleep when Adrian lay next to her. As usual, he did not touch her. His body hovered so close, they shared heat, but he did not touch her. She'd been so tired, but now she was wide awake. Adrian slept. She could tell by his breathing. He really and truly slept.

Why did he never touch her? He wanted to. She inched closer to him, so close that her breasts touched his back. Her nipples stiffened; in fact, they ached. If he woke now, he would know her desire.

But he slept.

Damn him.

She moved alongside him fully. She would pretend to be sleeping if he woke. Which he didn't. Slowly, she wrapped her arm around his middle. If he woke, she'd pretend to be asleep. She didn't want to move; it felt so good to be this close. She pressed a kiss to his shoulder.

He jerked slightly, inhaled, and leaned back against her with a sigh as if enjoying the feel of her, but he slept on. That was alright. She'd be able to sleep now.

"Sara Anne."

She started and opened her eyes. Adrian was crouched down. It was morning, already, and he'd woken her.

"Time to go," he said.

# Chapter Seventeen

They were less than half a day's ride from the Forth of Firth. The original plan was to take a boat to Stonehaven, but now, fearing an ambush, they'd decided they would ferry from North Berwick to Pittenweem, and continue by land. They would lie low until they got a sense of what had happened.

No one spoke as they traveled. A melancholy had settled over Sara Anne, and Adrian didn't know what to say to her. He hated the thought of her with Carmichael. What he wanted to do, needed to do, was dissuade Carmichael from wanting her at all. Or what if he gave up his part of the reward in exchange for her? Except she was worth more to them than what he was due. Unless he could convince them otherwise.

Sara Anne didn't want to return home, but he could not give her the sort of life she'd had. She'd known wealth and privilege. In truth, he had no idea what Carmichael looked like. What if he was handsome and agreeable besides being rich?

Tension mounted as they rode into North Berwick. The Crown's troops were thickly posted, far more so than Adrian had imagined. Edmund rode apart from them, but if either of them were searched or questioned, they were dead men.

"We shouldn't be here," Sara Anne said quietly. She was riding behind him. "We should go. Just turn and go."

"They'd come after us. Best tae stay calm an' go about our business. Yeh see how they're watchin' us."

"Yes, of course, I see it. That was my point."

"This is not the time tae argue, woman." He heard her huff and could well imagine the roll of her eyes, but he was right. He kept his gaze straight ahead and they made it to the harbor without being questioned.

174

His knees felt springy as he dismounted. Sara Anne could have made a ruckus and been released at any time. What choice would he have had? Instead, she was fretting for them. As he put his hands around her waist and helped her down, he searched her eyes for the reason why. "Dinna fash," he said quietly. "We'll ferry tae a village across the firth. There willna be so many of them there."

She glanced around and then nodded. "Let's hope."

Edmund was negotiating with the ferryman as they approached. The ferryman looked Adrian and Sara Anne over and then named his price. Edmund paid the man, and they all followed him onto his flat-bottomed boat. Adrian's stomach knotted as he waited for them to shove off. It had been a mistake to have come this way.

They shoved off, the ferryman and two burly assistants, each armed with their long poles. Sara Anne swayed, and he reached out to steady her. He positioned himself behind her and slipped his arms around her. It felt as though she relaxed as she leaned against him — or was it wishful thinking on his part? Her arms folded over his, and her hair blew in the salt-tanged wind as she turned her head to speak to him discreetly. "Is the plan still the same?"

"I dinna' want it tae be."

She squeezed his arm. "Nor I."

He longed to press a kiss to her cheek.

"So, let's agree it's changed," she said.

Oh, things had changed, alright. He just hadn't quite worked out how to manage what came next. Seabirds flew by squawking. Sara Anne lifted her chin toward a rock island that jutted straight up from the sea. "What is that?"

"Bass Rock. There was a prison on it fer years. It was destroyed not long ago."

"It looks inhabitable."

"Aye. Both a dreadful an' perfect place fer a prison. That over there, the ruins on the cliff, that's Tantallon Castle. Cornwall destroyed it a hundred years ago."

"A hundred years. And yet the walls—"

"Aye. They'll be there fer another hundred years or more. Long after yeh an' I are gone."

It grew quiet between them.

"Why didn't yeh insist on bein' let go back there?" She turned to face him fully and he saw her eyes had filled.

"How can you ask that? Do you think I would trade my freedom for your life?"

The pain he felt served him right for involving himself with the abduction scheme in the first place. It had been a crime and worse. It wouldn't turn out well because it couldn't. There was no good solution. Even if he saw her freed and he got away with his life, which seemed unlikely, he'd never see his heart again. She'd have it. She'd never even know, but she'd have it. "No," he replied. "But yeh could have forced me tae release you. We both know I would have had no choice."

She studied him. It looked as if she wanted to say something, but she merely sighed and turned back around.

~~~

The boatman watched his passengers thoughtfully. This had to be the party he'd been questioned about. They fit the description too perfectly not to be and yet this couple was in love. The English had claimed the woman had been abducted and brutalized, but this woman was not afraid, nor did she look to be hurt. He'd been ordered to inform on the party if he encountered them, but he was sick and tired of being told what to do. Besides, no reward had been offered.

~~~

When they disembarked from the ferry, Adrian and Sara Anne went in a different direction than the Shadow. "Where did Edmund go?" she asked conversationally as they walked through the bustling fishing village leading the horse behind them.

Adrian sighed in disgust that she'd picked up on the name. "Yeh dinna ken his name," he breathed in her ear.

The sensation sent a shivery thrill through her, and her nipples stiffened. "Fine. I don't know his name. I don't know your name. I

176

don't know anything much at all, Iceman." He gave her a cross look and she smiled sweetly at him. "You must admit it's somewhat silly since we have lived within, what, ten feet of each other for these last very long weeks?"

"It hasna' been weeks," he retorted. "As tae it bein' long, yeh dinna have tae—"

"Yes yes. To be here in the first place. You may have mentioned it."

He hitched the horse outside a seedy-looking inn, and Adrian looked around before leaning close to her. "We'll goin' tae get a room as man an' wife."

Her breath thickened and her nipples suddenly ached.

The innkeeper was unsteady with drink. He handed a key over. "Upstairs, number three." His breath reeked of liquor, and his words were slurred. His gaze went to her.

Adrian nodded and they walked away. Number three was as dingy as the rest of the place. Adrian went to the window and peered outside. "I've got tae get yeh somethin' else tae wear." He turned back to her. "If we're questioned, yer my wife. Yer name is Mary McDuff an' I am James McDuff from Kinross. Say it."

"I'm Mary McDuff from Kinross."

He grimaced. "Can yeh not say it like yer a Scot, woman?"

"I'm Mary McDuff," she tried again with a Scottish accent.

He ducked his head as if her accent was painful to hear.

"Mary McDuff," she tried again, trilling her r's so that Mary came out as med-de.

"Better," he conceded. "Although it might be best tae claim yer dumb."

"I am Med-de McDuff from Kinross," she repeated, beginning to get the knack of the accent. "This man, my husband, yeh ask? Aye, he is. James."

Adrian fought back a grin.

"He is mean an' hateful, yer right about that, although I think yer mistaken when yeh say he's ugly." She smiled sweetly. "I dinna' find his looks all that offensive. Although yer right when yeh say he could use a bath."

177

He gave her a look. "I have tae tie ye up while I'm gone. Yeh can lie on the bed an' I'll try not tae make it uncomfortable."

"How considerate," she said dryly.

He retrieved ropes from his pack. He tied her hands together, secure, but not too tight. He fastened the rope to the top bedrail, then bound her feet together and secured them to the bottom bedrail. He looked around for something to gag her with that wasn't too repulsive. He lifted her skirt. "I'll take a strip from where it's cleanest."

"Is this really necessary?" she complained.

He tore off a piece. "It is."

"Haven't I shown that—"

He sat on the bed beside her. "I kin yeh dinna want me hurt. But yeh might choose tae slip away quietly thinking yeh could gain yer freedom an' extricate me an' Edmund from this mess. Am I wrong?"

Her eyes widened with surprise and a flash of guilt.

"Why don't we say that was a rhetorical question," he said tenderly. "I dinna blame yeh."

She frowned at that.

As he bent over her to gag her, he was conscious of her vulnerability and his own odor. He secured it and stood back up. "I won't be long," he assured her.

~~~

He looked into her eyes as if searching for a reaction. Was she giving him one? She had often been accused of giving away her every thought and feeling in her expressions, especially through her eyes. Caroline had often teased that she needed a fan to hide behind. "You give away everything you are thinking and feeling right there," she'd observed, gesturing at her eyes.

It had become such a recurring theme between them that Caroline was eventually able to gesture the opening of a fan with her fingers to indicate that Sara Anne should better guard her expression. "You should always carry a fan in public and *use it,*" Caroline declared one day, thrusting a fan into her hand. "Barely peek over and pretend you're feeling some strong emotion, and I'll guess which one it is."

From amused to furious, Caroline had correctly guessed eight times in a row. "Don't worry," she's finally said. "There's one technique that will help you. Hold the fan," she had reached over and readjusted the fan to cover Sara Anne's entire face, "just so."

"Yeh could sleep awhile," Adrian suggested.

Sara Anne narrowed her eyes and tried to say that she couldn't sleep while gagged, but he just shook his head and left. What would she have revealed in her gaze? Frustration. She certainly felt frustrated, although not specifically at him. Fear? Yes, that had definitely begun to take root. Hope? Desire?

She breathed out slowly, realizing how much she wanted to know him. She wanted to know about his home and his family and what he'd been like as a child. Had his beautiful brown eyes affected everyone around him? Had he ever fallen in love? She imagined a pretty Highland girl — imagined Adrian laughing with her, kissing her, and an overwhelming jealousy took hold.

*Stop it! How ridiculous you are.*

But she couldn't help it. The day he pulled her from the water and saved her had changed her forever. He'd held her as if he hadn't wanted to let her go. She would never get that moment, that feeling, out of her mind. Never.

~~~

A middle-aged man walked into an alehouse called the *Cock's Crow*. After the brightness of the daylight, it took his eyes several seconds to begin adjusting to the dim light inside, which suited Aaron Waldron. It was a tool he had been taking advantage of all day. He was able to observe a man without his being aware of it. He was looking for a loner, two men together or, best case scenario, the two men with Sara Anne.

Edmund Tully was one of the two. He was said to be a nondescript middle-aged man, which was not a lot to go on. The younger man was a Highlander by the name of McGoldrick. The others called him Iceman. He was said to be a comely man with brown hair, and they'd be able to verify his identity by a long scar on his torso.

Tully and McGoldrick were taking Sara Anne to a Scottish nobleman outside of Aberdeen. Of course, they would never make it there. He would see to that. Or, if they did make it there, they would make it no further.

The search for Sara Anne had been interesting and not as difficult as he had feared it might be once they'd discovered the location of Leith Kinnaird, one of the Scotsmen behind the failed plot. Kinnaird had been strong and defiant at first and beating him hadn't altered his resolve. Dripping blood and sweat, he'd sworn he would never tell them anything and he'd meant it. He was the kind of man who would have been tortured to death before uttering a word of information to his enemy. That was when Aaron had been allowed to step in and take over.

He'd brought in Kinnaird's young nephew and made him scream for a while. It had worked. Kinnaird had told them everything. Too bad for him it hadn't saved his life.

Aaron watched the new arrival sit at a table, motion for service, and then look around the room. When their gazes locked and the man registered alarm, Waldron felt a tightening in his gut. "Edmund Tully," he called.

The man did not acknowledge recognition of the name.

After he'd broken Kinnaird, the general had assigned a dozen men to assist his efforts for as long as he needed them. Now, their heads snapped toward him. "Do you see him, sir?"

Aaron got to his feet. "I may."

A barmaid approached the man he suspected of being Tully and the man ordered whiskey, bread, and meat. He looked sharply at Aaron as he sat across from him. "What do yeh want?" he asked, frowning at the intrusion.

"Waldron's the name."

The man squinted at him. "I dinna' ask yer name."

"You're Edmund Tully," Aaron said, watching for a response.

The man shook his head looking no less annoyed. "Yeh got the wrong man, mister. Yeh mind?"

The barmaid was back with the food and drink and the man bent to eating.

"What is your name?" Aaron asked conversationally.

"I dinna see wha' concern that is of yers."

"You see that table over there?" Aaron pointed to the table he'd come from.

The sight of soldiers altered the man's defiance. "I do. My name is McKnight," he said, giving in. "John McKnight."

"Do you have proof of that?"

The man looked taken aback. "Proof?"

"Yes, proof. Does anyone here know you?"

"No." The man thought for a moment. "I am not from here."

"No? Where are you from."

"Dundee."

"What are you doing here?"

"Conducting personal business. An' I mind my own business."

"I have business," Aaron stated. "Finding a criminal named Tully."

"I wish yeh luck with it." He took a bite.

Aaron waited, never taking his eyes from the man.

The man sighed with disgust. "I have a letter with me, if that would help yeh go away and leave me tae my meal." He reached into his dirty coat pocket and fumbled for something. He pulled out a creased letter and handed it over. It was addressed to John McKnight of Dundee. "Read it if you must. I dinna' need trouble with the English."

Aaron took it and read.

~~~

Adrian walked into the dress shop feeling as out of place as he'd ever been in his life – and he'd just come from a public bath house, the first one he had ever been to. The silks and perfumed air of the shop was nothing like he'd experienced. A lady came toward him and asked if she could be of assistance.

"I need tae purchase some items," he said hesitantly.

"I rather assumed," she replied, although it wasn't said unkindly. "What sort of items and what size?"

181

"Clothing an' … underthings." He held his hands out. "Her waist is—"

The lady called for someone named Abigail, and a young woman emerged from a back room. She was slight and dark haired, perhaps sixteen years of age or so.

"Is the lady larger or smaller than Anne?" the lady asked.

And he thought he'd been uncomfortable before. "Ah, she's taller, by so." He gestured with his hands. "And she's, uh—" he hesitated, wondering how to gracefully state that she had better breasts.

"Larger in the bust?" the lady asked.

He heaved a sigh of relief. "Aye."

"You have no measurements?"

"No. I'm sorry."

"An' she's not able to come in fer a fittin'?"

"No. It's a gift," he said hesitantly.

"I see. Do yeh have a color or particular style in mind?"

He shook his head.

"What about cost? Is there a price yeh must keep to?"

He had spent Kinnaird's money on supplies they'd need for the remainder of the trip. Dried beef, unleavened bread, cheese, wine, whiskey, a packet of tea, and a bar of soap. Of course, he had his own money. "May I just see wha' yeh have?"

"Of course." The woman patiently helped him select a new skirt, shirt and shift for her. His last stop was to purchase some new clothing for himself. All of his had far too many miles on them.

~~~

Sara Anne was impatient for Adrian's return. He had only been gone a short time, but being bound and gagged was miserable. She was planning to glare at him from the moment he walked through the door to express her vast discontent.

The doorknob jiggled and then door opened. She raised her head to fix Adrian with a look, but it wasn't him blinking back at her. It was a squirrelly looking stranger. Sara Anne's muscles tightened as he crept further in, leaving the door ajar.

"She's here," he whispered, his eyes never leaving her face. His face and clothes were filthy. He had thin hair and a beaklike nose.

A second man with long, dark hair and a narrow growth of hair in the center of his chin stepped in next and closed the door shut behind him. "Look at that," he said with a smirk.

Sara Anne was shaking as the men came closer, staring as if she was a foreign object. They were filthy and sickening, but she couldn't look away. Their necks were black with caked filth and their body odor turned her stomach.

"It's her," the dark-haired one said to his friend. "What was the reward?"

The question made everything painfully clear. It was over, although this was not the way she had wanted to go free. Not at the expense of Adrian being caught. Edmund had barely tolerated her existence, but she didn't wish that end on him, either. He'd never been unkind to her. Perhaps they could still get away. Perhaps she would be asked to point out her captors. If t she had any control, she would make sure they went free.

"Fifty guineas," squirrely man replied. He licked his lips obscenely.

She shivered with revulsion.

The dark-haired one pulled out a small dagger and tossed it from hand to hand, enjoying the fear in her eyes. "Dinna' worry, lass," he finally said. "I'll not cut yer pretty skin." He leaned in to cut the rope that bound her hands to the bed. "It's worth too much."

"Wait," squirrely stopped him. "Cut the rope from her legs ferst."

The other grinned obscenely. "Yeah, awright," he whispered.

She cried out, although the sound was too muffled to serve as an alarm. Still, the dark-haired man lunged at her. "Shut yer hole," he threatened. He narrowed his eyes, silently daring her to defy him, then bent to cut the rope around her feet.

Squirrely man was doing a little jig as he removed his trousers. "A reward on top of the reward," he sang gleefully.

The pain in her stomach intensified. She was going to be sick. She was utterly trapped.

Squirrely man was inching up her skirt slowly, tittering with anticipation. Dark hair watched, his mouth agape. Sara Anne squeezed her eyes shut and clenched every muscle, willing herself to be stone. It was with horror that she felt her pantaloons being dragged off. The bed sagged with the man's weight as he began to crawl over her.

*No, no, no. Oh, God, no,* she begged.

But his hands were on either side of her arms; he was on top of her. She kneed him with all her might. With a guttural *huuuuhg,* he fell sideways off the bed, clearing her view of the room – and of another man with a knife in hand, his face dark with rage.

"Who sent yeh?" he demanded.

With a gasp, she realized it was Adrian, only clean and shaven.

Squirrely reached for his breeches.

"Don't move," Adrian threatened.

Dark hair still held his dagger. "It's only the reward we want, highlander. Dinna be foolish."

In a move so fast, she almost missed it, Adrian hurled his knife at the dark-haired man. It buried itself in one of his eye sockets and the man let out a blood-curdling scream as he dropped to his knees. Adrian was suddenly on him, and the scream was silenced.

The other man was scooting away frantically and making a terrified whimper as Adrian went after him. There was a roar in Sara Anne's ears. Her sweat-soaked body felt ice-cold. Adrian was suddenly there, removing her gag and cutting her hands free. She twisted and bent over the side of the bed and vomited.

"I'm sorry," Adrian said, hovering close. "I'm so sorry."

She saw that both men were dead. There was blood everywhere. Adrian had done that in a matter of seconds. She squeezed her eyes shut.

"We've got tae go. Dinna' look upon them."

She wasn't even sure she could even stand on her own, but he got her up and embraced her tightly. She clung to him until they heard the sound of raised voices in the hall questioning the source of the scream. They heard a distant knock and then another, followed by demands to open up.

Adrian cursed under his breath, and then lifted her chin until she met his eyes. "I have tae get them off our scent." He pressed a kiss to her forehead, hesitated a moment and then left.

She listened to Adrian asking who had screamed. Within moments, it was clear that he'd joined the search and was indicating the direction it might have come from. They had to get out of there!

She started toward the window determined not to look at the corpses, but she couldn't help it. Squirrely man's head was turned so that it looked as if he were staring at the door in surprise. His throat had been cut and his blood was inching across the floorboards. The other man stared blindly with his one eye. Blood had covered most his face, his shirt, and the floor around him.

Adrian hadn't gotten any blood on him. That realization sent a painful shiver down her spine. He'd slit the throats of two men and yet somehow avoided it.

She tried to open the window, but it would not budge. It had not been cleaned or opened in years. Although everything viewed through it was muted in a filmy haze, she thought saw Edmund coming. Was it him? She went after Adrian's telescope and hurried back. It was Edmund, and he seemed tense. Her heart pounded. Would he come here and doom both himself and Adrian? Was he aware that a reward had been posted for her? She watched with her breath held as he passed the inn by without even a glance to indicate recognition.

*Thank God!*

She gave the street a sweeping glance and noticed English soldiers pointedly following Edmund. Did he even know he was being followed? There was no way for her to know or to warn him. She dropped the telescope to her side realizing their situation was only going to become more dangerous and out of hand as time went on.

The English were looking for her. They were here looking for her. She could alert them right now and this would all be over and done with. In the long run, it would be best for everyone. She could claim to have gotten free from her captors days ago.

Adrian would go free, as would Edmund' she would see to it. She would return to Middlesbrough and make her uncle and aunt understand the truth. No matter what Aaron had claimed, she was their blood. They knew her. They would believe her.

A figure on the street below grabbed her attention. It was his square shoulders and the way he moved. "No," she breathed, yanking the telescope back to her eye so violently that she hit her cheekbone.

Aaron glanced at the inn. She jerked back and tripped over the body of the dark-haired man. She tried to regain her balance, but she fell onto wet, sticky blood. She scooted away frantically, leaving the telescope behind. When she came into contact with a man directly behind her, she cried out, but a hand clamped down on her mouth stifling the sound.

"I dinna think we can risk another scream," Adrian breathed into her ear.

He helped her back to her feet, his eyes ablaze with concern.

"I saw Edmund go by! He's being followed."

Adrian went for his telescope and knapsack. He pulled the blanket off the bed and came back to Sara Anne with it. "Wipe yer hands," he said gently. "We've got tae go."

They walked to the door, and he opened it and peered out. He took hold of her hand and led the way down the hall and down the narrow back stairs.

~~~

They reached the side door to a courtyard just as commotion erupted above them, someone screaming about bodies and blood. "We have tae go separately," he said urgently. "Yeh take the horse and ride west."

She nodded.

"Clear town by at least a mile an' find a place tae conceal yourself until I find yeh. Alright?"

She nodded. "Yes."

"Take this," he said, handing her his pack.

She took it and looked at him longingly.

"Yel be fine. Should yeh be stopped, you were the victim."

"I'll wait for you," she pledged.

"Just ride. Keep yer head down. Dinna' encounter anyone if yeh can help it."

She pressed a kiss to his cheek before hurrying away. It was bewildering to watch her go. Once she was out of sight, he went north to skirt the main streets of town. He felt utterly conspicuous, like he was being watched, but he kept going. He walked briskly at first, but then he forced himself to slow so as not to draw attention to himself.

# Chapter Eighteen

**A**aron was agitated as he rode back through town. He'd been so certain he'd spotted Tully back at the *Cock's Crow*. His conviction had wavered as he spoke to the man who called himself McKnight, but enough doubt had lingered that he followed the man when he left the alehouse.

McKnight had ridden nearly to the edge of town before stopping at a dwelling and speaking with the elderly woman who lived there. After a short exchange, he'd continued northwest toward Dundee. When he was gone from sight, Aaron spoke to the woman to find out what he'd wanted. She claimed McKnight had stopped to pay an outstanding debt owed by his recently deceased brother. It corroborated the man's story, which chafed at his pride.

There was commotion at an inn Aaron passed, something about murder. It piqued his interest enough to investigate. In an upstairs room, two bodies lay in puddles of blood. Waldron cocked his head realizing they'd spoken with the men. "Whose room was this?" Aaron demanded, looking around for whomever was in charge.

"A man an' his wife," the proprietor of the inn, replied nervously. He smelled of body odor and spirits.

"What did he look like?"

"Brown hair. He were a fine looking man," he said with a tense shrug.

Aaron's pulse raced. "And the woman?"

"Oh, now she were a beauty."

"Light brown hair, green eyes?"

"Aye. The palest green, they were."

"Get the men together," Waldron shouted. "They couldn't have gone far!"

His men hurried out and Aaron felt high with vindication. He'd been right about everything, including Edmund Tully. The letter he'd produced had been a long-planned evasion device. Tully had paid that old woman to cover for him, knowing they were onto him. Clever, but he should have seen through it.

The group reconvened at the *Cock's Crow.* Aaron sat studying a map. "A few of you will go north," he said. "Williams, Peters, Ogglesby. You three," he jabbed his finger in the direction of three men, "head southwest. You four," he pointed at others. "Due east. You four, northwest and pick up the trail of the man who claimed to be McKnight."

"You think he's actually Tully," Ogglesby spoke up.

"I'd bet his life on it."

The men laughed.

"And us?" a man who had yet to be assigned spoke up.

"The rest of us go west. I have a feeling."

Sara Anne could only go so fast through town, although nothing would have felt better than to spur the horse into a dead run and put some distance between herself and Pittenweem. When she finally got beyond town, she did just that. Action helped and, for a while, she didn't think, she just rode. By the time she slowed and turned back to make sure no one was pursuing her, she had lost track of time. No one seemed to be following.

How far had she gone? Fear and freedom had occupied and driven her, not calculating distance traveled. How long would it be before he could catch up? Would it even be possible for him to find her? What if he chose a different route? All he had said was to go west, and that covered a lot of area.

A streak of lightning caught her eye. The sky was quickly becoming ominous looking. She walked the horse in a circle, considering what to do. She had passed a grove of trees some ways back. It would make a good place to conceal herself and the horse while she waited for Adrian.

~~~

Edmund heard them coming. It was a disappoint but not a surprise. Ever since he'd spotted the tall, dark stranger in the tavern staring a hole through him, he'd experienced a feeling, a *knowing*, that he was soon to die. The only questions were how soon and by whose hand.

He realized that he'd been followed when he left the tavern. Stopping at a lodge was a ploy to buy him time and it had worked; it just hadn't bought enough.

The American had been armed with information that he could have only gotten from one of the brothers Kinnaird, which meant the scheme truly was over. The men who had taken part in the abduction were either dead or would be soon.

The men of Jedburgh had a different battle to wage with the English than the Highlanders who wanted to restore a Stuart to the throne. Jedburgh was dying a slow, poverty-stricken death due to punitive taxes imposed by the English. Everyone who could move away from the border town had done so, but not everyone could. It had been wrong to abduct young women and hold them for money, but it was wrong to squeeze the life from a town, as well.

He thought of the elderly woman. "My name is McKnight," he'd explained. "My brother owes yeh a debt that I have come tae pay." He'd held out all the money he had, and the old woman had blinked in obvious confusion. She had been slow to catch on or perhaps she'd just been honest. "*McKnight*," he'd repeated, his eyes beseeching. "In case, anyone asks."

She'd seem to catch on then. "McKnight," she repeated, glancing around to see who was watching. She had looked down at the money he was offering. "Was it all that much?" the woman asked.

"Aye," he said. "It was. Take it."

"Stop!" voices shouted from behind him now. "Stop, Tully, or we'll shoot!"

It was over. The only question that remained was how well he would die. That knowledge came with a calmness he wouldn't have expected. He reined his horse in and turned about to face the enemy. There were four of them and they all had pistols leveled at him. He held out his hands as the rain began falling. "I am not armed."

190

"I would think not," one of them said facetiously. "Carrying arms is illegal."

Everyone snickered at the comment, even Tully, which seemed to displease the men. One of them came closer. "Open your jacket," he ordered. Tully obeyed, and the man nodded, satisfied there was no weapon.

"You'll come with us," another ordered. He was stocky with a thick neck and mean, squinty eyes. It would be a pleasure to kill him. "We have questions for you."

Edmund tipped his head in acquiescence and the thick-necked soldier took the lead. Edmund followed and the other three fell behind him. As he rode, he discreetly reached inside the flap sewn into his jacket where a pistol was concealed. On the inside of his leg was a sheath with a dagger.

When an ear-splitting shot rang out, Edmund slumped over. The man in the lead veered sharply left and slipped off the far side of his horse. The others looked around in panic and confusion.

"McGoldrick!" one of them shouted out.

"Where?"

Another shot rang out, and the soldier in the center was suddenly missing half his face. Edmund's ruse was exposed. He jumped down, knife in hand and ran for them. They fired and the bullets caught Edmund in the head and chest.

"Bloody hell!" one of the men cried.

The other survivor walked to Tully's body and kicked it. "Bugger! Slimy, Scottish bastard!" He kicked the corpse again and again to annihilate the contented look on its face.

# *Chapter Nineteen*

A drian crouched at the edge of woods, breathing hard and staring at the open field in front of him. There was a grove of trees ahead and then more pasture. Rain tapped the leaves and ground around him. Would he find her? It was possible she'd never had any intention of stopping and waiting for him.

~

It was becoming obvious to Sara Anne that she'd either gone too far or in the wrong direction. Daylight was waning and soon there would be nothing to do but to wait for another day. She had the bedroll, the flasks, and the food. Adrian had no provisions, and he was on foot. She walked to the edge of the grove and peered out in hopes of spotting him.

~

Adrian watched the light steadily snake from the earth like a great curtain being dragged across the land, leaving dusk in its wake. The small grove of trees was momentary lit in an almost blinding aura of gold – and his heart began to hammer as something caught his eye.

~

Sara Anne peered through the telescope. If no one were in sight, she would ride further back toward town. It didn't matter if the decision was born of bravery or fear; she needed action and purpose. She swept the landscape slowly, taking in the trees, the distant blue hills, more trees and ... *Adrian.*

She jerked so hard; she nearly dropped the telescope. Adrian was in the woods opposite her, looking directly at her through the veil of silver rain. She laughed aloud, her heart pounding at the discovery. She lowered the telescope and discovered that, with the naked eye, she could barely make him out. She peered through the lens again to better see him.

There was no doubt that he saw her. He was waving, no, motioning. She studied his movements and his mouth. *Stay there.* He was motioning for her to stay. She nodded dramatically and backed into the cover of trees thanking all of heaven above that they had found one another.

~

Adrian battled with himself. Go now, or wait until dark? If he ran flat out, he could make to her in a matter of two minutes or less. She was waiting for him, just as she said she would, and that knowledge made him jubilant. She cared for him, otherwise she would have kept going. Perhaps now, he could begin admitting how much he cared for her. It was hell when the mind battled the heart, particularly when the heart had been numb for as long as his had.

Gut instinct warned him to stay put until dark, but the desire to be with her was too strong and he set out running.

~

She felt a tightening in her chest at the sight of him running toward her. She was ecstatic until a strange rumble filled her with fear and then terror. A group of riders, seven or eight of them, were headed straight toward them. It was as if they had come from nowhere. Adrian jerked to a sudden halt in the middle of the field.

*Go, go!* She wanted to scream, but it was too late.

~

Adrian stopped. It was too late to turn back and if he continued forward, he would give her position away and he would not do that. He would not jeopardize the woman he loved.

~

As she watched, a series of telling expressions crossed his face. Fear, despair, sadness and finally acceptance. It happened in a matter of seconds and then the most beautiful smile came over his face.

*I love you,* he mouthed.

Her view through the telescope blurred, first by tears, then by the horses that had surrounded him.

"Please, God," she whispered. "Please, please—"

The telescope dropped from her hand, and she unwittingly took another step backwards. She looked around frantically, wondering what she could do. She had a knife, but no pistol and there was a group of them.

The men, seven or eight of them, had circled Adrian and were taunting him.

"Did you really think you could escape us, Highlander?"

"McGoldrick, isn't it? McGoldrick with the lovely scar? Lift your shirt and show us."

"Where's the woman?" Aaron called out.

Sara Anne put her hands to her chest. Her heart was pounding mercilessly. She crouched, horrified by the thought of what they might do to him. The crushing realization he would be hurt because of her was almost more than she could bear.

"A long way from here," Adrian replied calmly.

"Where?" Aaron demanded.

"Why should I tell you?"

Several riders dismounted, including Aaron.

"No, please," Sara Anne whispered. Her fists were pressed to her face. "Please, God, help him."

"Because I might let you die quicker," Aaron replied.

Two men grabbed and held Adrian while another lifted his shirt. They discovered his pistol and took it. They commented loudly on his scar.

"I might have given you that. I hope I did," one said.

One of them hit him in the stomach. Another hit him again. A third jumped in. Sara Anne buried her face and stopped her ears, moaning softly. More than anything, she wanted to jump out and stop them, but if she did, they would kill Adrian. There would be no reason not to. His only chance at survival lay in having the information they sought. They would hurt him, but they would not kill him.

She looked up and wiped her face with both hands. They were doing something. *What?* Adrian was lying on the ground. *Oh, God!* Had they killed him? They were getting back on their horses. Leaving! They were leaving! Her prayer had worked. She couldn't believe her eyes as they began riding off.

*Please let him be alive.*

She felt stunned and weak with relief—until his body jerked in an unnatural way and began sliding across the ground. They had tied his feet and were dragging his body. The horror robbed her of breath. She would kill them! God help her, she would kill them all!

The riders headed for the very woods that Adrian had been in when she'd first spotted him. He had only revealed himself because he'd seen her. It was her fault.

*"Don't be ridiculous!"* Caroline said in her mind.

"What do I do?" Sara Anne muttered in a low voice. But she already knew the answer beyond question or doubt. She had to go after him.

# Chapter Twenty

A drian sensed the severity of his situation even before he'd fully surfaced from unconsciousness. There was pressing heaviness in his chest and his head and midsection burned with throbbing pain. He was vaguely aware a man was shouting at him, the same few words over and over. What he was saying, Adrian didn't know. Were they friend or foe? His guess was foe, but he couldn't recall what had happened. He moaned and focused on surfacing, on understanding the muffled voices.

"Think we killed him, then?"

"Not quite. Not yet."

Self-preservation kicked in and, with it, the knowledge that he needed to continue to look lifeless until he could make sense of his situation.

The voices were fading as the men – definitely foe, walked away. His back was on fire. His ribs, in fact, everything hurt except his arms, which he couldn't feel at all. He was upright and there was bark at his bare back. He tried to open his eyes, but one wouldn't. His head was slumped forward, and he first searched the ground for feet before daring to lift his head a bit.

A group of men, the ones who had overtaken him in the field were a short distance away, gathered around a campfire. He remembered now. The night was as black as pitch, except for the light from the fire, which meant hours had gone by since the men had captured him.

He was tied to a tree, his hands extended out from his body, bound to thick limbs. He couldn't feel his arms because they had gone numb.

*How will I be able to free myself?*

He wouldn't.

They would torture him for information and eventually kill him. They were talking about it even now.

"—cutting him in the opposite direction," the dark-haired leader with the American accent was saying. "In crisscross fashion. Or, perhaps, we just reopen the old wound. Slowly."

Adrian felt his respiration increase. The threat made his bowels stir with fear.

"Burning works, too," a Brit said. "Once I saw—"

"I've branded many a man in my day," the leader interrupted, his voice calmly cutting through the other without so much as raising it. "And women as well."

"Women, as well?" another asked. "Do they scream?"

"Everyone screams," the leader replied. "Don't flatter yourself. You'd scream, too."

~

Sara Anne had been creeping toward the makeshift camp, but the woods were deeper than she'd realized, and the men had gone a good way in—dragging Adrian.

She'd gone after the group as soon as they were out of sight, riding as far into the woods as she dared. She'd secured the horse and continued on foot, intermittently rushing and then creeping, rushing and then creeping, listening for sounds that would give away their position.

There was a possibility that Aaron and his men had merely cut through the woods and then continued on, dragging Adrian to his death. Or perhaps, he was being tortured as she searched. The fears came unbidden, tormenting her with every step.

Finally, voices gave them away. Relief flooded her body like white light, weakening and then strengthening her. She started forward carefully, tensing to a stop at every soft crunch of cursed ground cover.

When she finally spied the group from the cover of foliage, her first realization was that she'd approached from the worst possible position. Aaron and his henchmen were in between her and Adrian, who was strung up against a tree. His face was bloody, and he looked unconscious. The rush of blood to her head made her dizzy. She had to get to him!

She withdrew and worked her way around camp listening to Aaron, the deviant bastard, holding court. The men around him were half drunk and completely engrossed in his story. She finally made it all the way around and crept up behind Adrian's tree. "I'm here," she whispered softly, hoping against hope he could hear her.

~

He couldn't believe his ears. She'd come for him. He was euphoric one moment, terrified the next. What if they caught her? What if they made her watch as he died?

He knew she was cutting the rope that bound one of his arms and he tried to brace himself in order to hold his arm up after she had cut through it, but it was impossible. The arm was totally numb and came thudding down against his side, heavy and useless. Shaking pathetically, he held his breath and looked to see if any of his captors had noticed.

Apparently, they hadn't.

Grotesquely animated in the firelight, they were totally absorbed as the American told a gruesome tale about breaking slaves.

Adrian struggled to lift his arm back up, but he couldn't. It didn't even feel like his own body anymore. His second arm was suddenly released and he stood rooted to the spot for a moment, not trusting his balance or the strength in his legs. She touched his back, which reminded him of the risk to her. His upper body was useless, but he took a sidestep and then another, eventually rounding the tree. She kept a hand on his back the whole time, moving with him just as they had moved together on the rocks that day. When they could not see the others, she pulled one of his arms over both her shoulders and supported him as she led the way.

She moved in a wide arc around the group. He resisted, wanting more distance between themselves and the men, but she seemed sure of herself and surprisingly strong.

"Trust me," she begged.

~

Her heart ached for him. He was badly injured, but she could not think about that now. She could not give in to the emotion that beckoned and would surely cripple her and condemn them both. They had to make it back to the horse.

They had fully worked their way around camp when Adrian's disappearance was noticed and shouted out. For a terrible instant, they froze in their tracks, but then pushed on, harder than before. His body had been put through such trauma, but she had to keep them moving, despite his pain. They had to find the way out of the woods.

She'd never felt so grateful for anything as she did when she spied the horse.

"Go ferst," he said, just above a whisper. He was hunched forward, his arm held in front of his body, shaking hard.

She didn't know how they would manage, but she mounted, and Adrian found the strength to mount behind her. They maneuvered through the woods and when they made it to the clearing, she kicked the horse into a dead run. Getting away was all that mattered. The ride was hurting him, but the men behind them would hurt him far worse. Rain poured. It was miserable, but it would be the same for those that pursued them.

She rode for dark hills, not knowing what direction she rode in. Occasional flashes of lighting provided illumination that allowed her to negotiate hills and, finally, to discover a series of caves. She didn't know how long they'd ridden or far they had come, but she was soaked and freezing. Her hands were completely numb.

They dismounted clumsily, and she helped Adrian into a cave. Inside, it was too dark to see anything. When she let go of him, he stood hunched and shaking. She hurried back for the bedroll and knapsack. Back inside, she pulled off the oil cloth and stretched the bedroll out. It was damp, but the wool would keep them warm. "Here," she said.

He lowered himself to a sitting position slowly, cradling his ribs protectively.

She fetched his plaid and the flasks mostly by feel. She needed to light a fire, but how when everything was so wet? She draped the blanket around him and brought the water flask to him first, then whiskey to dull his pain. One of his eyes was swollen shut and there was dried blood beneath his nose and one ear, but his ribs seemed to be causing him the most distress. There was a line of perspiration across his upper lip and forehead and his face seemed stark white, but she couldn't be sure with only flashes of lighting cutting through the inky black.

She eased him back and then stretched out alongside him before pulling the cover around them both. She held him tenderly, trying to provide warmth without weight. She didn't know what else to do. Bet had used brandy, laudanum, and love. His wounds were worse than hers had been, and she only had the whiskey to dull the pain.

"Rest," she whispered, desperately wishing it for him.

~~~

Aaron held a torch as he squatted to study the footprints. They were small. They were *hers*. She had somehow managed to sneak into their camp and rescue McGoldrick. A choking rage took hold of him. This was one insult too many. He would find her, by God, and he would punish her and punish her and punish her until she was sorry she had ever defied him. And then he would punish her some more. She would not break easily, but she would break. Everyone did.

He stood and attempted to make sense of the tracks, but they had been trampled over. "There are tracks," he called out. The idiot blunderers couldn't have destroyed all of them. "Find them!"

# Chapter Twenty-One

S ara Anne woke abruptly and sat with a gasp. He stood in the entrance of the cave, silhouetted by sunshine, watching her.

"Are you alright?" she asked, her voice raspy from sleep.

She was sleep tousled, a real mess, and so beautiful, it almost hurt to look at her. He had thought of so many things to say to her, so many questions he wanted to ask, but every one of them had vanished from his mind.

"Are you in much pain?" she asked.

"I've been in werse."

"That says quite a bit about your life, Adrian McGoldrick." She got up and walked toward him.

"I got a rabbit." He was being economical with his words because it hurt to speak. "It's skinned."

"Well, good, but please sit down. I'll collect firewood and cook the rabbit. You need to be still until you heal."

He moved out of her way, allowing her to step past him and out of the cave. He continued standing because it had taken him a long time to rise as pain shot through him. Twice he'd thought he was going to pass out.

Getting the rabbit had been a gift from heaven. It was sitting near some brush, and it stayed there as he slowly reached for his knife, aimed and threw.

Sara Anne came back with an armload of kindling, and then left again. He lowered himself carefully and went to the task of starting a fire, and then she was back with the saddle. She left again for more firewood and later for wild blackberries. He'd started the fire and fashioned a spit for the rabbit.

"I'll do this," she said.

He acquiesced. She frowned with concentration as she seasoned and adjusted the meat to cook it all around. It smelled delicious. Despite everything, he was hungry. "I canna' believe yeh came fer me," he finally said.

She huffed with insult. "Of course, I did." He saw her emotion get the better of her. She turned her face away from to wipe a tear. "Idiot."

"Sara Anne—"

She shook her head. "We just have to concentrate on getting you well," she said thickly. When the meat was cooked, she removed it carefully. She sat and they ate in silence, not counting the breathy grunts from sharp waves of pain that came over him.

"Do you think they'll follow?" she asked when they'd finished.

"They'll try."

"But the rain—"

"Helps our cause."

She rose to clean the dishes.

"That man," he said. "The leader—"

She sighed and nodded grimly.

"The one incapable of mercy," he said.

"I am so sorry, Adrian. I would have killed every last one of them if I could!"

"It's naugh yer fault. None of it. I dinna' remember much of it anyway, only bits. How did yeh find me?"

She blinked in surprise. "I—"

He waited, confused that she looked hurt. As if he'd hurt her feelings.

"I found a grove of trees to hide in," she said haltingly. "You had found another across a clearing from it. You don't remember?"

He was stymied for a moment. He'd meant that he didn't recall all the torture they put him through, but she was talking about before. About his admission of love. Or had she understood what he'd whispered? If she had understood and was glad that he didn't recall it, he certainly didn't need to make it clear now. "Perhaps when my head herts less," he hedged.

"You saw me," she continued, unwilling to let it go. "You were coming to join me when the riders converged. It happened so fast."

"I should have heard them," he said bitterly.

"There was thunder," she said.

"I should have waited."

"So, you do remember?"

He hesitated. "Some of it. Not all." He took a drink from the flask.

"You should lie down and rest." She came closer and got on her knees beside him. "Let me help."

Once she'd eased him back and the agony of movement had subsided, he said, "As soon as we can, we'll make fer my home." His words were halting, his voice strained. "We'll be safe there while I mend."

She reached for the edge of the cover and pulled it over him. "Are you warm enough?"

"Cold then hot," he admitted. She gently brushed back his hair, which felt good. She was so soft and womanly – and so courageous. She'd risked her life coming after him. He was overwhelmed by it. "After I mend, I'll take yeh anywhere yeh want tae go," he pledged.

A momentary expression of pain crossed her face and her eyes suddenly glistened with unshed tears. Had his words hurt her?

"It's a generous offer," she said stiffly.

He didn't understand her tone or her expression. "Sara Anne—"

"No more talking. You need to rest and get well. Otherwise, how else am I ever to get back home?"

Of course, that would be her concern. It was the reason she'd come after him. She was in a strange country at a dangerous time, and he'd proven she was safe with him. At least, he'd proven he would not hurt her. He wished he could sleep. Wishing he didn't feel all that he did. Pain in his head and back and ribs – and a wrenching ache in his heart. He'd brought it on himself, he thought bitterly. He had brought every bit of it on himself.

His misery was eased by the feel of her fingertips gently stroking his forehead. "I'd like tae hear about yer life."

"Alright. I'll distract you for a while."

"Nothing humorous," he said.

"I'm not that cruel." She was a good storyteller, and he became enraptured and enlightened by the window into her world. It was a world she'd willingly given up to be free of a man who would never stop hunting her, who would stop at nothing to get her back.

"The day we left for Scotland, I received word that Aaron was coming after me. Not only that, but he wrote to my uncle, claiming we *were* married."

"Married?"

"It's a lie, but I was ... startled by it. Panicked by it, I suppose. I had no idea what he was up to, but there was no time to think it all out because we were leaving, and Ginny so wanted to go. I intercepted the letter before my uncle saw it. I burned it and left with the others. I know it wasn't the right thing to do. I should have stayed. At least long enough to be truthful with my aunt and uncle. At the very least, I should have done that."

He realized her aunt and uncle must have sent Waldron after her believing he was her husband.

"But when we were taken," she continued. "I realized it provided a ... a sort of opportunity to me to disappear."

He gawked in disbelief. *Opportunity?* "Disappear?"

"Yes. I knew Aaron was coming and I wanted him to think I was gone forever. I certainly wouldn't have chosen for us to be *abducted*, but since we were—"

She made it sound as if she'd been offered a stay in the country. "Yeh were bein' offered tae another man!"

"I knew you didn't want that."

"That has nothin' tae do wi' it!"

"Stop getting angry," she snapped back. "You'll aggravate your injuries."

He shook his head in frustration at her thickheadedness.

"I believed we would come up with a different plan in time," she said reasonably.

"We?"

"Yes, we. You and I. And I still think we would have, even if nothing had gone wrong."

She had more faith in him than he deserved, and it loosened a wave of remorse and regret. "Yev got nerve," he muttered. "I'll give yeh that."

"Thank you," she returned flippantly.

"I dinna mean it as a compliment."

"Just because you didn't mean it that way, doesn't mean I can't take it that way. Now, be quiet and rest. Story time is over."

"Good. I'm not sure I can take any more of yer stories."

# Chapter Twenty-Two

During the next eight days, Sara Anne scavenged for food, collected firewood, brought back water, kept Adrian's fevered head as cool as possible, and helped him up and down. Occasionally, she sponge bathed most of him and combed his hair until he complained she was trying to make him pretty. "You are pretty," she said. It was a statement he did not care for.

She tried to behave matter-of-factly about the business of washing him, but it was anything but. Even with his bruises turning colors, his well-defined chest, arms, and legs gave her feelings she didn't know how to deal with, as did the deep scar on his torso. It proved how close to death he'd come at Culloden.

It was ridiculous to have fallen so deeply in love with him. If he had truly fallen in love with her before his capture, he'd lost the memory of it. Naturally, he was grateful that she'd come to his rescue, but he was prepared to repay the debt by returning her safely home. The thought of it was heartbreaking.

"Will you shave this again?" she asked, running the backs of her fingers along his beard.

A corner of his mouth quirked. "Unless yeh like it. I certainly want tae be handsome fer you."

He said it teasingly, of course, not having any notion how his words made her feel. "How very kind of you," she replied drolly.

"I will miss this," he said a moment later.

It so mirrored her own thoughts; it took a moment to respond. When she did, it was to feign ignorance. "What?"

"Lying here with you … like this. Just being. Not the sore ribs. I willna' miss that."

"I'll miss it, too," she admitted. She could own to that much. "It's as if the rest of the world doesn't exist. As if time has stopped."

It was quiet except for the hooting of an owl. "What do yeh think the wise owl is sayin' tae us?"

"That he wouldn't miss the sore ribs either."

"Oh, woman. What made yeh as are yeh are?"

She cocked her head, wondering what he meant. "What am I?"

"Courageous, for one thing," he replied without hesitation.

She pressed her lips together and resisted the urge to cry.

"So many dunderheads think that women are weak and helpless, but anyone with a woman in their life sees it's naugh true. They bear children an' endure their men goin' off tae wage war, sometimes despite good sense." He paused. "Enduring is harder than doing. That's what I think."

She stared out the mouth of the cave as the last light of day waned. The birds were quieting. "I think you're right."

"But you are more courageous than most," he added.

"So much of what seems courageous, was really just desperation."

"Feeling desperate may have been the motivation, but action requires courage."

She thought about the statement. Maybe it was true. "Growing up, I measured most everything by the way Caroline did it or what she thought."

"She sounds remarkable," he agreed.

"She was. She was funny and sometimes irreverent, but she was always a lady when it counted. She made it look easy. I never found it so easy."

"I'm glad she looked out fer yeh."

"Aye, she did at that," she said in her best Scottish brogue.

He grimaced. "Dinna' make me laugh, woman."

"Yer sayin' my accent is laughable?"

"I suppose it's naugh so bad."

"Tell me about your sisters."

"Colline is the eldest and then Miriam. Then there is me and Shae is the youngest."

"Your parents have passed?"

"Aye, as has my grandfather who raised us after."

"Do you have a favorite among your sisters?"

"It varies by the day," he teased. "No, I love them all. They're quite different. Colli is warmth an' love. Verra' maternal. Never a bad word fer anyone. Like our mother. Miriam is … loyal an' strong. Hert someone she loves, an' she will come after yeh tooth an' nail. She'd go' opinions on everythin' an' she's no' afraid tae share them."

"And Shae?"

"Pretty and kind. A soft heart. Yel' love her. She teases she was raised by Colli as her mother and Miriam as her da. Grandda was grandda and I was big brother." He paused. "She doesn't much remember our parents."

Sara Anne chewed on her bottom lip and then took the plunge. "Did you leave a sweetheart behind when you left?" she asked, trying to keep her voice light. He drew breath but stayed silent, which filled her with dread.

He turned his head slightly. "Yer heart's beating faster."

Her face suddenly burned. "It is not."

"Aye, it is!" He sat up with a grunt and turned to face her, his eyes searching. "No, I dinna' leave a sweetheart behind."

She gave a slight shrug, doing her best to feign indifference. "Oh."

"Oh? That's all?"

"Yes, that's all. Of course, that's all. I was just curious."

"Just curious, eh? Then why did yer heart beat faster an' why are you blushing?"

"It didn't and … that is … this is ridiculous," she complained hotly, scooting away from him so she could get to her feet. "It's time we go to sleep."

"Where are yeh goin?"

"Out. I need some air."

"Sara Anne, when yeh asked, I was tryin' tae think of something clever tae say."

She left the cave, feeling exposed. He knew she cared if he had a sweetheart.

"How's the air?" he asked, having followed.

She narrowed her eyes at him. "Just what I needed. Sometimes the air gets close in there. Must be all the hot air we're putting out."

"Wha' if I promised no' tae mention again how yer heart was beatin' harder when ye thought I might have a sweetheart? Will yeh come back in?"

Her jaw dropped in astonishment. "You are exceedingly vain, Adrian McGoldrick. Especially for someone in your condition."

He shrugged. "My condition will improve."

This was foolish. It was dark, she was cold, and he was being conceited. She walked back toward the cave saying, "I don't care if you have a sweetheart or not. Have one. Have two. Have a whole passel of them."

"Would yeh be part of my passel?"

Having stopped short and lifted her chin. "I would not be part of anyone's passel," she declared. She attempted to walk on, but he grabbed hold of her arm.

"Nor will yeh ever need tae be. No man would have a passel when he could have you."

Her face tingled in a strident warning that tears were imminent, and so she walked on.

She was lying in the bedroll, curled on her side away from where he would lay when he returned. She'd stripped down to her shift and covered herself, as had become her habit.

"All better?" Adrian asked, as he sat beside her.

"Better than what?"

He chuckled. "I want tae say something."

Reluctantly, she turned over to face him. "You really don't ha—"

He touched a finger to her lips. "*Shhh.* I need tae say it. Please." He paused, struggling for the right words. "Yeh dinna' belong with someone like me."

She'd thought herself prepared for whatever he might say, but the statement leveled her, and tears rushed at her eyes painfully.

"No," he breathed, brushing back her hair. "Please dinna' look like that. I love you."

She sat straight up, pulling back from the bedroll so she could distance herself as much as possible. It didn't help when his gaze fell to her barely concealed breasts. She covered her arms in front of herself. "How can you ... *say* that to me?"

He looked hurt. "That I love you?"

"That I don't belong with you!"

"Yev lived a privileged life."

"Yes, I have. In many ways. And I left it," she said, enunciating clearly. "Remember that part? I left!"

"Aye, but yeh dinna' plan tae be here."

"And yet here I am! Here we are."

His gaze softened. "Do yeh naugh think I'd give anythin' tae have yeh as my wife? But yeh dinna' ken how simply we live."

A tear ran down her face and she wiped it away angrily. "You think I object to living simply? You think *that's* what I care about?"

He found himself at a loss for words.

"I love you," she said. She heard his breath catch. Did he not believe it? Had he not guessed it?

Tears filled his eyes, but he blinked them back. "I was yer abductor."

"Are you under the impression I'd forgotten that?"

"Aye. Perhaps. Without realizin' it." His eyes looked almost feverish. "Let's be honest fer a minute. I had control of you, an' I *liked it*. Holdin' yeh against me, your body pressed tae mine, I liked it. I wanted yeh fer my own. From the first day, I wanted yeh fer my verra own. *That's* the truth of who I am." He paused to allow his admission to sink in. "But I also saved yer life, an' showed yeh mercy afterwards." He narrowed his eye as he shook his head. "Ye dinna' ken the hidin' I wanted tae give yeh that day at the river when yeh nearly drowned."

"I remember."

"Yeh do naugh remember, because it dinna' happen. It wasna' a spankin' yeh would have soon forgotten, I promise yeh that. My point is, it is no' a wonder if yer—"

"Confounded?" she supplied.

"Aye. Confounded."

210

She took a breath and exhaled. "I suppose you may have a point. On the other hand—"

"Is there another hand?"

"Oh, I think there is. Because while it is true that we were abducted, which was a terrible thing to do, it was you who told me, on several occasions, that I could simply admit who I was and where I belonged and be sent right back home." She stopped abruptly as a new fear took hold. "That was the truth, wasn't it? Were the others all returned to their homes unharmed?"

"Aye! No one was supposed tae get hert. I swear it on my life."

She sighed in relief. "Good. In that case, my point was, I had a choice. You gave it to me. I *chose* to go with you."

He frowned and shook his head. "Oh, no—"

"Oh, yes. It's true," she insisted. "All the time you thought you were in control," she paused and shrugged, "I had my own plan. I let you take me away because that's what best suited my purpose. I was going to give it enough time and then I was going to get away from you."

He drew back, thoroughly insulted. "Is that so? An' just how do yeh think ye wou' ha' managed that?"

"Carefully."

"Yeh wouldn't have gotten away from me."

"Oh, yes, I would have."

"Oh, no, you would not have."

"Well, it's unproveable, isn't it? Since I no longer want to escape."

"Yeh wouldn't ha' gotten away from me," he repeated stubbornly.

"You can say that until you're blue in the face, Mr. McGoldrick—"

"An' I may!"

"*You* have no idea the risks I took to escape home!"

He was quiet a moment. "Yeh would no' have gotten away from me, but I wou' like tae know about before."

"Well then, perhaps I'll tell you sometime. But if you'll allow me to return to subject at hand, I went with you willingly. And I liked being with you, too. You say you liked holding me? I liked being held. I liked it. So, there. That's the truth of who I am."

His expression was searching. He wanted to believe her, so why couldn't he just allow himself? What was holding him back? What did she need to say or do to make him believe it? Because she couldn't lose him. "It's true you saved my life," she said tenderly, "but I saved yours, as well."

"Aye, yeh did at that. At great risk tae yerself. But how cou' yeh ever forget how this started? How cou' yeh ever truly forgive me?"

"You gave me a choice, remember? And I'm not sorry for going with you. How could I be?"

He pulled her into his arms. This time his heart was also beating fast.

"I don't want to hurt you," she said, anxious of his bruises.

"Then give yerself tae me," he said in a husky voice.

She pulled back to look at him, to be sure of his meaning. It was there in his eyes, in the intensity of his expression. "I do," she breathed.

"Now," he said. "This night."

It was a frightening thought, but only because of the unknown. But he was the man she loved.

"But naught just fer tonight," he said slowly. "I can naugh allow myself tae have yeh once, if I canna' have yeh fer always. I may be askin' too much, but—"

"You're not. I feel the same."

He studied her, wanting to be certain.

"I love you," she said. "And I feel the same."

He exhaled slowly, then eased her onto her back and hovered over her. "Say that again."

She ran her fingers through his hair and looked deeply into his eyes. "I love you."

He leaned in and kissed her and then pulled back to look at her. He stretched her arm out and up and his hungry gaze traveled the length of her body, making her quiver with anticipation. "Do yeh know how I've wanted you?" He didn't wait for an answer, but moved in for another kiss, a more demanding one. His tongue teased her lips apart and his velvety tongue plunged, explored, and withdrew. He pulled away to nuzzle along her jawline and up to her ear before whispering, "Yer my woman now."

Warmth surged between her legs and a long sigh escaped her. "Yes," she breathed.

His mouth moved back to hers and a mutual exploration began. His hand caressed her side, her hip, her thigh and back up again. By the time he pulled away to slowly lower himself down her neck, alternately kissing and tasting, she had abandoned all thought. There was only this moment and the man she loved. He hovered over her breasts, teasing her taut nipples with his breath, tongue and teeth through her shift, making them jut out maddeningly.

"Take it off," he said huskily.

"Are you sure you're well enough—"

"Sara Anne," he warned.

Trembling, breathing hard, she maneuvered the shift off. Her breath caught as he looked her naked body over with undeniable desire.

"Yer so beautiful," he whispered. "Sometimes I canna' take it in."

The words touched her, and her eyes filled. She would admit that it was the same for her, but he wouldn't believe it.

He got up, still watching her, and took off his clothes. She averted her gaze as his trousers were removed.

"Look at me," he said.

She resisted.

"Sara Anne. Look at me. I am yours. What I am, what I have, it's yours."

Slowly she looked, keeping her gaze on his although she could still see his erection. Her pulse raced at the size of him. How in the world was this supposed to work? Holding her breath, she allowed herself a quick look. It was astonishing. His man parts were not what she'd expected. They seemed alive.

He lowered himself next to her again. "I never want yeh tae be shy with me," he said gently. "Making love is both pleasure an' need. It's love an' it's desire. Shame does naught belong in the same bed with us."

"It's not... I ... I'm not accustomed—"

His hand slowly moved downward to the heated wetness between her legs. "I want tae please my woman."

Please her? The words were shocking, and things were moving too fast. Was she ready? She closed her eyes and felt him prop up one of her knees. He stroked her most forbidden zone gently, knowingly, and a moan escaped her.

"Look at me," he urged.

Reluctantly, she opened her eyes, although it took a moment before she could focus on him.

"I want yeh tae look at me."

She wasn't sure she could do that. Her skin was on fire. Her insides, as well. She wanted him so much. She hadn't known it was possible to want a man so much, but to watch him while he touched her there? He stroked again, and she turned her head.

"Look at me," he said in a husky whisper.

Grudgingly, she looked back at him.

"Yer my woman. My woman tae please."

He stroked faster making her breath catch. She wanted to look away, but his gaze held her now.

"My woman, who feels like this, so warm and wet, because she wants me."

He slipped a finger inside her and she gasped. His finger withdrew, dipped again and explored. The sensations could not have been more foreign to her.

"This is mine," he said darkly. "Mine and no one else's."

A small cry escaped her as he hit a certain spot. How was it that he seemed to know her body better than she did? She'd had no idea.

"Is that good?"

She couldn't possibly answer him, and so she turned her face away.

He leaned in to nuzzle her ear. "Wha' did I say about that?"

When he pulled back, she looked at him, loving him completely. She wanted him. Had things unfolded differently, it might have been Aaron claiming her, and she could have never, ever loved him or felt this way. Even if he had been kind, her heart was meant to belong to another. To Adrian. Which meant that everything had happened for a reason. It was a powerful, unexpected realization that left her profoundly shaken.

Adrian moved atop her, and the head of his hardened shaft teased her opening. It felt good, but then the pressure began. She began to panic and then gasped sharply as he pushed inside. She cried out, and he stopped.

"Did I—"

She shuddered.

He looked aghast. "Was that—"

She was shaking and she couldn't stop. She began crying because she felt entirely too much to contain.

He lowered his forehead to hers. "You were a virgin," he breathed. It wasn't a question. He knew it now. "Oh, God. I just broke through your maidenhead."

She wrapped her arms around his back, unable to speak. She just needed to hold him and have him hold her. Tears slipped from her eyes, over her temples and into her ears. "It was yours," she whispered.

"Mine?" he whispered back. He moved again inside her, tentatively, slowly. And then faster. He buried his face in her hair, and she held onto him. She couldn't think; the feeling was so overpowering. When he cried out and jerked in climax, it was a relief of sorts. Or was it?

"Why dinna' yeh tell me the truth?" he asked apologetically.

She took a shaky breath. She didn't want to cry anymore because he would think she was sorry when she wasn't.

He pulled her into his arms and cradled her. "Di' I hert you?"

She shook her head, but the tears were still coming. She could not hold them back.

"I'm sorry," he whispered.

"No. I n-never expected it to be like that."

"Like what?"

"Good," she said with a shrug, only to break out in fresh tears.

He smiled. "What did yeh think it wou' be?"

"Duty," she stammered.

"If it ever comes tae just being duty, we have a problem." He rose up on an elbow to wipe away her tears. "Why did yeh tell me yeh weren't pure? I wou' ha' been more careful."

"You asked what to tell Lord Carmichael. You said it was a matter of establishing a price for me."

He cringed at the recollection.

"I said you could *tell* him I wasn't—"

"I'm sorry. I thought yeh meant it. An' then yeh cried—"

"I don't want to think about that. It's all in the past. Please don't be sorry. I'm not."

He smiled. "I will love an' protect yeh all my life," he pledged.

"And I will love and protect you."

"In my heart, yev just become my wife, an' may God help any man who tries tae step in the way of it."

A calmness settled over her and she pressed a hand to his chest. She could feel his heart pounding. "Sara Anne McGoldrick," she said. "How does that sound?"

"Except fer the funny accent, yeh mean?"

She laughed. "Aye, except fer that."

"Like the most wonderful thing I've ever heard in my life."

# Chapter Twenty-Three

The first thing she became aware of the next morning was a soreness between her legs. Adrian was lying next to her. He loved her and he had made love to her. She would marry him. She would marry the man she loved, just as it was supposed to be.

Her father would be highly displeased by the turn of events, but Caroline and her mother would have approved. Bet would approve, not that she would ever meet him. The thought made swing from blissful to melancholy.

Making love. The sensations had made her lightheaded. He'd changed her in so many ways, but touching as he had, he'd turned her insides molten. There had been pain, but there had bliss as well—sweet, heady bliss she had never imagined.

Adrian's eyes opened. He breathed in sharply, waking fully, but, rather than joyful, his expression reflected regret.

"What is it?" she asked. She wouldn't be able to bear it if he regretted what had happened between them.

"I woke earlier—"

She waited.

"Yeh were turned away from me. An' yer back—"

"But I told you. I showed you."

"The light hit it and … I canna' believe yer father did that tae yeh. Damn the man. God damn him!"

"It doesn't hurt now."

"No one will hert ye again."

"I'm fine," she swore.

"Oh, yer fine, alright," he said tenderly. He kissed her forehead, her cheeks, and her lips. "Yer so very fine."

~~~

217

They traveled on, always climbing upwards. She knew the journey was hard on Adrian, but he never uttered a word of complaint. The scenery was spectacular. He called the mountain range *am monadh ruadh,* the red hills, but the peaks of the mountains, which were blue, soared thousands of feet high. It felt as though they were the only ones on earth, but in a matter of days, they would reach his village. He would be home.

"What will they think of me?" Sara Anne asked as they rode.

"Who?"

"Your family. The people you love."

"They'll think yer beautiful an' good. They'll see yer the woman I love an' that yeh love me."

"Can't we just go back and live in the cave?"

He laughed. "They'll love yeh. I promise."

~~~

Their homecoming was most the joyful event Sara Anne had ever witnessed. From the first child's yell to the crowd of people who surrounded Adrian embracing him. Tears flowed without shame or restraint.

"Adrian! Adrian's home!"

"He has a girl with him!"

"Adrian! He's home!"

An adorable freckle-faced girl of about five or six reached him first and thrust herself into his arms.

Laughing joyfully, he lifted her up and whirled her around before turning to introduce her to Sara Anne. "This ferocious creature would be my niece, Barbara."

"Yer favorite niece," Barbara exclaimed into his face.

"My favorite niece," he repeated. "Except fer all the others."

"Aye? Well, yer my favorite uncle, except fer all the others!"

"Barbara, this," Adrian gestured to Sara Anne, "is Sara Anne. Soon to be yer aunt."

Sara Anne beamed. The words were sweeter than music.

"Adrian!" a male voice boomed. "Thank God! Where have yeh been, man?"

"Andrew," Adrian exclaimed, putting his niece down. "Yer alright!"

"Adrian!" a woman wailed. "Oh, Adrian, we've searched everywhere for yeh!"

Sara Anne was jostled as the throng closed in around Adrian. The villagers were laughing and then crying then laughing again. She received curious looks and polite nods, but mostly, she listened and watched.

A few of his clansmen had survived Culloden. Several women were crying; children were jumping for joy, and Adrian was struggling to hear who had survived and endure confirmation of those who had not. "Where is Thomas?" he asked, swiping at his moist eyes.

"Oh, he's off after a gerl but he's fine!"

"I'm Colline, Adrian's eldest sister," a woman said.

Sara Anne turned to her. She had a considerable amount of gray in her hair and the warmest, deep brown eyes Sara Anne had ever seen. "Hello."

"Wonderful tae meet yeh," Colline said. Then she turned on her brother. "Where have yer manners gone, Adrian?"

"Beggin' yer pardon," he directed to Colline. "This is Sara Anne Aldridge from America, soon tae be Sara Anne McGoldrick."

A cry of celebration went up all around them and Adrian hugged Sara Anne to him. Her heart felt as though it might burst with sheer joy.

"So that's where yev been," someone called, which was followed by laughter.

Sara Anne became aware of something at her side and looked down at a young girl, perhaps four years of age.

"Ah, Jinty," Adrian said, kneeling. He held his arms out to the small girl, and she came to him with a shy smile. He scooped her up and stood, bringing the child to eye level with Sara Anne. "Jinty neither hears nor speaks." The girl buried her face in the crook of Adrian's neck and he patted her back. "She's my gerl," he said affectionately.

"And that is my sister, Shae," Adrian said, pointing to a woman who looked very like him. She was making her way toward them, but before she could reach them, the group began moving, carrying Adrian and Sara Anne with it.

"And, that one is Miriam," Adrian said, pointing at a woman Sara Anne had seen him embrace earlier. "She's two years older than I, though she sometimes confuses herself with bein' my mother," he said with amused affection.

They moved into a shelter where Shae caught up to them. She took Sara Anne's hands and welcomed her home. The word hit with a strange force. This would be her home now.

It was a rambunctious group, completely overwhelming to Sara Anne. There were so many discussions going on simultaneously, she wasn't able to concentrate on any one of them. Adrian, on the other hand, was totally in his element. He was able to take part in one discussion then seamlessly switch to another. Occasionally, he'd break from all of it and point out various people to Sara Anne and explain who they were. What a change from Iceman the Jedburgh men had known.

"Adrian!" a man roared.

Adrian turned and embraced a man. "I didn't think anyone survived," Adrian said in a choked voice when he was able to speak.

"Not many of us did."

"I'm Miriam," came from Sara Anne's immediate right.

Sara Anne turned to Adrian's middle sister.

"Yeh love my brother, then?"

Sara Anne was momentarily taken aback at her bluntness. "I do."

Miriam glanced up at her brother, who was engrossed in his conversation with his clansman. "He looks different tae me." She chortled and shook her head as she looked back to Sara Anne. "I have tae admit, I thought he'd never fall in love, though enough gerls have tried tae make it happen."

"It's high time we hear from Adrian," someone called.

"We should eat first," a man complained. "I listen better on a full stomach."

"Pipe down," a woman retorted.

The group quieted in expectation, and Adrian began to speak, stunning and silencing the people. When he finished the explanation, Colline shook her head. "Yeh *abducted* Sara Anne?"

His expression was grim, his hands folded together in front of him as if awaiting sentence. "Aye."

"An' somewhere along the way tae bringin' her tae this Carmichael, the two of yeh fell in love?"

Adrian looked at Sara Anne, as if wanting to confirm the truth of it himself.

The intensity of his gaze stole her breath. Suddenly the most important thing in the world was to reassure him of how much she loved him. She smiled.

People shook their heads. It was a bizarre story, but the bond between them was clear to see.

"The men who were after her tried tae kill you, yeh say?" Miriam spoke up.

Sara Anne thought of his still bruised ribs. It occurred to her how they must have hurt from the many enthusiastic embraces he had received. He'd never said a word or even winced that she had seen.

"They were after both of us," he corrected. "Her, tae take back an' me—"

"Not tae take back," Miriam provided cryptically.

"Are they still after yeh?" Shae asked.

Adrian shook his head. "They dinna ken where I'm from."

"That's enough fer now," a young man standing next to Shae spoke up. Andrew. Adrian had called him Andrew. "We have our answers. He's home wi' his new bride, an' we can all see they're tired."

Those few words were all it took for the noise level to surge and the group to either break up or press toward Adrian again. Feeling a bit lost in the crowd, Sara Anne looked around at the simple but sturdy lodges and the passionate people in their plain garb. This would be a very different existence than any she had known.

~~~

Adrian watched Sara Anne look around his lodge for the first time. His sisters had kept it clean, but Sara Anne was used to fine houses made of brick with carpets on the floor. "I'll build a bigger one," he pledged.

She turned to him, her eyes twinkling. "When we *need* a bigger one."

An overpowering sense of love and gratitude filled him, clogging his breath. He pulled her into his arms. "Do yeh know how I love you?"

"I do. And I love you."

His body responded to her nearness and so he exhaled slowly and pulled away the necessary few inches. "I should get yeh tae my sister's," he said with a lift of his brows "before we cause any more scandal. Not fer long, though. Only until we can get a man of the cloth here tae marry us proper-like."

She smiled and nodded.

~

Hovering in the doorway of Colline's lodge, the McGoldrick sisters watched the couple coming closer, oblivious to anyone but themselves.

"Look at him," Shae marveled. "I've never seen him so happy. Have yeh ever?"

Colline shook her head. "No."

"This is one of the greatest days ever," Shae declared. "Adrian home an' in love!"

Miriam sighed. "Suppose I best go tally up all the promises I made tae God pleadin' fer this day."

Colline chuckled. "Do that later. We've got a celebration tae pull together."

~

"Do yeh recall me mentionin' a great castle nearby?" Adrian asked Sara Anne as his sisters ducked back into the lodge.

She nodded. "Ruthven Barracks."

"That's right. I just learned it was destroyed in the rebellion."

She stopped. "Oh," she replied gently.

"Tomorrow I'll go wi' the others who fought tae honor what was lost. I'll be a day or two."

"I understand."

"When I get back, we'll be joined. I don't want tae wait. I want tae live an' rebuild. I want a family with you."

"I want that, too."

They started walking again. "I wish Thomas was here, but I dinna want tae wait when our life beckons." Two young boys ran by, grinning at them, and a dog followed. "Can you see yourself here?" he asked worriedly. "Happy, I mean?"

She stopped and turned to him, placing her hands on either side of his face. "Of course, I can. I do."

He kissed her lightly, then glanced around and kissed her again.

# Chapter Twenty-Four

S ara Anne stirred the next morning, having slept hard after an evening of celebration. The room she'd been given in Miriam's lodge was small, and the bed narrow, but it was wonderful after sleeping on the ground for so many nights.

She began to doze again but the sounds of voices, tension-filled voices filtered through her consciousness. She frowned and listened. It was a man and two women talking in the next room. She heard Adrian's name and then her own. "English an' one American," the man said.

She bolted upright in alarm and hurried to get dressed, but her trembling made it difficult to manage the borrowed clothing. English and one American could only mean one thing. When she stepped out, all conversation stopped between Miriam, Shae and a strapping, young man Sara Anne had not seen before. Their faces drawn and pale. "What is it?" Sara Anne asked quietly. "Is Adrian alright?"

"He's fine," Miriam replied. "As far as we know," she added hesitantly. "He left with the others. Sara Anne, this is Thomas, our cousin."

"Thomas," Sara Anne said, nodding politely.

Thomas nodded back, but he looked uncomfortable, embarrassed even.

"Thomas was in another village," Shae said shakily. "He just returned."

"He heard about men lookin' fer Adrian McGoldrick," Miriam interjected. "English soldiers."

*And one American.* Sara Anne felt a sharp pain in her belly.

"They know his name," Miriam whispered, as if it was too frightful to say aloud.

Sara Anne moved woodenly to a chair and sat. Aaron was still coming for her, closing in on her, and he wouldn't stop until he had her back. Not only that, but he was backed by a group of soldiers who would be keen to kill the highlander who had escaped them.

What could she and Adrian do? It wasn't as if they could keep running. This was his home. And sooner or later, someone would reveal where the McGoldricks lived. She had thought they'd escaped, but she'd been wrong.

A tremor passed through her because there was only one answer, one thing to do. She had to give herself up. It was the only way to save Adrian. She bowed her head and squeezed her eyes shut, agonized at the thought of leaving him. But what else could she do?

"Sara Anne?"

Sara Anne opened her eyes. The tears on her face felt cold and she felt oddly removed from the scene. "I have to tell you, but you must swear—" she was having difficulty getting it out.

"What?" Miriam prodded.

Shae crossed to Sara Anne and sat. "Sit down," she urged the others. "We're listening."

"They want me," Sara Anne stated.

"Who? The English?"

"The American. He leads the others." She took a shaky breath and conveyed the story. "I can see now that he won't stop until he has me back. Only I can convince him that Adrian is dead."

"Dead?" Shae burst.

Sara Anne looked at her. "That's the only way they won't come after him."

"What are yeh sayin'?" Shae asked, aghast. "You would turn yerself over tae this man, Waldron?"

"Yes. I have to." Sara Anne turned to Miriam, her eyes pleading for understanding. "Can't you see that?"

"But yeh can't," Shae appealed. "Yeh love Adrian."

"I have to because I love him."

Miriam rose. "Wha' will happen tae yeh?"

Sara Anne shook her head. She couldn't think about that. All that mattered was saving Adrian. "He'll take me back home," she said flatly. "When I left Charles Town, I made a fool of him. That's how he sees it. And his pride is more important than anything, so he'll take me back to show that he's won. But the important thing is' he'll call off the others. I will convince him Adrian is dead." She swallowed. "You'll have to prevent Adrian from coming after me. Please. You have to swear it."

Shae began crying, but Miriam, barely holding her emotion in check, nodded stiffly.

"I can endure anything if I know he's alright," Sara Anne whispered.

"But he willna' be alright without you" Shae exclaimed. "There has tae be another way!"

"What?" Sara Anne asked, praying that there was.

The room filled with an anguished silence.

Sara Anne looked at Thomas. "Can you help me find these men?"

He looked miserable, but he nodded.

"This is wrong," Shae cried.

"Shae," Miriam said sternly. "If she doesn't go stop them, they'll find us an' they'll kill Adrian. They're callin' him a criminal."

Thomas cleared his throat. "It's true. They're postin' rewards, threatening, anythin' tae get information on the McGoldricks." He paused and looked at Sara Anne. "They're half a day's ride from here."

"Only half a day?" Miriam repeated, clearly frightened they were so close.

"They won't still be there," Shae argued, frowning.

Miriam glowered at her. "Shae, yer not helpin'!"

"Adrian will be so angry," Shae warned.

"Aye, he will. He'll hate us an' we'll hate ourselves," Miriam retorted. "Now do yeh want tae help save his life or no?"

"Of course, I do! But I don't want Sara Anne tae sacrifice herself, nor do I want either of them tae have tae sacrifice their love."

"No one does," Miriam cried. "But what's our choice? For God's sake! What's the choice?"

Sara Anne looked at Shae, who was unable to stop crying. "If I could avoid them forever," she said tenderly. "I would. I would stay here, marry Adrian, have his children and—" Her voice broke, and she took a moment to compose herself. The crying had to stop. It was accomplishing nothing. "But I must find them before they find us. I could not survive it if they—" Abruptly, she rose, having made up her mind.

Thomas looked uncertainly at his cousins and then rose, too.

"Now?" Shae asked, her eyes full of alarm.

"Aye, now," Miriam agreed, standing. "Adrian will never let her go. She has tae go now if she's goin'." Tears tormented the backs of her eyes, but she blinked rapidly and held them in check.

"It isna' right," Shae said in a choked whisper.

Miriam placed her strong hands on Sara Anne's shoulders. "God willin', yel' find yer way back tae us." She pulled her close and held her. "I believe yeh will," she said just above a whisper.

# Chapter Twenty-Five

In a crude café, Aaron stirred a rice and mutton mixture and took a bite.

"Waldron! We've got her!"

Aaron looked up as a man named Peters closed the distance between them.

"She was delivered to us," Peters said. "Because of the reward."

Aaron felt a stirring of excitement like he hadn't felt in weeks. "What about McGoldrick?"

"Dead," Peters said victoriously.

"Dead?" Waldron repeated.

"Yes. Dead. Miss Aldridge was trying to get back to England, but her guides brought her to us instead. Quicker reward that way. Shall I bring them in? She's under guard, of course. I had her put in your lodge."

Aaron shoved his plate away. After the long search, it seemed too easy. "Take me to them."

~~~

"Where is Sara Anne?" Adrian asked.

It was the first time Miriam had been asked and so she was surprised by the edge to his voice. Sara Anne and Thomas had left two days ago, but Thomas had not yet returned, so she had no way of knowing what had happened. "I'm sorry, Adrian. I truly am, but she's gone."

His eyes narrowed. "What do yeh mean *gone?* Gone where?"

This wasn't going to be pleasant, and Miriam tried to brace herself for the row that was sure to follow. "I canna' say. I promised."

"What are yeh talkin' about?" He took two threatening steps toward her. "Tell me!"

Miriam took a deep breath and let it out before speaking again. "She went off tae find the men after yeh both. I willna' give yeh details because I respect what she did. She loves yeh an' she's tryin' tae save yer hide." She watched him pale before her eyes.

"What are yeh talkin' about?" He grabbed hold of her arms. "What in God's holy name have yeh done?"

"Yeh can shake me till my teeth rattle, but I will not tell yeh!" Miriam suddenly began crying as if her heart were broken. "I swore it."

He released her and stepped back. "Miriam—"

She wiped her face, "We found out the English were close by an' lookin' for you," she said, speaking more calmly, although her voice still shook. "By name, Adrian! Callin' yeh a criminal. It was only a matter of time until they found yeh."

"Where did she go?" he asked beseechingly, looking into her eyes which bore such a resemblance to his own.

She shook her head slowly and a tear ran down her face. "We thought we'd lost yeh once before an' I willna have a part in seein' yeh killed now. Hate me if yeh will."

He bowed his head and then turned and walked away without another word. Outside, he walked blindly, trying to clear his head. He'd taken Sara Anne across the county and claimed her for his own in the doing. He couldn't lose her now, *unless*—

He stopped short and swallowed hard. Was he being punished for taking part in an immoral scheme in the first place? He felt physically ill at the thought. He'd found love with Sara Anne. She would be the only woman he ever loved. Surely, he couldn't have been given such a gift only to have it yanked away as punishment. God wasn't that cruel. He couldn't be.

He began walking again. He had to find someone who knew and would tell him her whereabouts. He had to find her.

~~~

Thomas lay on his belly on a hillside perch above a village watching the activity below through Adrian's telescope. He saw Waldron striding toward the place Sara Anne was being held. His stomach tightened at the grim intensity on the man's face. Sara Anne had been brought into camp over an hour ago, placed inside a lodge, and kept under guard as if she were an important prisoner.

Since leaving home, he and Sara Anne had worked to set the trap he saw being sprung before his eyes. How frustrating and ironic that was since it would yield a result no one wanted other than Waldron.

To successfully extricate Adrian, Waldron had to believe Sara Anne's story. He also had to be convinced of the sincerity of anyone who delivered her, which meant those people had to be legitimate.

Thomas and Sara Anne had begun with a man Thomas trusted, who had passed on word about Sara Anne seeking a guide to Middlesbrough. She was described as an American beauty promising a significant reward on arrival in the north of England.

When two men approached and offered to take her to England, Sara Anne and Thomas were hopeful she would be taken to Waldron. When the men took her due southeast, it was confirmed. It was wretched to see the trap ensnare Sara Anne, but Thomas kept reminding himself of two things. The purpose was to save Adrian's life, and it was Sara Anne's sacrifice to make.

As Waldron entered the lodge, Thomas felt a heavy gloom settle over him. Whether Sara Anne was right or wrong in this decision, and he didn't personally think she was wrong, he hated to think of what she'd go through now.

~~~

Aaron stepped inside the lodge he'd taken for his own during their stay and shut the door behind him. Sara Anne was curled up on the cot, dozing. He walked toward her with deep satisfaction welling in his chest. He'd spent some time making certain the men who'd delivered her had been telling the truth. They were now a hundred guineas richer, but minus half a left index finger in the exchange. He'd had to make certain he wasn't being set up.

Sara Anne looked thinner. Her clothes were worn and dirty, and yet somehow, she was more beautiful than ever. He heaved a sigh, thinking of all the things he was going to do to her. She'd given him a chase he would not allow her to soon forget. It didn't matter that he had enjoyed the challenge. This moment, this final victory, was perhaps the sweetest feeling he'd known, but that was beside the point.

They had a long, hard ride ahead of them before they reached Middlesbrough again. By the time they arrived, Sara Anne was going to confess to her family that she had lied to them, that she was indeed his wife, and then she was going to beg their forgiveness. That was his first challenge. He had between here and there to convince her of the wisdom of such a confession.

The convincing would take different forms, physical punishments and mental ones, as well. "These punitive measures are for your own good," he would tell her. He would think up a new punishment each day and make her ask for it. Beg for it, if necessary. If she refused to do this, which, of course, she would at first, the penalty would be harsher than the punishment. Ah, yes—pain and humiliation were the order of the day and, with every one, he would remind her that she had brought it on herself.

"Wake up," he said, kicking the cot she slept on.

She stirred and moaned, loath to wake, and so he kicked the cot again. Her eyes fluttered and opened. It took a few moments for his presence to register and then she sat up with a gasp.

"Hello, darling," he said.

She blinked in astonishment. "How ... are you here?"

She was so beautiful, and her voice was raspy. He turned and walked to a table in the center of the room, drew back a chair and waited for her to join him. She rose, not yet fully awake enough to be thinking clearly. "Come," he instructed.

She moved forward uncertainly. "How—"

"How did I find you? I've been on your trail for some time. From Charles Town to London to Middlesbrough and all across this cursed country." He lifted and banged the chair on the floor. "Sit."

She started at the noise, stared at him in confusion, and then did as he bade.

He moved to the chair opposite her and sat. "You act surprised, but you must have seen me when you stole my prisoner from camp."

Tears sprang to her eyes. "What are you talking about? What camp?"

She seemed confused and lost. It wasn't without impact. "Tell me everything that's happened from the moment you were captured. We'll go back and cover the time before that later."

She crossed her arms. "Did my father send you?"

"You are not asking questions," he snapped. "You are answering."

She was taken aback. "You have no right—"

He lunged forward, leaning on the table threateningly. "I have every right!"

"You're mad," slipped out in a frightened whisper.

"From the moment you were abducted," he repeated, enunciating slowly and clearly.

She frowned, insulted, and beginning to get angry. "I don't have to tell you anything. Who do you think—"

He backhanded her and sent her reeling onto the floor. He watched dispassionately as she glared at him, her lip bleeding. "Get up," he said.

She pulled herself up and moved back to the chair shakily. "Continue."

"We were taken to an encampment of some kind," she said resentfully.

"Where several men were waiting for you."

"Yes. From there, they took us in different directions."

"They wanted ransom but you," he cocked his head, "you claimed to have no connections in England that would pay. Why is that?"

She huffed. "Because I didn't want my family to—"

He stuck a finger in the air. "Be careful," he warned. "I've calculated punishments for every offense up to now. But for every lie you speak, I'll add one."

"You have no right to talk of punishment," she objected, trying to sound forceful and failing miserably.

"Answer my question!"

"I was trying to buy time," she blurted. "I thought I could get away from them."

"Perhaps that I believe. You really are quite," he searched for the perfect word, "confident in your abilities. Overconfident, I fear, but we'll work to correct that."

Her jaw dropped momentarily and then she closed it and pointedly looked away from him.

"Let's have a drink," he said. His chair squeaked against the wood floor as he pushed back. He rose and walked to a cupboard saying, "They make excellent whiskey here." He rummaged, found a bottle, and poured two glasses. "We must take some back with us," he said as he walked back to her. He set one of the cups in front of her.

She glared at him. "No, thank you."

He shrugged, downed his, and then set his glass on the table. Moving with speed, he grabbed her hair with one hand and pressed the glass to her mouth with the other. She swallowed and choked, although most of it went down her front. He went back for the bottle and poured them each another. "I said to drink."

She lifted the glass in a shaking hand, and he returned to his seat. "Go on with what you were saying. Who was it that took you?"

"Two men," she bit out, keeping her eyes on her glass. "One's name was McGoldrick, and I never heard the other man's name."

"Where did you go?"

"I don't know. We stayed in the countryside. Eventually, we came into a place called North Berwick."

"Where you crossed to Pittenweem."

She hesitated. "Yes."

"You seem surprised I know this," he observed. "I'm not sure I believe that but continue. You were taken to Pittenweem … and?"

"I was kept there for more than a week."

It was the first unexpected statement. "Kept by whom?"

She shook her head. "I don't know their names. There was a man and two women. I don't know who they were. I was blindfolded most of the time."

He downed his drink. So, it hadn't been her that had snuck into camp and freed McGoldrick. He should have guessed as much. She had no experience that would have allowed her to carry out such a thing. "Go on."

"Something happened to McGoldrick while we were there." She hated using his name, but Aaron already knew it and she had to appear truthful. "He was wounded. Beaten."

Aaron nodded slowly.

"He died the day after they brought him back."

"After who brought him back?"

"The man and one of the women."

He thought about this. "What happened to the second man, the one with McGoldrick?"

She shook her head. "I never saw him after Pittenweem."

"I see. And then?"

"I told the people holding me about my uncle. I told them there would be a reward if he would only return me to Middlesbrough." She paused. "I was trying to get back there. I have been trying to get back."

He considered everything she'd said. "What happened then?"

"The man took me. I thought he was bringing me back to England, but then two other men took me. And here we are."

It was an interesting tale. Not what he'd been expecting.

"Do you know about the others who were taken? About my cousin, Ginny?"

"It's my understanding that none of the women were harmed. We'll soon see for ourselves as we leave for England tomorrow."

"Good. My family must be worried."

"But that hasn't stopped you from pursuing whatever ends amused you at the time."

Her eyes grew wide. "Amused me?"

"Something else we'll work to correct."

She huffed. "There is no *we*, Mr. Waldron."

"Oh, but there is, my sweet. And tonight, we'll have our long overdue honeymoon."

She jerked at the pronouncement. Her jaw had dropped.

"Oh, that's right," he said, feigning amazement. "You don't yet know that we're married."

She shook her head slowly. "You are mad."

"It's done, Sara Anne. Sanctioned by the church, signed off by witnesses."

She clutched at her stomach. "What witnesses?"

"Your father and aunt."

She stood, rigid as a post. "How did we get married without a ceremony or my presence?" she asked breathlessly.

"How forgetful of you. There was a ceremony, and you were there. Admittedly, you were barely visible beneath the veil. You see, I explained to the minister how your father had beaten you and bruised your face—"

She shuddered and closed her eyes.

"Everyone at home believes we're on our honeymoon. When we get back, we'll tell our family and friends all about it. First, of course, we'll stop in Middlesbrough for a few days where you will inform your family that you lied about not being married."

She shook her head, clearly panic-stricken.

"Oh, yes," he continued, enjoying himself immensely. "Then you will tell everyone at home about our delightful honeymoon trip. Since the wedding was so small, just a simple family ceremony, the reception and the parties in our honor will begin when we get back."

"I will not tell my—"

In a flash, he was up and had grabbed her. "You will say exactly what I tell you to say. No more and no less." He seized the back of her neck and pressed his mouth to hers. Pulling back, he sneered. "All of your running was a waste of time. Nothing

235

changed. You're mine. You were mine from the moment I decided I wanted you." He released her.

She'd been pushing against him and now, unbalanced, she stumbled backwards, nearly falling.

"I want you to tell me your name," he uttered. "And then I want you to take off your clothes."

She stood silent and motionless a moment too long and he looked around the room for his first instrument of punishment. He spied a razor strop on the far wall and walked toward it. He took hold of it and started back toward her. "I asked your name."

"Sara Anne. You certainly aren't a very considerate husband not to remember it."

Clever girl. "I'm afraid you'll find it's not the worst of my faults." He let the strop drop to his side, impressed that she had depleted his will to use it for the moment. She really was an excellent match for him. "I rather meant your last name. Your full name. I'd like to hear it."

"Mrs. Aaron Waldron, you mean?"

"That is what I meant. Now, take off your clothes."

She hesitated a moment, but then turned and began to unfasten the buttons of the simple bodice.

"I didn't say to turn away."

She turned back, but an insistent rap on the door interrupted them. He strode to the door and yanked it open.

"Someone shot at us," an alarmed voice reported. "Wilkins is hit."

"I'll be right there," he snapped before slamming the door in the man's face. He turned back. "When I get back, you will be in bed, naked, waiting for me. Do you understand?"

She nodded jerkily and so he let her go and left.

~~~

The door was slammed behind Aaron. "Make certain she stays put," he ordered.

Sara Anne released a shaky breath. She was beyond exhausted. She was weak and she felt so sick. All she wanted to do

236

was to fall into a deep sleep that she never had to wake from. She quivered with revulsion knowing he was coming back, determined to have and hold and break her. It would be better to die than to stay his property, his prisoner—his wife.

The only bit of relief she had was that he believed Adrian to be dead. It's what she'd set out to do. Now, if only she could be free, but there was no way out. Not with his men watching to make sure she stayed put.

*When he gets back...*

What? What could she do then?

*They won't be watching, then. Not closely.*

She began to pace. "If I can get away from him—" she said under her breath. She went to the utensils by the stove—pots and pans and *knives*. She picked up a long knife and inspected its blade before setting it back down knowing it wasn't in her to use it, not even against him.

She went to the cupboard and rummaged through the sparse contents, but she saw nothing that could help her. She turned and surveyed the room, unclear about what she was looking for. She moved to a chest of drawers and frantically pawed through the top drawers. It contained personal items—clothing, blankets, hair powder. In the bottom drawer was more clothing and some small, dark bottles in the back corner. She picked one up to study its faded label.

Foxglove.

It was medicinal, she was certain, but what was it used for? Perhaps she could put something in his drink and incapacitate him long enough to get away.

The label of the second bottle was too faded to make out. The third had Henbene scrawled across the label. Henbene, Henbenon ... why was that familiar to her? It was from a passage by Shakespeare. Something about the *juice of Henbenon*. Something about sleeping in the afternoon, and a vial containing the juice of Henbenon. If it was a medicine used to aid sleeping, that was exactly what she needed.

She pried open the small cork and smelled the contents. It was not odorous. Quickly shutting the drawer, she brought the bottle to the table. Her hands were shaking as she tipped the bottle to get some of the tincture into his glass. She waited, but nothing happened. Then one brownish drop of liquid fell. Two. Three. She shook the bottle and got a slow fourth drip, but that was all there was. Would it be enough to affect him?

She hurried back for another vial, depositing the first. The fourth and last bottle had Powdered Thornapple written on the label. She had to try. She shook some in his glass, then poured more whiskey and mixed the solution with her finger. She stared and held her breath as some of the powder settled at the bottom of the glass. She set the glass down and backed up, praying for it to dissolve completely.

She glanced out the window and then looked back at the glass. This wouldn't work. He'd notice and he'd punish her for trying to poison him. She started forward to dump it out, but the door flew open, and she froze, her heart in her throat.

"I told you to be in bed," he said.

She felt ill, so very ill. "I thought you'd be longer," she replied breathlessly, stammering from fear. She still had the bottle in hand and wasn't sure if she'd shut the drawer. She turned to face him keeping the bottle hidden in the folds of her skirt. "I needed another drink."

He grinned and turned to shut the door, and she quickly stuck the bottle in her pocket. As he came closer, she went back to the table and poured whiskey into her glass. Or perhaps she would switch the glasses.

"Those men never touched you, did they? McGoldrick or the others?"

"No."

"Good. I knew they weren't supposed to. They were delivering you to a great lord. Did you know that?"

"Yes."

He reached for his glass. *Oh, God!* Would he notice? "What happened to your friend?" Sara Anne asked urgently, hoping to distract him.

"Who?"

"The man who was shot."

238

"Hardly a friend," he scoffed. His hand had closed over the glass. "But he's dead." He lifted the glass to his mouth but stopped before drinking. "What is this?"

She tried to speak, but her throat was too tight.

"You look horror-stricken." He guffawed. "You didn't even know the man." He downed the whiskey in two gulps.

Her heart was pounding because it was done. He'd consumed the drink with whatever she'd put into it. Would it make any difference? She watched as he walked to the edge of the cot and sat. "Pull these off," he said, sticking up a dusty boot.

She came forward, took hold of his boot, and pulled. He stuck up his other foot and she pulled that boot off as well.

"Take off your clothes," he ordered.

"I need a drink first."

He shrugged. "Make it fast."

She walked back to the table, picked up her drink and drank it. Then she coughed. She wiped her mouth with the back of her hand and poured them each some more. Anything to buy time. "You never said how you came to be here."

"I came for you, of course. Wife. But that is quite enough small talk," he slurred. "Come here. I... want you to ... to—" He sniffed in a long breath as he looked toward the ceiling. A look of confusion crossed his face and then he began breathing in shallow pants. "You—" came out in a great gush of air.

It had worked! She breathlessly glanced out the window. It was twilight. Soon it would be dark.

"What ... did ... you—" His eyes lost focus. He tried to get to his feet but couldn't manage it. He collapsed back onto the bed, his stocking feet still resting on the floor.

She hurried to the window and carefully looked out. She didn't see of his men posted. She glanced back at Aaron, and then went to the door and opened it a crack. No one was posted outside the door, but villagers went about their daily activities. If she did not wait until dark, someone would see her leaving. She'd come this far; she had to get away.

# Chapter Twenty-Six

Thomas jerked awake because of the shouting and commotion below. It was just past dawn. He rubbed his eyes and fumbled to retrieve the telescope he'd set beside him, nearly jumping out of his skin when he came face to face with Adrian, who was on the ground beside him.

"If I dinna' ken yed meant well," Adrian said, "I would never forgive yeh."

"Meant well? I meant tae do my part tae save yer life. But I suppose I'm glad yeh ken I meant well."

"Where is Sara Anne?"

"Down there."

Adrian looked through the telescope, growing more and more confused by the moment. A sickly-looking Waldron was agitated, waving his arms and shouting. "... got away!" he bellowed.

Adrian's pulse raced. "She got away."

Thomas shook his head. "When? How?"

Adrian was striving to make out what was being said. The soldiers were looking for tracks, preparing to go after her.

"They had her under guard every minute unless Wa—"

Adrian looked at his cousin. "Unless Waldron was with her?"

Thomas nodded. "Aye."

"How long was he with her?"

"The first time it was only minutes. Then one of his men came after him. Because someone had mysteriously shot one of their men."

"You?"

"Of course, me. But not from here."

"Then what? Waldron went back tae her?"

Thomas nodded grimly.

"How long was he with her then?"

"I don't know. It was growing dark by then."

240

The men below were preparing to ride out. Waldron mounted, but then quickly dismounted. He took two wobbly steps, dropped to his knees, and vomited.

"I wonder what's wrong with him?" Thomas mused.

"Everything," Adrian replied bitterly, getting to his feet. "We'll have tae follow."

Thomas got to his feet. "Well, I've got tae relieve myself ferst, if yeh dinna mind."

All day long, Adrian and Thomas followed the group, keeping just enough distance not to be noticed and growing increasingly anxious about how to get ahead of them. At this rate, they might see the men overtake Sara Anne and not be in position to do anything about it.

At dusk, Waldron and his men rode into Stirling, and Adrian and Thomas were forced to fall back. Crown troops were still thick in the cities, especially this one, the site where William Wallace had defeated the English some four hundred and fifty years before. If they entered, they would be stopped, detained and who knew what else.

"They'll stop for the night," Thomas reasoned.

Adrian knew he was right. "Let's get tae the rise an' see where they go."

~~~

"You're certain?" Waldron asked.

"Dead certain," the soldier confirmed. "She passed through a short time ago on an old nag. You can easily overtake her."

His men exchanged looks. Very soon, they would have Miss Aldridge in custody and, this time, they would see her broken before their very eyes. The men spurred their mounts to a faster pace. They were ready to apprehend her and then move on to the next phase and a celebration dinner. Waldron was buying.

~~~

Sara Anne rode onto an ancient, stone bridge that spanned a river some fifty or sixty feet below. Daylight was nearly gone, and she was sensationless with exhaustion, but the height of the bridge provided a grand view of the old city.

Someone crossing the bridge stopped and gawked at something behind her. She looked back to see Aaron and his men closing in on her. Sara Anne kicked the horse forward, despite knowing she could not outrun them.

If she jumped over the side, could she survive it? She had to try. There was nowhere else to go. Hooves thundered on the bridge. They were almost to her. She edged her horse to the side of the bridge, lifted herself in the stirrups, and then hoisted her left foot onto the top of the saddle. She was aware of a hand coming at her. Terror filled her but she pushed off with all her might and then began a dizzying fall toward the water below.

~~~

Watching from a ridge, a quarter mile away, Adrian cried out and stretched out his hand in reaction.

Thomas jerked. "God Almighty! She jumped! Off the bridge!" He looked at Adrian, who was stunned speechless. "Can she swim?" he asked in desperation.

Adrian hadn't seen Sara Anne surface, so the question was slow to penetrate. "Aye, she can," he finally replied without pulling the scope from his eye. Was it possible to survive such a fall, or had he just witnessed her death? No! She couldn't be dead. He loved her. She couldn't be dead.

Thomas stared at the gathering crowd on the bridge. People were running toward the bank, looking for her. "Jesus, Mary and Joseph, my stomach feels like a bottomless pit. I canna' believe she jumped."

"Where is she?" Adrian agonized. "Where is she?"

"Oh, Adrian. I'm sorry. I'm so sorry."

~~~

Aaron was spurring his horse into a run to get to her. The noise and the crowd were infuriating. First there had been screaming. Now, they only wanted to gawk at the spectacle and get in his way.

His men kept pace, one of them jerking his thumb northward. "The current pulls toward the sea."

"Can she swim?" someone called from behind him.

Aaron didn't bother to reply. He didn't think so, but he couldn't face that fact yet. He reached the bank, jumped off his horse and stepped into the river, scanning the surface. In two steps, he was in knee-high water, three steps brought the water thigh-deep and he could feel the pull of the swift current. He squinted and stared but saw no sign of her.

"She's gone," someone said from a short distance away.

"But her body—"

"It'll float, though not at first."

Aaron ran both hands through his hair. He wanted to scream. He finally let loose. "Sara Anne!"

The name echoed from the arches of the great stone bridge and traveled over the surface of the water.

"She's got to be this way," Peters was saying. "The current would take her—"

Waldron went for his horse and followed. He'd come all this way and found her. It wasn't possible that he'd lost her now. It just wasn't possible.

~~~

Air sliced through her, and her stomach contracted from terror as she plummeted toward the river. It took mere seconds and then she hit the water. The impact hurt terribly, and the force of the fall drove her deep. She kicked manically toward the surface. The color of murky, gray water lightened before she broke through and gulped air.

She was underneath the bridge, being pulled with the current. It was too strong to fight. She'd need to go with it. She's already been swept to the other side and was about to be clear of the bridge

243

and in plain sight. She took a few deep breaths before submerging herself and swimming under water as hard and fast as she could. She had to surface again but was conscious of keeping her head down. Another few gulps of air and she swam on, keeping under the water's surface as much as possible. Exertion warmed her and fear and adrenalin lent her strength.

~~~

Adrian crouched to the ground to catch his breath. They were on foot running toward the River Forth, and they could both see and hear the search party combing the bank. So far, there was no sign of Sara Anne.

"Let me see it," Thomas gestured to the telescope. He was too out of breath to say much more.

Adrian handed it to him, and Thomas brought it to his eye. Adrian watched Waldron searching the river, screaming Sara Anne's name. He looked truly stricken. Was it possible the bastard loved her?

"Hey," Thomas said. He was focused on something downriver. "It's her!" He offered the telescope to Adrian. "She's trying to get away, only surfacing for air. There," he pointed to an area not far from the search party.

Adrian looked but didn't see her. "She's alive?"

"Aye, very much so. But they're not far away."

Adrian started off again. "Let's go."

~~~

Muscles cramped in her side and in her back, and the pain was paralyzing. She tried to surface but an undertow tugged her down. Consumed with panic, she fought with all her might and surfaced. She sucked in breaths and tried to get her bearings. She had just rounded a bend, which prevented anyone from seeing her for the moment, but voices were calling, and they sounded close. Her strength was gone. She had to get out of the water while she had a chance.

She made it to the bank and used the last of her strength to get out. She crawled away and into some brush a split second before a man on horseback came bounding down the opposite bank. She breathed in choked gulps and shook violently. A second rider was right behind the first and they were shouting back and forth.

"See anything?"

"I thought I did."

She began scooting backwards. When she backed into the body of a man, she lacked even the strength to cry out, she simply crumpled.

~~~

She smelled his scent as she came to.

No, it couldn't be. He was gone. No, *she* was gone. Aaron had caught her again. She was worse off than dead. *Oh, God.* She couldn't open her eyes. She would simply will herself to die.

"Sara Anne?"

The voice sounded like Adrian, which was nothing but a cruel tease. It was too much. She began sobbing with wracking, heart-broken abandon.

"Sara Anne!"

She opened her eyes and blinked in shock and horror at the image in front of her. It was Adrian. They had caught him, too. All her effort had all been for nothing. Nothing!

He lifted her and held her against his chest. "Stop yer crying, love. Yer safe."

It was a trick of some kind. She looked around and didn't recognize where they were. There was a crackling campfire — it was dark. They seemed to be alone. She was confused, but his body was warm. He was real. She began crying again, only softly this time.

He pulled her close. "*Shh.* Yer worn out."

She breathed his scent and clung to him.

"I've got yeh," he murmured. "An' I'm goin' tae keep yeh, this time."

"Are they after me?"

"No. Yer safe. They're convinced yer dead."

Could it be true? She buried her face in the crook of his neck and grabbed the fabric of his shirt in her fist. She had never felt so weak.

"Thomas is followin' them. He's determined tae see them gone."

"You came after me."

"Of course, I did. I love you."

Scalding tears leaked from her eyes.

"I canna' believe yeh jumped off Stirling Bridge," he said, holding her tighter. "My heart stopped."

"Tell me it's over," she begged. "Tell me they're gone."

His eyes scanned the darkness outside the circle of light from the fire. "It's over," he whispered. "They're gone."

She exhaled slowly. "Remember what you said about wanting to live, to rebuild?"

"Of course, I do." He pressed a kiss to her temple.

Why could she not stop crying? Her heart was aching, and yet she'd never been as glad and relieved as she was at that moment. "I want to marry you and have your children."

"We will. I promise."

She sighed. She was limp with fatigue, but she was with the man she loved, and they were safe, at least, for the moment. She would fall asleep in his arms and wake to find him next to her. They *would* have a life with all the joy and the tribulations, the fear and hope that came with it.

Ah, yes. *Hope.*

With crickets chirping, the fire crackling, and the sound of the river in the distance, she gave in and slept deeply.

Jane Shoup is the award-winning, multi-genre author of Down in the Valley, The Restoration, An American Baroness, The Chronicles of Azulland, and many more. She lives in North Carolina with her husband Scott, over attached, rescue-pup, Gabby, and near her grown daughters and their families, including six grandchildren and six granddogs.

Visit her website at www.janeshoup.com